SPECIAL MESSAGE TO READERS

THE ULVERSCROFT FOUNDATION
(registered UK charity number 264873)
was established in 1972 to provide funds for
research, diagnosis and treatment of eye diseases.
Examples of major projects funded by
the Ulverscroft Foundation are:-

- The Children's Eye Unit at Moorfields Eye Hospital, London
- The Ulverscroft Children's Eye Unit at Great Ormond Street Hospital for Sick Children
- Funding research into eye diseases and treatment at the Department of Ophthalmology, University of Leicester
- The Ulverscroft Vision Research Group, Institute of Child Health
- Twin operating theatres at the Western Ophthalmic Hospital, London
- The Chair of Ophthalmology at the Royal Australian College of Ophthalmologists

You can help further the work of the Foundation
by making a donation or leaving a legacy.
Every contribution is gratefully received. If you
would like to help support the Foundation or
require further information, please contact:

THE ULVERSCROFT FOUNDATION
The Green, Bradgate Road, Anstey
Leicester LE7 7FU, England
Tel: (0116) 236 4325

website: www.foundation.ulverscroft.com

Debbie Howells is a florist and lives with her family and assorted animals in Sussex. Her first novel, *The Bones of You*, was a *Sunday Times* Top Ten bestseller and a Richard and Judy Book Club selection.

You can discover more about the author at www.debbiehowells.co.uk

THE BEAUTY OF THE END

Now living an aimless life in an isolated cottage, ex-lawyer Noah Calaway is haunted by the memory of April Moon, the beguiling young woman who left him the day before their wedding sixteen years earlier. Then one day he receives a troubling phone call: April lies in a coma, the victim of an apparent overdose — and the chief suspect in a brutal murder. Deep in his bones, Noah knows that April is innocent. Then again, he also believed they would spend the rest of their lives together . . . Ella is a troubled teenager who holds the key to finding the killer — but no one will listen. And as Noah's, April's and Ella's stories converge, shocking revelations come to the surface. The truth is obvious. Or so everyone believes . . .

Books by Debbie Howells
Published by Ulverscroft:

THE BONES OF YOU

DEBBIE HOWELLS

THE BEAUTY OF THE END

Complete and Unabridged

CHARNWOOD
Leicester

First published in Great Britain in 2016 by
Pan Books
an imprint of Pan Macmillan
London

First Charnwood Edition
published 2017
by arrangement with
Pan Macmillan
London

ISBN 978–1–4448–3172–6

Published by
F. A. Thorpe (Publishing)
Anstey, Leicestershire

Set by Words & Graphics Ltd.
Anstey, Leicestershire
Printed and bound in Great Britain by
T. J. International Ltd., Padstow, Cornwall

This book is printed on acid-free paper

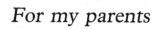

For my parents

I believe in everything until it's disproved.
So I believe in fairies, the myths, dragons.
It all exists, even if it's in your mind.

Who's to say that dreams and nightmares
aren't as real as the here and now?
                                    John Lennon

I do believe in an everyday sort of magic —
the inexplicable connectedness we sometimes
experience with places, people, works of art and
the like; the eerie appropriateness of moments
of synchronicity; the whispered voice, the
hidden presence, when we think we're alone.
    Charles de Lint, author of *The Onion Girl*

And I wonder — if everything's connected,
does that mean that everything can be
manipulated and controlled centrally by
those who know how to pull strings . . .
                                Malcolm Margolin

I want to live forever . . . We were standing on top of Reynard's Hill, where the ring of trees seemed to reach up, their branches tangling with the sky; where you could breathe, April said, as though air alone was not enough for her.

The steep climb took my breath away, but as we reached the top and looked down, for a split second I saw what she saw, the entire world seeming to stretch out from beneath our feet.

'Look how beautiful it is . . . '

At her side, I hadn't noticed the tinge of sadness in her voice. I was mesmerized, as much by her presence as by the towns below, so insignificantly small from where we were, the dark lines scored into the patchwork landscape linking them.

She'd taken a step forward to where the ground dropped precipitously away, her long red hair damp from the mist, her eyes gone to that place where I could never follow. As she stretched out her arms, for a moment I imagined she could fly.

Reality caught up with me. I remember lunging forward to stop her, my clumsy movement sending a shower of stones tumbling over the edge, almost carrying me with them. Far from my coming to her rescue, it was she who pulled me back, holding on until the ground stopped moving.

It was one of many times I tried to save her. But by the time I did, it was too late.

1

May 2016

You think you know what it is to live. Those moments seized, battles fought, love yearned for. But you don't. Not really, not until the end, when it's slipping away from you. When your body no longer listens to you, has become a prison inside which you can't move, can't breathe, can't reach out.

When the person you need most isn't there . . .

The memory is bitter-sweet, splinter-sharp. A transitory flash of long red hair damp from the mist; bone-chilling cold, the starkness of trees in winter. My heart quickening, as it always did. A girl I knew once, when the world was different, who filled my every waking thought, my dreams.

Did you know, we're like stars? At their brightest, most vibrant, before they die; a trail fading until the naked eye can't see it; the brilliant crescendo of a life that builds to silence.

Just as quickly it fades; a memory I've buried since I arrived here, four years ago, when my aunt Delilah died and left me her cottage. I'm questioning what's triggered it, glancing up from my desk just as the old black phone rings, past and present overlapping for a moment. As it continues to ring, though I'd rather not, I have to answer it.

Sliding my chair back, I get up and walk over to the windowsill. Feel behind the heaviness of the curtain to where it sits untouched. Unaware, as I answer it, of the hope that flickers, like the flecks of dust stirred, caught in the dull glow of my reading light.

'Hello?'

'Hello? Noah? Is that you?'

I pause, startled, as fifteen years fall away. The clipped, precise tone is instantly recognizable, making my skin prickle as I'm jolted back to the present, because the phone isn't part of the memory.

'Hello. Yes.'

There's another brief silence before he speaks again, clearer this time. 'It's Will.'

I watch the moth that's taken refuge, camouflaged perfectly against the stone of the inglenook, as the fire I lit earlier sparks into life. My cottage has thick stone walls that hold fast to the chill of winter.

He adds, 'Thank Christ. I thought I'd got the wrong number.'

It can take a lifetime to learn that appearances are deceptive. Take the forest that's three-dimensional in the black depths of a still lake, each branch defined, every subtle shade perfectly mirrored, the sun looking out at you, so that if you stare for long enough, you forget. It's just a picture; hides the cold darkness that can close over you, that's silent.

Will and I were friends — once, a long time ago. But too much has happened, things that belong in the past.

As this, and much more, flashes through my head, common sense kicks in because I owe Will nothing. I'm about to put the phone down, when he says two words that alter everything.

'It's April.'

It's reflexive, a knee-jerk response that, even now, my heart skips a beat at the sound of her name.

And there are moments when a few words, the single thought they provoke, can be devastating. Shatter what you've painstakingly constructed. Reveal who you really are.

'What about her?' I keep my voice neutral, my eyes fixed on the fireplace, on the moth's wings, twitching unevenly.

'There was an accident.' He follows it up with, 'She's in hospital. It's not looking good.'

He speaks fast, impatient, his voice level, unemotional. I wonder if calling me is an inconvenience. And I'm sorry, of course I am. April and I were close, but it was a long time ago. Accidents happen every day. It's sad, but I've no idea why he's calling me.

There's only so long you can do this. Fake the pretence, dance to the piper's discordant tune. Hide an agonizing, unbearable truth that's been

5

silent too long, that's hammering on the door,
screaming to be heard, for someone to listen.

'I'm not sure what happened, exactly. Look . . . '
He hesitates. 'I only called you because it'll be all
over the papers. A guy was murdered — in
Musgrove, of all places. Knifed to death in his
car, parked behind the pub. The North Star
— can you believe that?' He pauses again. 'The
thing is . . . Well, it looks as though she may have
killed him.'

I'm struggling to take in what he's saying,
because the North Star was once our local.
There's a sick feeling in the pit of my stomach.
Then I dismiss the possibility outright, because
some knowledge is instinctive and I know this,
with a certainty that's blinding, absolute. Will's
wrong. I watch the moth launch itself into flight,
its wings beating a slow undulating trail that
circles the room twice, before battering itself at
the closed window.

'That's impossible. She couldn't have.'

Only no one comes, because no one knows that
you're bound and gagged, invisibly chained to a
monster. There is no escape. There never can
be, because wherever you go, he finds you.
Won't let go of you.

'The police think there's evidence.'

But as I know, it isn't always that simple.
'They could have missed something.'

And what about hope? That eternal optimism of

the human mind, as vital as blood and lungs and your beating heart, that carries you through suffering and heartbreak? Because when hope goes, you have nothing.

My jaw tightens. 'When did it happen?'
'Last night. Late, after the pub . . . '
'Exactly,' I flash back. 'It's far too soon. They need to carry out forensic tests. They can't possibly know.' I pause. 'How did you find out?'
'They were seen together in the pub. The police found a woman's glove in his car, along with the murder weapon — and her phone. They traced it to her address, but by the time they got there, she'd taken an overdose.' His voice is low. 'They called an ambulance — then they called me. They must have found my number on her phone. Anyway, she's in St Antony's, near Tonbridge.'
'Why's she there?' I ask stupidly.
'It's where she lives. Of course — I'm forgetting. You wouldn't know.'

Suddenly your whole life is like a car crash: no brakes, gaining momentum, piling up behind you. Your mistakes, missed opportunities, all the time you've wasted, a twisted, rusting heap of scrap metal that can't be salvaged. Overwhelming you. Crushing you.

Even now, even though he once loved her too, I hate that Will knows all this, how dispassionately he speaks, the condescension he barely conceals. That all these years on, he's still in touch with her, when I'm not.

7

'She's hardly going to want to see me.'

He hesitates. 'She's not exactly up to seeing anyone. She hasn't come round, mate. She's on life support. God only knows what she took.'

The *mate* is automatic, a throwback to our friendship — and out of place. But as I listen, I'm shocked, trying to absorb what he's saying, unable to picture April as someone who isn't vital and beautiful and brilliantly alive.

'The police are looking for witnesses. People who were in the pub, CCTV . . . If she's guilty, it won't be hard to prove,' he says.

'*If* she is,' I say pointedly.

'It's almost a foregone conclusion.'

I used to think he was confident, not arrogant, but he really is so fucking arrogant. 'Will. You know as well as I do. She wouldn't hurt anyone. She couldn't.'

You can play the part for so long. Wear the mask, say what people expect you to say. Fight for as long as there is air in your lungs. Fly if you have wings.

But you can never be free from someone who won't let you go.

He makes a sound, a staccato laugh shot with cynicism. 'When you haven't seen her for all these years, how can you possibly say that?'

He's a bastard, Will. Uses his surgeon's precision to dig the knife in, but he's forgetting, I knew her soul. I stay calm.

'The same way you know who you can trust.'

He understands what I'm saying. An uneasy

silence falls between us.

'Fair enough.' Will sounds dismissive. 'I thought you should know, that's all.'

'Fine. Hey, before you go, who was the guy?'

Will hesitates again. As he tells me, I watch the moth spiral into the flames.

★   ★   ★

It's surreal. My flashback, seconds before Will's call; that April is suspected of murder. The tidal drift of willow seed across the fields as I step outside now, but then it's a warm spring after the wettest winter in a decade. Pollen levels are high, willow seed prolific.

As I drive the half-mile to the run-down garage that stocks a few basic groceries, I'm strangely removed from myself, the countryside I know so well suddenly unfamiliar under the onward, imperceptible flow of the willow seed, to the soundtrack of Will's words replaying in my head. I'm waiting for my brain to slot them into place, only it doesn't. Instead I'm trying to work out why, after years of silence between us, after everything, Will should be concerned that I know.

None of it makes sense — unless there's something he isn't telling me. I found that out about Will, too late. The half-truths; the lies-by-omission that were no less lies for being unspoken, set in a past I can't change, that's woven into the essence of who I've become — just as April is.

And whether I want him there or not, so is Will.

9

★   ★   ★

That evening, I'm still thinking, trying to decide what, if anything, I should do, aware of old scars that were long forgotten, newly inflamed by Will's call; by the thought of April, unconscious in a hospital bed, like the memory of an amputated limb.

I'm wondering if anyone's with her. I never met her family. By the time we were together, it was as though she'd moved on, shedding them like a skin. There'd been a brother she didn't speak to. Her mother had died shortly after April left home, but she'd never mentioned her father.

Not that I can help her. I'm in Devon, April's in Kent. Anyway, if Will's in her life, he'll have it covered, which should fill me with relief — only Will made no attempt to disguise it. I heard it in his voice. He thinks she's guilty.

I stare through the window into the darkness, my feeble excuses reflecting back at me. That I'm so far away; that I left my London law firm four years ago; that apart from the occasional day's work for Jed Luxton's small local practice, I'm ill prepared to defend a murder suspect; that my one suit is pushed to the back of my wardrobe. I'm not even sure it still fits. Then a fleeting image comes to me of April driven to an extreme of desperation I can only guess at, plunging a knife into someone. An image so inconceivable that just as quickly it's gone.

For so long I'd believed she was my future. My sun, my stars, my April Moon, I told her once, carried away by the moment, by being alive, by the depth of my feelings for her.

Believing love was enough. That we were meant to be together. Never expecting it to change.

2

1991

I was fourteen when I fell in love with a goddess. Goddesses have that effect, even on teenagers such as I was. Being plump or uncool has no bearing on the ability to fall in love — and my fate was sealed.

It was the beginning of my first term at Musgrove High. We'd moved to Musgrove at the beginning of the longest, hottest summer I could remember, when my father started a new job. The first I'd heard of it was when he proudly showed me the car he could now afford, a shiny silver BMW 3 Series.

I'd climbed in excitedly, inhaling soft leather and a faint petrol smell. Things were changing, my father told me, as he got in and showed me how the seat adjusted. We were moving up. I didn't really understand what he meant. A job was a job as far as I could see, but I pretended to share his enthusiasm — until he told me we'd have to move.

The thought filled me with a horror I couldn't talk about, but the opinion of my fourteen-year-old self was of no consequence. In my small, sheltered, middle-class world, adults made decisions, children did as they were told. But it didn't stop me dreading it.

I distinctly remember packing up my things

— reluctant, resentful, overwhelmed by a need to hold on to the familiar, the childish, the outgrown. My mother's insistence that this was a good time for clearing out clutter, whatever that meant, and that there was no sense paying the removal people to take what I didn't use. As if it wasn't enough dragging me away from my friends and my home; by the time she'd ruthlessly been through my books, my model car collection, my secret cache of Action Man weapons, half my childhood had been ripped away too.

As we drove off from everything that defined me, my very identity seemed in question. Swotty Noah Calaway, with his small dark bedroom and nerdy friend next door, was gone forever. I'd no idea who I was.

Musgrove was an uncomfortable four-hour drive away, four hours that I filled with hostile new classmates and dread. My face turned to the open window, I fought off waves of nausea in the back of my father's new car, a car I'd come to hate as symbolic of unwanted change.

The first I saw of our new house was as we slowed down and turned up a wide, quiet road, and my father pulled up at the roadside. It wasn't unattractive, a red-brick Victorian house surrounded by others that were similar, and after the modest terraced street we'd left behind, it was big. Big doors leading into big rooms. Big windows. It was OK, I supposed, it just wasn't home.

The first thing I did was run round the back to look at the garden, which disappointingly wasn't big at all but long and narrow, though a massive tree right at the end made up for it. But as I stared into its branches, so high they almost tangled with the clouds, in the faintest hint of a breeze I felt myself shiver.

What tortured me most was the thought of school. If only I could have changed my name — to a memory of someone important, perhaps, or a meaning that I could wear, like strength or slayer of dragons. But I mean, *Noah* . . . What were my parents thinking? My mother said they had liked its biblical connotations and that it meant rest or comfort, which was nice, she told me. Nice and solid and reassuring, which was no good at all when it made you a figure of fun.

Over the years, I'd lost count of the number of times so-called friends turned up in their waterproofs on my doorstep — even when the sun was shining and there wasn't a cloud in the sky. Crapping themselves laughing, while I was forced to endure yet another episode of ritual humiliation. I knew that here, it would be no different.

The first morning, I was so nervous that after I'd eaten my breakfast I threw it all up. Inside, I was silently crying out for my parents to leave here and move back to our old house, for my father to give up the new car and return to his old job, to take me back to my old school because I knew from experience that the devil you knew was a whole lot easier to live with than the devil you didn't.

But in my heavy heart, I also knew that it wasn't going to happen and instead somehow found myself keeping my eyes down and staying out of everyone's way, as I shuffled along the corridor to my classroom.

As I was teenage and awkward, with an odd name and old-fashioned hair to boot, my expectations were at an all-time low. Being a nerd further handicapped me. I was as incapable of not handing homework in as I was of keeping my arm from springing up whenever the teacher posed a question.

Today was no exception. It was my first maths class here and, short of nailing my hand to the desk, there was no stopping it.

'Yes? Your name, boy . . . '

'Noah. Calaway. Sir,' I added, pulling my arm down and waiting for the titter. I wasn't disappointed.

'Noah, eh? Don't think we've had one of those before,' boomed Mr Matthews. Completely unnecessarily, I remember thinking. 'Well, speak up, boy. Better still — get up here and write it on the board.'

How I hated that arm. I hated, too, feeling everyone's eyes boring into me. I'm sure I detected a sadistic gleam in the teacher's eyes as he relished my discomfort. As I scrawled scratchily on the board, my hands clammy, my heart thumping in my chest, the piece of chalk snapped in two. I reached down to pick it up, completely mortified, but as I straightened up again, something extraordinary happened.

The classroom door opened and a girl walked in. She was slender, with this way of walking, her head held high, her long red hair falling in heavy waves down her back. I felt my jaw drop open as I stared at her.

'*Boy,*' roared Mr Matthews, completely ignoring her. '*In your own time . . .* '

I felt my cheeks turn scarlet as the sniggers and mutterings behind me started up, but I didn't care. Suddenly my head was filled with the image of that girl. I'd never seen anyone like her. Quite simply, she was a goddess.

3

2016

I don't notice darkness falling, or the past creeping ever closer. Instead I'm thinking that even now, April can still do this, exert an invisible pull across hundreds of miles.

Throwing another log on the fire and closing the curtains, I walk along the narrow hallway to the kitchen, wondering why Will really called me, because it wasn't out of the goodness of his heart. His heart is rotten. But if he's right, if April's a murder suspect, there's no question that she needs a lawyer.

I float the idea of leaving April at the mercy of a system that, when she comes round, will assign her a lawyer. Maybe a good one, who'll believe in her — or maybe not, because I know the system. I'd come to hate, too, that it was a gloriously complicated game, with so-called defence and prosecution, with their twisted words and questionable rights and wrongs that should have been black and white, but were in fact every shade of grey; the lines that seemed to blur and move every time your back was turned.

But the more I think of Will's words, heavy with the weight of his cynicism, and then of April, unconscious, the memories are back, of the girl who was my first love, now defenceless, needing a voice to speak for her. Sweeping my reluctance to one side because I know also that she needs someone who absolutely believes in her.

My heart sinks slightly as I realize what this means, because it would be so much easier not to do this. To stay here in Devon and let the legal system run its course. To leave the past silenced under the multiple layers of years. To never speak to Will ever again.

4

I glimpsed the goddess after school again, outside in the stifling heat as we blinked in the sunlight. She was with two other girls, one with fair hair, the other mousy brown with a bleached streak in it, their socks rolled down and skirts hitched up, whispering to each other before pointing and giggling loudly.

'Oi! Tosser!' yelled the brown-haired one above the general level of chit-chat. Across the road, a group of boys turned round, terrified. 'Yeah — that's right, you! 'As it dropped off yet? Yer *cock* . . . '

Everyone must have heard. Though I stared in awe at the girls, at the red-haired one who looked astonished, I couldn't help my heart going out to Tosser, who'd turned a shade of beetroot, wondering what he'd done to deserve such a public lashing. The girls, meanwhile, were teetering up the road on their wedge-heeled shoes, still giggling.

'I'd stay out of their way if I were you.' The voice, friendly, came from beside me.

Surprised, I turned to see that he was talking to me.

'Farrington,' said the boy. Slightly shorter than me, he had ginger hair and freckles. I'd noticed him in my English class. 'William. You can call

19

me Will. Those are scary chicks, believe me. There's this rumour they're witches — well, except for the long-haired one. She's new. But the others meet on Reynard's Hill after dark and cast spells and shit. I've seen them.'

I was even more enthralled. Spells and shit sounded awesome and as I walked home, already I'd conjured up this picture of the three of them sitting in the woods, lit by an eerie, greenish light as they stirred a cauldron and muttered incantations, unleashing their mighty powers across the whole of Musgrove. Of course, the goddess with hair the colour of autumn leaves, she'd turn out to be the chief witch. I could tell she was no ordinary mortal. Already I was under her spell.

'You can come and swim in our pool, if you like,' he continued cheerfully. 'I'll get my mum to phone yours. What's your number?'

I scribbled it on a scrap of paper, hardly believing my luck. This was turning out way better than I'd expected.

With a new friend and a major crush to take my mind off things, I settled in quite quickly after that. Will and I started hanging out and I was thrown into a whole other world, where money was plentiful and success seemingly effortless. Will's parents held flawlessly orchestrated parties in their large, elegant home. There was the lure, too, of their pool, with its crystalline depths through which we'd plummet to the bottom, holding our breath, the blood rushing in our ears, until one of us raced to the surface gasping for air.

It was a world I wanted a piece of. And meanwhile, each day I lived in hope of catching another glimpse of this living, breathing deity with the long red hair, though she proved somewhat elusive. I would go several desolate days without seeing her, then suddenly, she'd be there, round every corner.

In my head I'd constructed her entire life story. It was obvious that though she was born of mere mortals, there was a higher purpose to her being here. The raucous piss-taking by the other two girls was just a cover, so that no one suspected. I would have to be patient, and in time, all would be revealed.

On the downside, I was sure she hadn't even noticed me, but there wasn't really anything that set me apart. Until one extraordinary, magical day the following week, she walked into my chemistry class and looked directly at me — or so it seemed at the time.

'Good of you to join us, Miss Moon,' our teacher, Dr Jones, said drily. 'For your information, class started five minutes ago. Kindly take a seat over there.'

And as he pointed at the bench next to where Will and I sat, her green eyes flickered towards me. Then, in a heart-stopping moment that I knew I hadn't invented, she caught my eye again and winked.

At last . . . I had her name. Her surname, at least. I'm amazed the whole class couldn't hear my heart ricocheting inside my chest. Out of the corner of my eye, I watched her as she arranged herself on a stool, breathing in the alien spicy scent that seemed to come from her general direction, as if it were the most sublime perfume on this earth.

'You got a cold or something?' Will muttered at me. 'Only your breathing's gone funny.'

I shook my head and tried my hardest to concentrate on the lesson and Jones's briefing. When he'd finished and a low-level, general mumbling started up, Will stared at me.

'What is wrong with you?'

'What do you mean?' I could feel my cheeks growing hot under his scrutiny.

'Usually,' said Will, who unlike me was completely unabashed at being in the presence of a goddess, 'you're like, jumping up and getting shit organized before I've even worked out what we're doing. Something's weird.'

'It's not,' I said hastily, leaping up to prove him wrong and promptly knocking over a tripod, which clattered noisily to the floor. Picking it up, I tried to pull myself together.

But as Will titrated sodium hydroxide with hydrochloric acid, for the first time I let him get on with it, instead eavesdropping shamelessly on the conversation going on behind me. As I listened to the goddess's soft voice, finally I learned her name. April. Her friends were Beatrice and Emily.

By now, I was totally in awe, not just of her beauty, but also of her confidence, which was surely yet another manifestation of her other-worldly status. And as for her name . . . It seemed the most exotic, most beautiful name I could imagine. *April Moon*.

As I whispered it over and over, I knew I was madly, irrevocably in love.

5

April Moon, April Moon, April Moon . . . Over and over I silently repeated her name, in time with my footsteps as I walked home after school, not caring about the rain that was soaking into me, almost getting knocked over by a car. I would remember this day forever, I decided. She'd seen me. She'd even winked. It meant something.

After that, she appeared in more of my classes, near enough for the spicy scent of her to torture me, but always with others sitting between us, and so I learned to be content to worship her from afar. But such was the lot of lowly creatures like myself, I decided, wallowing in my misery. It was enough to know she was there.

It made perfect sense that April was a witch — a good one, of course. I knew they existed, but when I pushed Will on the subject, I got nowhere.

'You've seen what they're like,' he said, looking at me as though I was mad. 'What if they put a curse on you?'

I couldn't tell him that I'd been under April's spell since the first day I saw her. That was a secret, even from Will. In the end I took matters into my own hands.

It was autumn, dusk falling earlier by the day, the air rich with the scent of woodsmoke, when I decided to follow them. Just as Will had told me, they were headed towards the woods below Reynard's Hill.

Staying far enough back to remain unnoticed by them, I didn't see how it happened, just that a car sped past, too fast, sending a cloud of feathers into the air as something somersaulted onto the pavement. I heard April's cry, saw her run, then crouch slowly, reaching towards a small bird.

I watched as she picked it up, careful not to move its awkwardly outstretched wing. After that, their pace slowed and the chatter became quiet. Suddenly I realized what they were doing, and that as witches, they were taking the little bird to their magical place where they'd weave a spell and heal it. I knew also that this was something I had to see.

I followed in the shadows, as far behind as I dared without risking losing them, trying not to think about the rumours that for centuries, Reynard's Woods had been grassland, until a tragedy had befallen the village, wiping out most of the children with a terrible disease. It was then that the woods were said to have sprung up. It was said also that those trees were the spirits of the dead.

Now, darting among their shadows, I shivered, wondering if it was true, imagining wraith-like beings that I couldn't see, hearing the wind catch the leaves, keeping April and her friends in my sight, until in a split-second moment of distraction, they slipped down a path and disappeared.

In a panic, I ran. I couldn't come this far and

not see what they did here. But just as suddenly, I heard their voices again, close by; felt myself freeze. Then through some bushes, in the last glimmer of daylight, I saw them.

Edging closer, I crouched under a bush, listening to the hiss and crackle of twigs as they lit a small fire. The other side of it, I could make out April's face, the bird still cupped in her hands. Her voice gentle, with one finger she stroked it. Then she rested its head in her other hand; I held my breath as her fingers closed round it. This was what I'd come to see. The moment she'd weave a spell and heal it. I waited, my heart thudding in my chest, for the extraordinary kind of magic that was about to happen here.

There was a brief pause in which none of them spoke. Then its wings fluttered and I gasped. From across the fire she looked up, seeming to look straight at me, before she turned her attention back to the bird, laying it carefully on the ground in front of her. The three of them started chanting, a soft, eerie sound, and as I watched, transfixed, it soared up towards the sky.

★   ★   ★

That night, in my bed, I worked out I'd seen a miracle. That April had healed a mortally wounded bird. I wondered how many others there'd been, that the trees had been witness to, thrilled that it was proof of what before I'd only guessed at. I now inhabited a world where anything could happen. Where April had a power, a magical connection with the universe that most people didn't have, and my fantasies intensified. Away from her, I dreamed of the day she'd open her eyes and see beyond my name to the real Noah Calaway, fellow slayer of dragons, for the first time. She'd hold her hand out to me and together we'd save the world or whatever our higher purpose was. And once it was done, we'd share a kiss, as myriad stars swooped down on us to take us with them, together for all eternity.

It didn't happen, of course. Several times after that, I crept back to the same part of the woods, but I never saw them. The last time, however, a murky afternoon that cast the woods in a persistent state of twilight, something nearby caught my eye.

As I turned, my gaze was drawn to a young tree set on its own. It was about twice as tall as I was and even in the half-darkness, a strange movement I couldn't identify drew me closer.

As I started to focus, I heard myself gasp, unable to believe what I was looking at, feeling my eyes widen, fixed on the slow rotation of a squirrel, hanging from a branch by a length of ribbon round its neck.

Horrified, I stepped back and my shock intensified. The more I looked, the more I was able to see of the tiny, desiccated bodies which were strung there as they came into focus. There were birds, the leg of what I guessed had been a rabbit, and butterflies too, as if they'd settled on the branches and never again moved.

It was gruesome, a kind of hangman's

Christmas tree, especially when a feather fluttered down in front of me, followed by another; looking up, I spotted the magpie hanging from wire looped round its neck.

I stood there, transfixed, then out of the corner of my eye saw the body of a kitten, its eyes fixed open in death as they had been in life.

The silence was broken by the squawk from a nearby crow, followed by the crashing of its wings through branches. I turned and ran, not wanting to imagine how they'd all got there, banishing unwanted images from my head. It was only much later, when the initial horror had receded, that I worked out that the death tree, as I thought of it, had to be a monument. It was the only reasonable explanation. A place where April and the others could bring innocent victims of the carelessness of man to finally rest.

★　★　★

In the way these things do, over time it had grown less shocking, eventually melting into the background of my mind. Meanwhile, as I was thrust back into the mundanity of everyday life, it rained perpetually, day in and day out. The land was saturated, the roads flooded; under the cover of darkness one night, the brown, swollen river invaded the town.

I awoke the next morning to a watery hinterland. In my imagination, it was yet another manifestation of the universe's power, unleashed against some nameless victim — I'd no idea who. I wondered if this, too, was connected to April, but I didn't have a chance to find out.

An impromptu holiday was forced upon us and school was forgotten, but my joy was fleeting as this presented also an insurmountable barrier between me and April. Just as the excitement of it died down, winter blew in. Then before I knew it, Christmas loomed.

As the term drew to a close, I faced a new problem, finding myself reduced to a nervous, jabbering wreck as I endeavoured to pluck up the courage to give April the present I'd made.

It was a tape. One I'd poured every last, tortured drop of my teenage angst into. There were Madonna tracks, Berlin, the Human League, interspersed with emotive strains of Puccini and Debussy. It was a desperate, hopeless attempt to touch her heart and reveal my true self to her.

But however much I wanted to, I couldn't do it. I racked my brains for a way to give it to her anonymously, but found none. It was only as the last chemistry lesson on the last morning came to an end, and with just minutes before the final bell of the term, that I'd simply pretended to pick it up off the floor and, with my heart hammering in my chest, walked over to her.

'I think you must have dropped this,' I said, avoiding her eyes as I handed it to her. It was the closest we'd ever been. The effect was intoxicating.

She looked at it, puzzled, as she took it from me. 'I don't think so — it must be someone else's.'

I shook my head. 'It has your name on it.'

She turned it over and read it, and I saw her genuine look of surprise. Then her eyes lifted to meet mine.

'Thank you.' She said it softly. If she'd guessed, I couldn't tell.

★　★　★

Term ended, Will went skiing with his parents, Christmas came and went. Usually I loved this time of year, but not seeing April for so long was making me restless. I'd never much liked walking for walking's sake, but that winter I went for cold, meandering walks in the afternoons, hoping that I might randomly bump into her; that we'd fall into conversation, a meaningful one, of course. She'd have played my tape and really loved it, never for one second giving away that she'd guessed it was from me. Then I'd hold her hand and we'd carry on walking, together.

I even checked out Reynard's Woods, seeking out the death tree where, dusted with ice, the little bodies that still hung there had taken on a ghostly form. But there was no sign of her. Like the embers of the fire she'd made here, her presence had been washed away.

Several times I went back. Once I even lit my own small fire, sitting crouched beside it, warming my hands over the damp, smouldering wood, just waiting. Not once did I see her. Then the new year came blasting in with a fall of snow that stopped the world in its tracks, before melting just as rapidly to slush. And before I knew it, we were back at school.

The holiday had painfully magnified my feelings. I was condemned, it seemed at times, to drown in unrequited love, consoling myself with the thought that I was in the company of many great lovers whose affections were unreturned, who must have suffered just as I was suffering. But comparisons with the likes of Romeo and Juliet, Tristan and Isolde, provided small comfort from my torture, which steadfastly refused to go away.

It was about that time I started to notice April's absences. A week, sometimes two, before she'd walk into school as if she'd never been away. A little pale, perhaps, which wasn't surprising if, as I guessed, she'd been ill. But she gave no explanation, simply borrowing books to catch up on what she'd missed and acting as though nothing had happened.

Other than that, nothing changed. Another term passed. My fifteenth birthday arrived, a dull, unmemorable occasion unlike the noisy parties my classmates bragged about. My parents bought me a camera — a little one, with several rolls of film which I wasn't to use up too fast, they cautioned, because of the price of developing them. My mother took me and Will to the cinema, then out for pizza. And then I worked out we'd been in Musgrove an entire year.

The summer holidays arrived, which I could see only as an unwanted barrier keeping me from April, and I was saved from their unbearable endlessness by the long, hot days which I spent at Will's, where the pool was a welcome distraction. Under the sun, my skin tanned and as I set myself the goal of swimming an ever increasing number of lengths, I imagined my body defined by the faint outline of muscle that would transform my chances with the opposite sex.

It appeared to work. By the autumn, when we returned to school, occasionally, miraculously, April and I would talk. It was mostly about school and homework, it had to be said. If she'd missed classes I'd lend her my notes, but I knew how these things worked. That girls like April didn't go for boys called Noah. There were plenty of Daves, Johns and Simons out there, with cool hair and cool clothes, who knew how to kiss without squashing your nose or cricking your neck. And, as it also turned out, there was a Pete.

Right from the start, I didn't like Pete. Not because he was older and smoked and wore leathers and gave April lifts on the back of his noisy motorbike, roaring off into the distance leaving a trail of noxious fumes. I'm sure he was a perfectly reasonable guy — if only he wasn't seeing April.

No matter that I never really had her, suddenly it was like I was losing her. I saw her out with him, once or twice — an extra shirt button undone to reveal the swell of pale skin beneath, her jeans skintight to her ankles, with black Cleopatra-style eyeliner that gave her a feline sexiness I was uncomfortable with. I wanted my schoolgirl goddess back, not this siren.

'Forget it, buddy,' Will told me one day, as I stood defeatedly watching her walk past hand in hand with Pete. 'She's out of your league. I read somewhere that girls like guys they can look up to. Like Pete.'

'I don't know what you mean.' In my heart, I knew he was right but I couldn't bear to think of April and Pete like that. I turned and stalked off. Even now, no one was allowed into the fantasy.

Early in the summer term as exams loomed, the atmosphere in our year changed, from one of false bravado to abject fear of failure. There was no more putting off the inevitable. The time had arrived. Heads were down, books were open, pockets crammed with revision notes.

And then, out of the blue, April vanished.

ELLA

I'm the beneficiary of my parents' unrelenting wisdom. They know everything, from how to run the world to exactly what's best for everyone. Including me.

'Are you looking forward to meeting her?'

She's talking about the latest in the long line of therapists she believes will unlock the person I really am, somewhere inside. This one's good. She has to be — why else would my mother spare the hour it takes along narrow East Sussex lanes before blasting round the M25 to get me there? Only my mother's questions aren't really questions. No Answers Required.

'Abigail's told me so much about her. She's helped Toby terribly.'

Twelve years old, six foot two, tidal waves of testosterone raging against his whiny, irritating mother. It's always poor Abigail, never poor Toby, who has to live with her. Ten out of ten for her choice of word, though. Terribly.

'Try not to be too long though, darling, will you? I've an appointment at five.'

That'll be hair — or was that yesterday? Maybe it's nails — but there's always something far more important to her than I am.

'It isn't normally up to me.' Sarcastically polite, which she never gets.

'You know what I mean. Just be straightforward. Answer her questions.'

What she really means is no bullshitting, just tell the shrink what she wants to hear. Cool. Not like we're wasting anyone's time.

* * *

'Hi. It's Ella, isn't it? Come and take a seat.'

Therapists use a socially acceptable code. Out of a million ways to start a conversation, like let's cut to the chase because we both know there's something we need to talk about, they all use exactly the same words.

'Nice to meet you.' I hold out my hand — firstly, because of my upbringing and secondly, because there's no reason not to be polite. Anyway, apart from the fact that she studied psychobabble at uni, it's hardly her fault she has to talk to me.

She gestures towards a set of chairs arranged round a coffee table, which I kind of smile at, only in an ironic way, because it's the modern-day version of the shrink's couch. Her arm is really tanned — hasn't anyone told her about skin cancer?

She sits opposite me. Out of the corner of my eye, I notice she's younger than they usually are, the edge of her left ear punched with sparkly studs.

'So.' She picks up her notebook. 'Why don't you tell me a little about yourself.'

I shrug. 'I'm fifteen. I live with both parents. Big house with land. In Ditchling. I go to school at the Lester Academy.'

I say 'both parents' on purpose so she doesn't

35

have to ask. I don't tell her it's a stupidly big house, because she doesn't need to know — just watch the large silver ring on her right hand catch the light as she writes.

'You're into drama?'

Everyone's heard of the Lester Academy, source of future megastars of the stage and screen — and uber-wealthy parents.

I shake my head. 'Music, mostly.'

She looks interested. 'Which instrument do you play?'

'Guitar,' I tell her. 'Electric and acoustic — I did keyboard for a bit. I dropped the saxophone last year.'

Figuratively, you understand. I dropped the keyboard too, which pissed my mother off, because she has her own vision of how my dazzling future's supposed to blow practically the entire world away. I watch her pen hesitate, then write it down, waiting for the old joke about how I'm a regular one-girl band, but it doesn't come.

'Wow. I'd love to be able to play just one of those,' she says, looking wistful.

I sit back and fold my arms when she says that, warding her off, because icebreaking I'm used to. The dancing politely round each other, like we're on a first date. The walking on eggshells when it comes to the trickier stuff. Issues, you'd probably call them. But 'wistful' makes her sound like a normal person.

'Do your parents enjoy music?' she adds.

I'm not sure how to answer that one. Actually enjoy? I don't really know.

I shrug. 'I guess. My mother plays classical all the time. I don't really know about my father.'

She moves on. 'So, tell me what else you like to do — when you're not at school.'

OK. Only some of them ask this one, mostly because it's not on the checklist they tick off before totting up my final score and telling me there's nothing wrong with me. Which I already know.

'Swim.' I shrug again. 'We have a pool. And I read.'

Most of the books in the house are mine. My parents don't read, except for Sunday papers or interior-design brochures. 'And I write.'

That fell out without my meaning it to, because what happens then is people ask what I write.

'What do you write?' she asks, right on cue.

I look at my shoes. 'Just stuff.'

I could lie and tell her I write bleak, dark love songs, such as therapists' dreams are made of, just to wind her up, but instead find myself gazing across her office at the large, abstract canvas hung on the wall. Trying to find something to like about it.

She watches my gaze. 'Are you interested in art?'

'I don't really know anything about it,' I say.

'I think what matters is knowing what you like.' She glances at the canvas. 'You like that?'

I look her straight in the eye. 'Not really my thing.'

She bites her lip, says conspiratorially, 'Not really mine, either.'

I feel us connect, briefly, kind of like a needle prick, before I get it. She's smart. She hangs the ugliest painting she can find to give her common ground with everyone but the guy who painted it.

Then she really does surprise me. She puts down her pen and notebook.

'Can I say something, Ella? Only I get the feeling you've done this before. Am I right?'

By 'this' I'm guessing she means therapy. So the dancing thing's over already. I raise my eyebrows. 'Quite a few times, actually.'

She looks puzzled. 'Can I ask you why you think you need to come here?'

She says 'you'. I sit back, hearing breath drawn out in a long sigh, wonder why she's doing that. Then realize it's mine.

'Well . . . It's complicated.'

'I have time.'

'Yeah . . . '

I know she has time. They're paid by the minute or something.

'It's like this. I don't personally think I need to be here. My mother does. We don't really get on. Mothers and daughters don't always, do they?' *I glance at her, but she doesn't respond.* 'She thinks that a bit of psych-washing and I'll turn into the daughter she wants me to be. No offence, by the way. But that's about it.'

Skipping the part about how my mother doesn't get me because I don't slot into her neat and tidy life; how her plans for my future take no account of what I want, how nothing I say interests her. How that is the measure of my worth. There's more, like how even when I'm so tired my eyes close on their own, I can't sleep, and when I do, I have these dreams, so vivid that when I wake up, it's like they're real. Like I said, it's complicated.

'I see.'

She really doesn't, but then I haven't told the half of it. It'll take more than a crap painting before I do that.

'I ought to explain about my mother,' I add. Breaking the unwritten rule, answering questions she hasn't asked. Deflecting her while I still can. 'Because everything she and my father do, is like a-maz-ing.'

Giving it the full benefit of its three syllables, then rolling my eyes to make sure she gets it. 'They have their amazing jobs, incredibly expensive clothes, and they're always travel-ling . . . '

Only the problem is, I'm supposed to be amazing too and I'm not allowed to cut my hair and buy cool T-shirts from the market stall, with Guns N' Roses on them.

'Really? Where do you go?'

'I said they,' I point out, frowning. 'They don't take me with them. Half the time I'm in school, anyway. It kind of makes sense.'

Wondering if she'll work out the real reason, because it's obvious. They don't want me with them.

She looks faintly shocked.

'It's fine,' I tell her. 'It really is,' I add, because she looks as though she doesn't believe me. 'Anyway, they're probably not the kind of holidays you're picturing.'

'Oh,' she says, like a question. Oh?

'They go to cities, mostly. They like boutique hotels and shopping and art galleries and opera. Boutique hotels . . . not my thing,' I add, shaking my head, because you've seen one of them, you've seen them all and because I'd rather be lying in our garden reading a book.

'So who looks after you?'

'Gabriela — our housekeeper.'

Her face is confused. Clearly I'm not her regular fruitcake. 'It's cool. Actually, when my parents are away, I like it a lot.'

That bit's actually true, because I can wear shorts and the cheap clothes my mother doesn't know I have; because when they heave suitcases in the car and drive away, their demands and expectations go with them.

She pauses, then looks at me again, quizzically. It's when I know she's sensed she's missing something.

'It sounds good.' She says it quietly, then she puts her pen down. 'Shall we leave it there? For now?'

I look at my watch, then sit there, nonplussed, as she gets up, because we've another ten minutes. Is she a cheapskate, or is this a new therapist thing I haven't seen before?

She notices my hesitation. Pauses. 'Or was there something you wanted to talk about, before you go?'

I shake my head. It's one of the rules. I have to remember that. You give them what they're expecting. Enough, but that's all. No more.

40

* * *

On the way home, my mother plays Madame Butterfly turned up over the sound of the air con.

'How did you get on?' she shouts.

I reach forward to turn the volume down, just in case, for once, she actually listens.

'OK.'

'Good,' says my mother. 'We'll tell your father it went well. And I'll ask Gabriela to make another appointment . . . '

Turning the music up even louder, so that her voice is lost, but music's good for that. Gives her somewhere to hide.

' . . . for next week.' Shouting again. 'Abigail told me she's supposed to be good.'

I don't know what good's supposed to mean, but she's OK. Different to the others. She really listens, to more than just my words.

I turn my eyes away, thinking of Toby, with his thick tufted hair. He throws things and yells a lot, so my mother says. Mostly at Abigail. Poor Abigail. She says that a lot too, because she only ever talks to Abigail. Not poor Toby. But not everyone can do that. Imagine being other people.

As we leave the motorway, I lean my head against the window, gazing through the trees at the iron-clad sky. I'm not sure what I'm feeling, or if I'm feeling anything at all. Then the trees clear and there are fields, fading into the distance until you can't tell where they end and the clouds begin.

41

'What is all this stuff?' she shouts. 'You'd think they'd spray it. Don't open the windows. I don't want it getting in the car.'

I watch the stuff she's talking about, the tiny, weightless willow seeds that float until they settle on the ground like beautiful, ethereal snowdrifts. But in her orderly, designer world there is no place for such things.

I lean my head against the window, blocking out her voice and the music and the cold air whooshing in my face, thinking how there's so much I can never tell her, looking at the sky that's heavy, muggy grey.

Waiting for the rain.

6

2016

My thoughts are interrupted by a familiar voice.
'Noah? Hello? You're in there, aren't you?'

Clara lives next door. A close friend of my late
aunt, I've got used to her coming and going,
once I got over the way she'd let herself in when
it suited her and how I'd turn round to find her
standing there, just behind me, forced to listen
while she regaled me with some screwy
observation or other.

★ ★ ★

The first time it happened, I don't know how
long she'd been watching me. Lost in my work, I
hadn't noticed her until she spoke.

'*So you're Noah . . .* '

Startled, I'd glanced up to see a woman
standing there, with long, greying hair and sharp
eyes that looked me up and down.

'So you've come to put Delilah's things in
order then?' She broke off, scrutinizing me, as I
felt myself shrink under her gaze.

'I suppose.' I frowned. I hadn't really thought
about things being put in order. 'She left me the
cottage. I thought I'd stay. Well, for now, at least.'

She stared at me. 'You don't sound so sure.'
Her voice held a trace of an accent I couldn't

identify, her tone leaving me vaguely uncomfortable.

It happened a few times, before we slowly got to know each other. We'd never be friends. She was too disapproving, frequently and outspokenly critical of my solitary ways, but we rubbed along, Clara asking probing questions about subjects I didn't want to talk about, then sweeping aside my objections one by one, distaste written on her face, as though she was peeling the layers of an onion.

'You should get yourself out of here. Go to the pub. Meet people your own age.' By people she meant girls — I think Clara thought I should have been happily married off. I'd grunted something unintelligible, resisting the temptation to tell her that I'd come close — twice — but that was enough for anyone and I didn't plan on doing it again.

'It's better to be alone than with the wrong person.' I'd said it with the defensiveness that comes from being badly hurt, knowing that wasn't what she was getting at, yet again aware of her unblinking gaze.

I didn't want to drag myself out to make small talk with strangers. Even when I found myself a part-time role in a local solicitor's office, it wasn't good enough for her. But my reason for moving here was to write, I kept reminding myself. Clara hadn't approved of that, either.

'So whatever is it that keeps you in your books?' Words laced with disapproval, as on yet another occasion she'd caught me unawares.

Turning back to my work, I'd finished the

44

sentence I was writing, then looked up. 'I used to be a lawyer.'

Even I could hear how defensive I sounded, because it had been an identity I'd worn, like an expensive coat, which in the blinkered mindset of the society we live in, had set me apart as a recognizable someone who garnered respect. An identity I'd yet to replace.

'I know that,' she'd said impatiently. 'Not now, though, are you?'

She wasn't intentionally unkind, as I found out later. It was just her way, in part cultural, and maybe also the legacy of a difficult life that had left her direct, brusque, to the point.

I remember I'd hesitated, because most people didn't understand. I'd given up trying to explain, but then this was Clara. 'If you really want to know, it's research for my novels. Into the psychological profiles — of murderers, mostly.'

I'd watched her as she drew back. 'Sweet Jesus. Delilah didn't tell me that.'

'She didn't know. I don't really talk about it. But there are case studies, weighing up any number of possible causal factors. Like family background. Whether the father or mother is an offender, whether other lesser crimes are committed first. Even the structure of the brain. But there are other cases, less easily explained, where a solid pillar of society somehow undergoes a fundamental change and becomes a murderer. Like John Smith, who worked his whole life, until one day he jacked in his job, then went home and shot his wife . . . '

With my captive audience of one, I'd been

getting into my stride, enjoying myself because John Smith was my classic example, until the look of horror on her face stopped me.

'OK,' I'd said more soberly. 'Let me ask you something. About first impressions. What do you think of them?'

Clara loved to light the touchpaper and watch what followed. But that time she'd shaken her head. 'That's the trouble with you young people.'

Saying 'young' as though it was a bad thing.

' . . . you're in too darn much of a hurry to notice.'

'Notice what, exactly?'

'The difference,' she'd replied slowly, as if I were particularly stupid, 'between what people want you to see — and what's real.'

'Exactly!' I'd said triumphantly. 'That's what I was saying.'

Clara had glared at me; then, shaking her head, stared out of the window. 'You're talking about eyes,' she'd muttered. 'Eyes tell you nothing, don't you know that? You need to look with your heart.'

An awkward silence had fallen between us after that, heavy with irritation on my part at Clara's all-knowingness, because I didn't need her to tell me appearances could be deceptive; disgust on hers at my arrogance, as no doubt she perceived it.

Coming over, she'd picked up one of my books on the Jack the Ripper murders.

'And you . . . enjoy this?' Her face was unfathomable.

I'd thought about it before I answered. 'Not

46

enjoy, exactly. All murders are someone's tragedy. But think of the murderer for a moment . . . Some people just don't have boundaries, I know that, and there are some who claim to enjoy it. I know,' I added, seeing her face. 'But for me, it's the psychology that's so interesting, because if you knew what drove someone to such extremes, maybe you could do something to prevent it.'

'Oh, I wouldn't go getting your hopes up,' Clara had muttered darkly. 'Some folks have it in them, no matter what.'

I'd put my book down. 'Okay. Now you're talking about psychopaths.'

I'd caught her interest. Sitting down, she'd leaned towards me. 'I should know. I was married to one. Thought the world of himself, but he didn't give a fig about anyone — not even his own wife. Wasn't a killer, though. Tell you what I think. There's plenty of people don't think anything of it — raping and killing, for the sake of it.'

'Exactly.' I sat back and looked at her. 'And there's a reason. Upbringing, a constant diet of violence around them, the TV every time they turn it on . . . '

Clara grunts. 'Maybe. But folks like that don't change.'

'Do you really believe that? Isn't that a rather depressing view of humanity?'

'Yes, well, most likely you think it is. But you young people are all the same. Always looking for excuses, instead of facing the facts.'

'I don't believe that's true,' I'd started to

47

argue. But she'd taken offence for some reason, stomping off, slamming the door behind her.

I'd got used to her, and having no family to speak of, no friends, I found her inherent nosiness, her way of speaking her mind, vaguely companionable if somewhat abrasive. Even now, with a modestly successful published novel to my name, if it had given me credibility in her eyes, she'd never said.

'Haven't eaten, have you?' she says tonight, a statement framed as a question to which she already knows the answer, looking disapprovingly around the kitchen, unwrapping the dish she's carrying before placing it on the table.

'Thanks. I was just looking for something.' Tins of beans I bought at the garage. Maybe a drink.

She shakes her head. 'No point you even looking. You never have anything in them cupboards of yours. You need to get out, Noah. Find that new supermarket that's just opened. Go to the pub before you forget how to talk to people. Does you no good, shutting yourself away.' The familiarity of the years we've known each other, condensed into bluntness.

'It's not that bad. There's the vegetable garden, remember? The one you nagged me about looking after?' I point out, thinking of the plot in the garden that according to Clara had been so lovingly tended by my aunt; that now, however hard I worked on it, in my inexperienced hands was only minimally productive. 'I go to the office now and then. And I talk to you.'

'I mean young people,' she says sharply.

48

'Yeah. Well, it so happens I'm going away — '
I break off. 'You eating with me?'

She pulls off her jacket and slides stiffly onto
one of the wooden chairs. 'If you've something to
tell that's interesting, and not about them books
of yours, I may as well.'

'OK.' I rummage in a cupboard for two plates.
'Drink?'

'Whisky, you mean,' she says drily. 'Go on
then. But a small one. With a drop of water.'

I've poured her enough of them over the last
four years to know precisely how Clara likes her
whisky. Pouring another for myself, I join her at
the table.

'I had a call earlier. From someone who used
to be a friend.' I take a mouthful of her casserole.
'This is good.'

'Rabbit.' She continues eating, jerking her
head just once. 'You were telling me about a
phone call.'

'Well, there's been a murder in the town where
we grew up. He thought I'd want to know,
because a girl we knew at school is the main
suspect.'

I take another mouthful, still puzzled as to
why Will is so convinced of April's guilt. Feeling
Clara's eyes on me, unflinching.

'It's strange. We're not even friends. In fact, I
hadn't spoken to him for years. He's sure she's
guilty.' Frowning, I put my fork down. And as I
knew only too well, he'd been in love with her
too. 'Christ. How can he think that?'

Clara takes another mouthful. 'You don't,
then?'

I shake my head. 'I can't see it. I'd even go so far as to say I utterly, absolutely, know she isn't. She couldn't have done it.'

Clara frowns. 'You could be wrong.'

Sitting back in my chair, I shrug. 'I can see why you'd say that, but I'm not. I know I'm not. And you're forgetting something.'

She glances at me. 'And what might that be?'

'Well, firstly, I knew her — really well.' I don't tell Clara I was in love with her. 'But also, even if I didn't, I've spent years of my life trying to understand the criminal mind, as you know. I've profiled dozens of killers, male and female, from all kinds of backgrounds who committed all kinds of crimes. It's taught me something.'

'Ah. Those books of yours again. It hasn't taught you one thing, though, has it?' She raises her lined face, her rheumy eyes staring into mine. 'People act on impulse. Make mistakes. They're people, aren't they? It's not scientific method you're on about. It's judgement, pure and simple.'

Meaning my judgement, and I feel myself grow irritated, because every time we discuss my work, it ends like this.

'You know what?' I look at Clara. 'No disrespect, but you could just as easily be wrong, too.'

It's a good answer. She nods slowly; then her face crinkles into a rare smile, which just as abruptly vanishes.

'So, you're going to see her.' It's a statement rather than a question.

I hesitate, then nod.

But instead of the scathing retort I'm expecting, she surprises me. 'Could be a good thing, couldn't it? I mean, could be good for you. Don't look like that! Writers need life experience to draw on.' She stares across the table at me. 'Don't they?'

'You need imagination. And there's nothing wrong with my writing.' She's touched a nerve and I'm defensive again. 'Anyway, I've had plenty. And writers don't need people. People clutter your head. They take up too much of your time. I'd never get anything done.'

Telling myself that it was true and that the odd pang of loneliness was a small price to pay for the simple life that made writing easier. OK, so I'd kept up my occasional mornings at Jed Luxton's office, because until I made a name for myself as a writer, being a part-time lawyer meant I was someone. But if I was honest, apart from the occasional intrusion from Clara, I preferred to be alone.

I decide to tell her. 'I may end up staying for a while. If the police are going to charge her, she'll need a lawyer. I thought if there's no one else, it might as well be me.'

Clara snorts. 'You?'

But instead of being undermined, I feel my resolve strengthen as I sit back and look at her.

'Can you do that?' She stares at me.

'I still work,' I remind her, ignoring her derisive snort. 'And I know, before you say anything, that Jed Luxton only deals with the most minor offenders.' On top of which I only very occasionally show my face. 'But there's

51

nothing really to stop me.' I pause for a moment before adding, more heartfelt, the truth. 'Anyway, I can't not.'

Clara's long drawn-out sigh ends in silence as I wait, because there'll be more. Clara's never silent for long. But to my surprise, she doesn't ask why.

'You even look in the mirror these days?'

Words that are candid rather than insulting, but still startle me, even though I know what she's saying.

'I'll get a haircut,' I tell her. 'I'll even shave.'

But as she shakes her head, I know it's more than that. That physical neglect cuts deeper than just skin; that everything about me reeks of failure.

'So when are you going? To see the girl. In a prison, is she?'

'No. Actually, she's not. That's another thing. She took an overdose. She's on life support.'

Clara looks at me as if I'm insane. 'So you're going back to do the job you hated to defend an old girlfriend who's killed someone and then tried to kill herself.'

'It's not like that,' I tell her obstinately.

★ ★ ★

Having extracted what she wants from me, Clara doesn't stay long. Pouring another whisky, I take it into my office, where I power up my laptop and search for the address of the hospital where April was taken. Then I go upstairs and run a bath, scrutinizing my appearance in the glare of the light bulb above the mirror, forced to see myself through Clara's eyes, and that it's far worse than I'd thought. I knew my hair needed cutting, but as I examine my reflection, I realize I've aged, my eyes dulled and my skin puffy, the appearance of sharp cheekbones making me gaunt. All the more shocking because, until now, I haven't noticed.

I pack enough clothes for a few days, including my suit, before deciding that with a long drive ahead of me in the morning, and feeling suddenly tired just at the thought of it, I should probably have an early night.

Only my mind is too wired, sleep impossible. I toss and turn, restless, listening to the bark of a fox, then a lone owl and the last, blood-curdling death throes of its prey, until in the early hours, eventually my eyes close.

But even when it comes, sleep brings no relief and I'm flung into a vivid dream of a burning woman, her dark shape featureless, her face silhouetted against an orange sky. In the midst of the flames, she's holding something out to me.

'This is my gift,' she keeps saying, her voice urgent, over and over, thrusting it towards me.

But each time I reach to take it, the flames force me back so that I have to watch, powerless, as the fire consumes her, only realizing when I wake, my heart pounding and my skin coated in sweat. She never told me what it was.

7

1995

'Man, I need to get out of this dump.' Will was prone to exaggerating. He'd already packed, leaving his large bedroom empty, except for the pile of boxes and suitcases. I was putting off my own packing as long as possible, but then I wasn't leaving for another week. I felt exactly as he did, though. Since my father had died, my mother's anxious, neurotic ways were driving me mad.

'You'll miss having your meals cooked for you,' I remind him. 'And your washing done . . . '

'I won't. I'll be too busy partying and schmoozing with all those girls . . . ' Will closed his eyes and sighed lasciviously. 'Maybe I'll find one that can cook.'

'I wouldn't count on it. Uni students are all rabid women's libbers,' I warned him, thinking he was going to be disappointed. 'Pub? Or is that too boring for a budding Cambridge student such as yourself? Remind me, why are we both committing to some of the most complicated subjects known to man?'

'So we'll be rich and famous. Come on, let's get out of here.'

We walked the half-mile to the North Star, with the easy self-centredness of being eighteen

54

years old and on the brink of breaking away — from loving, but nevertheless constraining, parents on Will's part and on mine, from my increasingly overanxious mother.

'This is it, mate.' Will couldn't keep the excitement out of his voice. 'After this, it all changes. I know we'll come back, but we'll have our own places. No one looking over us. And *girls, think of all the girls* . . . ' He held up his hands to the heavens and pretended to sink to his knees.

Bizarrely, while I seemed caught in a stage of perpetual lankiness, Will had grown from a short, spotty kid into a babe magnet — but then Will had never lacked confidence. Even round here, he wasn't short of female attention, though his activities were somewhat inhibited by living at home. But all that, he was convinced, was about to change.

'It probably won't be quite how you're imagining,' I told him, as we walked up the steps.

'It probably will.' He pushed the door open and I followed him in.

I was going to miss him — for about a week — until I headed off too, to Bristol.

'There'll be lectures,' I reminded him. 'And you'll have competition. There'll be other ginger studs hanging around . . . '

'Yeah, but none with my charm and charisma. Watch and learn, buddy. Watch and learn.'

He ambled over to the bar, where a blonde-haired girl stood with her back to us, buying a drink. I watched as he exchanged a few words, his head bent towards her. I didn't need to see his face to picture the self-deprecating smile that girls seemed to find irresistible; the seemingly instant fascination that he adopted, as if she were the only girl in the world. He knew all the tricks. I was still watching, a little enviously, when from behind me, I heard my name.

'Noah?'

As I turned round, I felt the smile plastered on my face, even before I saw her.

'April! I don't believe it!'

So many times, I'd dreamed of such a moment. Struck by adolescent clumsiness, I felt the years peel away. I didn't know what to say. I just looked at her, dumbstruck. Still lovely, her hair in long red waves down her back, her eyes lit by secrets.

'You seem . . . ' She paused, her look teasing.

'Taller?' I said it jokingly; hopefully, too, wanting her not to remember the awkward schoolboy, and instead see someone altogether more worthy of her. Then as we stood there, in seconds, it was back. The old magic, its tendrils tightening round my heart, as I remembered myself.

'Look, can I buy you a drink or something?'

Or something . . . I took a deep breath. What was I thinking? Get a grip, man. You're not Noah the nerd, you're cool.

I bought her a vodka and Coke, glad that I really was eighteen, and no longer had to worry about John the landlord challenging me about my age; and hardly believing how shit the timing was, seeing her here, just when I was about to go away.

'So what are you doing here?' I placed our drinks on the table, trying not to spill them, and pulled out the chair opposite her.

'I came to stay with Bea,' she said, nodding over to the blonde girl at the bar still being chatted up by Will. That sophisticated creature was Bea? In the two years I hadn't seen her, she'd changed beyond belief.

'So where do you live?' All of a sudden, I had a million questions. 'What are you doing?'

'London.' Her eyes wore a slightly guarded look. 'I have a flat share. I just got a job in a restaurant there. Cindy's Diner. Nothing special but Cindy's really nice and it pays the bills.'

'Who do you live with?' Avidly trying to picture this new life she had, about which I knew nothing.

'Her name's Edie. She works at Cindy's too . . . '

As she talked, I hung on her every word, wanting to love what she was telling me, but in truth, what I felt was disappointment. She'd been so clever, so smart. And I knew there was nothing wrong with it, but she was destined for greater things than being a waitress.

'Tell me about you.'

Her smile made my heart turn over. 'There's not much to tell. I got my A levels and next week I'm off to uni. I'm reading law.'

She sat back and folded her arms. 'Wow, Noah! That's brilliant. But I guess you were always going to study something like that. I'm pleased for you.'

Her voice was quiet, her eyes bright as they

held mine. Suddenly, it was there. Right in front of me. The chance I'd been waiting for all my life.

'I have a week,' I said quickly, feeling a sudden heat in my cheeks, seeing Will and Bea coming over and knowing the time to do this was now, before it was too late. 'Before I leave. Can I call you?'

A look of surprise crossed her face, then she nodded. Hastily I wrote down the number she gave me. The rest of the evening passed in a blur, as did a long night in which sleep evaded me. I'd ended up lying there, gazing at the ceiling, hardly daring to believe my luck, wondering what tomorrow would hold, until eventually I must have slept, waking the next morning, my heart hammering in my chest as soon as I remembered.

The house quiet, I leaped out of bed and called her. In the seconds while the phone rang, before she picked up, imagining a million reasons why this wasn't going to happen. I could have written the wrong number down or she could have changed her mind, found any number of excuses. But then she answered and the same smile I'd seen last night was there in her voice.

We arranged to meet in town early that afternoon. Having chosen my clothes with care, I took enough money to buy lunch from the precious supply I'd earned over the summer and carefully saved, to take to uni. But then April was worth every penny.

I got there early, waiting on the bench outside

the shopping centre, checking my watch every few minutes, feeling the same fear I'd felt when I'd called her, still half expecting her to stand me up.

But my worries were unfounded. And as she walked towards me, her hair falling softly down her back, her frame small in loose-fitting jeans and leather jacket, I felt myself fall in love all over again.

'Hi.' I stood up, suddenly self-conscious.

'Hi.' She looked up at me, smiling as though there was something amusing her. 'You look nice.'

Awkwardly, I glanced down at my cotton shirt and neatly ironed trousers, which suddenly seemed wrong, but they were all I had. 'Thanks. So do you,' I added hurriedly.

'Thank you.' This time, her eyes smiled back at me. 'So, what did you have in mind?'

'I don't know.' I felt foolish. 'We could have lunch — if you haven't eaten? Or go for a walk? Or see a movie — if you like. Only I don't know what's on, but we could find out . . . '

As we walked across the street, I babbled on, until I felt her hand slip under my arm, and the softness of her skin on mine stunned me into silence.

We settled on Cornish pasties in brown paper bags, bought from a small corner shop, then made our way towards the park. We shouldn't waste such a beautiful day, April said, her hair glinting in the sun. So we walked, away from the parched flower beds, the chatter of the people sitting in groups on the grass, towards an empty bench under the shade of a tree.

I'd waited so long for this. Dreamed that it would be as if we were soulmates, who because of the bond each of us recognized, would instantly confide our innermost thoughts. But it wasn't quite as I'd hoped. The easy and relaxed banter of old friends was absent and the conversation stilted, skirting round the one subject that in the end I had to ask her about.

'I was really worried about you,' I said eventually, referring to the last time I'd seen her, just before she moved away. 'Before you left, you said you'd write.'

Her face was a picture of astonishment. 'But I did. Several times, Noah. When you didn't reply, I gave up. I couldn't see the point.'

'I never got them.' I was filled with relief because she'd written, but also anger that her letters had never reached me, as I imagined someone, who could only have been my mother, intercepting them.

'My mother,' I frowned. 'Since my father died, she does crazy things.' Which was true, but if I thought about it, she'd been strange before he'd gone. Today, however, was not about my mother.

'Well, I wrote to tell you I was fine. And to thank you for finding me, that time — ' She broke off, gazing into the distance, as if remembering. 'Anyway, then I wrote another letter when I moved again, to give you my new address.'

Which made two, at least. Possibly more, their contents to remain forever a mystery to me.

'I never got any of them,' I said hotly.

'It doesn't matter.' She shrugged, but her face

60

was turned away from me and I couldn't tell if she meant it.

'But it does.' I was quietly furious.

'Really, Noah. It's OK.' I felt her hand on my arm.

It wasn't. So much time had been wasted, time during which I'd believed I meant nothing to her, because someone who thought they'd known what was best for me had taken the decision out of my hands. That it was behind us, in the past, made no difference.

I continued eating in silence, not tasting the rest of my pasty but only the bitter tang of resentment, until April spoke.

'Tell me about your course.'

I was still angry, but not wanting to waste the day, I let myself be distracted. It was the last time we spoke of it — for many years. I'd wittered on about the course options I'd chosen, the work experience I'd done that summer, the reading list I was ploughing my way through, thinking she'd find it boring, but she listened intently.

'So, when you've qualified you'll be a solicitor? Hey! That's impressive.'

But I didn't want to talk about myself. 'I always thought you'd continue studying. You always did well — in school. Before . . . ' My voice died away.

Wondering from her silence if I'd pushed her too far.

'If things had turned out differently, then maybe I would. But now, I don't have time,' she said. Her voice was bright, but I liked to think there was regret there too. 'Now that I have rent to pay, I need to work.'

'It doesn't mean you never can,' I said, more gently. It seemed so unfair, in my eyes, that someone so talented should go to waste. 'You should think about training while you work.'

But she'd shaken her head and placed her small hand on my arm. 'You don't get it, Noah. It isn't always that simple. Not for everyone.'

★ ★ ★

We met the following day, lapsing into an easier familiarity; and then again, the one after that, on a glorious late-summer afternoon, the sun hot and the air still, when we walked up Reynard's Hill.

Her cheeks were flushed from the climb, the sun and, I wanted to believe also, from being with me. Then as the path levelled out, it was like standing on top of the world, the jagged edge of it softened by bleached grasses and the tiny pale stars that were dried scabious flowers. As we stood there, I felt the last few years fall away. The disappointments, the broken dreams, the hurt, so that I was like my fifteen-year-old self, alone at last with my goddess.

'I love it here.' Her voice was wistful. And as she spoke, I forgot all about my earlier anger. None of that mattered. She was here, now. It was suddenly so simple.

'I used to think you were a goddess,' I said humbly. 'That you were from another world.'

She turned to me, her eyes huge with astonishment.

'You didn't know?'

'I had no idea. No idea at all. *Oh, Noah* . . . '

In that exact moment, as I looked into her eyes, saw the flicker of her pulse in the skin of her neck, I knew I hadn't imagined it, that she felt it too, the magic between us that I had always known was there. Then she stepped towards me.

That was when I leaned down and kissed her. A long, sweet kiss that was everything I'd dreamed of and much more. Her lips were soft, her hair like silk between my fingers and, when she kissed me back, my heart became hers forever.

'For years, I've dreamed of this,' I murmured into her hair. 'Only if I'm dreaming now, I never want to wake up.'

'It isn't a dream,' she said, reaching a finger to my lips, as we stood for several minutes, not moving. Then she took my hand and placed it against her heart.

But all I could feel was her warmth through her clothes, the soft swell of her breasts. My fingers moving, searching, questioning. She didn't stop me.

This time it was April who kissed me. Who led me under the trees, where we lay on fallen leaves and very slowly she let me undress her.

⋆ ⋆ ⋆

It was dark by the time I got home. I crept in, wondering if anyone would be able to tell, just by looking at me. As I closed the front door behind me, my mother called out from the kitchen.

'Noah? Is that you? Where've you been?'

As I thought of April's letters, resentment coursed through me. I prepared to confront her, but then her face came into view, wearing the perpetually anxious expression that these days never left her. I couldn't do it.

'Do you remember that girl, Ma? The one I helped — from my school, a couple of years ago?'

My words were tempered, not just by her world-weariness but by the knowledge that she wouldn't understand, that she'd never known how love could truly make you feel. The rush that was joyous, tolerant, impulsive all at once. I knew she'd never loved my father that way. You couldn't know love and end up empty, as she was.

I watched her closely, not sure she'd even remember. Her medication meant that at best her brain worked slowly — and at her worst, she jumbled words and lost threads, hearing as if through cotton wool. Change had gradually crept up on her, unnoticed, the way it did with people you saw all the time; until the day I'd properly looked, shocked, seeing a stranger.

A troubled expression flickered across her face. 'The girl who was hurt.'

'That's right. It was strange,' I said slowly. 'Only she said she'd write. And she never did — or did she write to you, Ma?'

I watched her eyes flicker again, then shift towards the window. 'I don't remember,' she

64

said, more clearly than she'd said anything in a long time.

The helpless fury that rose up in me was pointless. The moment had long passed — almost three whole years ago. Turning away, I went to finish packing.

She was lying. She remembered, I was almost certain. For whatever reason, she'd taken the letters before I'd seen them. It reinforced why I couldn't wait to get away from here.

★　★　★

April and I had arranged to meet again the following day, our last before she returned to London.

This time, we would stay in touch, I'd decided. No matter what. London and Bristol weren't a million miles apart. I could get the train up to see her at weekends and she could come to stay in Bristol. But that night, I couldn't sleep, instead replaying every second of the afternoon. The incredible feeling of losing myself in April's body, the scent of her, as I lay there restlessly, hating the thought of us being apart.

In the darkest, most silent hours, the solution came to me, so obvious I wondered I hadn't thought of it before. The world wouldn't miss another lawyer. Instead of going to uni, I'd go with April back to London. Get a job. We'd be together. My mother wouldn't like it, I knew that, but I was eighteen. I was an adult and I was leaving anyway. It was up to me where I went.

Now I'd made the decision, sleep was out of

the question. I got up and found some paper, then sitting at my desk, wrote my mother a letter. It was cowardly, but it was the only way I could be certain she wouldn't stop me.

And with the letter written, as the dawn light crept through my curtains, at last I slept.

8

I slept until midday, lying in bed as the hazy recollection of the previous day drifted over me, the magnitude of what I'd decided only mildly shocking in the light of day. It was inevitable, that much was clear to me. Then seeing the time with horror, I'd leaped out of bed, afraid I'd miss April, imagining her reaction when I told her I was coming with her. As I showered, rehearsing what I'd say.

Uni's not for me . . . I can't stand more years of studying . . . I thought I'd go to London and get a job . . . I'd say it casually, as though it wasn't important to me, frightened she'd try to change my mind, when the truth was that the thought of being away from her was killing me.

And I knew she felt the same. After yesterday — I'd seen it in her eyes, felt it in the way her body responded to mine. I looked at the bag I'd packed the previous night. At all my uni stuff still piled on the floor, thinking only fleetingly of the law career I was turning my back on. Then glancing at my watch again, I tore down the stairs and out of the door.

In my haste, I was halfway down the street when I realized I'd forgotten my wallet, sprinting back and letting myself in, cursing the time I was wasting. It was as I came downstairs for the second time that, out of the corner of my eye, I saw it. The envelope on the hall table, with my name on it.

The handwriting was unfamiliar but as I ripped it open, almost as if I'd guessed, I'd felt my heart start to pound; then as I read it, stop altogether, as my dreams, my hopes, my plans for the future, all of them melted away.

Dear Noah,

I've decided to go back to London early. I think it's for the best. You are sweet, dearest Noah. The sweetest boy I've ever known, but even a goddess can fall from grace. I don't deserve your devotion or that pedestal you put me on.

There's too much you don't know about me. But I don't want you to know, I just want to remember what we had.

I read it again, hearing a sob that seemed to come from deep inside me. I couldn't lose her. Not now, after the last three days, when it had become clear we were meant to be together. I'd been heartbroken the last time she left, when I was fifteen — or so I'd believed at the time. But it was nothing compared to this. Wave after wave of utter despair washed over me, and as I drowned, I felt a new kind of pain grip my heart, then rip it in two.

ELLA

We weave the first strands of friendship like a spider's web. For a therapist, she's cool. But then I get caught.

'So what about when you have friends round?' Julia asks casually, the next time I see her.

I hesitate, because 'casually' is anything but; and it's the F-word. It was there the minute I walked in, because it always is. It was just a matter of time before we got to it. It's taken her three appointments. Mostly they get there in one.

'It's complicated.' I think how I'm going to explain that it's just like my clothes.

'My parents insist on the right kind of friends. The ones that get invited over to our house, that is.' I pause, then look directly at her. 'It doesn't work though, does it? I mean, you can talk about stuff with anyone . . . '

Like this crap, I'm thinking, but don't say.

'Only it doesn't make you close. They have to, like, really get you . . . '

Like laugh at the same stupid crazy things and share secrets.

'I do have those kind of friends. Proper ones,' I add hurriedly, before she thinks I'm a total loser. 'Only they're at school.'

She nods slowly. 'They don't come over to your house?'

I shake my head. 'I don't really want them to,

69

because then my mother would get to know their mothers, and she'd be in the middle of everything . . . And it would ruin it. School's different.'

What I really mean is, when I'm there, I'm different. It's the same when my parents go away. I'm more like me, or at least the me I want to be.

'So your mother organizes your life,' she says quietly.

Not just organize, she freaking controls it, that's why I like it when she goes away.

'She probably wants what she thinks is best for you. Is that so bad?' she adds, yet another question fluttering around, a little annoying fly I want to swat away.

There's a vase of stiff, scentless roses on the windowsill. Roses. Rose garden. My mother, every-fricking-where I go. I glance at my watch, thinking of her, perched on the grey sofa on the other side of the door, flicking through Vogue magazine or maybe the paint charts the interior designer brought her, checking her phone every few minutes. Inconvenienced, because Gabriela had to sprain her wrist, today of all days; that she's had to shoehorn my appointment into her diary yet again, when she should be somewhere else.

Feeling a jolt as another strand of the web gives way.

'Why don't you tell me about your friends — your school friends, that is?'

'Well, Sophie and Katarina are my closest friends. Sophie's like me, into music. Kat's on the drama course.'

'But you don't really see them out of school?'

'Not really.' I shrug. 'Kat's family live in Italy. I went out to stay with them — once. And Sophie's travel a lot.'

'You must miss them.'

Do I? I've never thought about it like that. Anyway, it's not like I'm on my own. I have Theo. And sometimes I'd rather be alone.

★   ★   ★

'You were a long time. Did you have a good talk?'

One of my mother's questions that doesn't require an answer. The seamless movement as she glances in her driving mirror, smoothing an imaginary strand of hair behind her ear and then changing gear, so that I'm pushed back into my seat as she pulls out and accelerates past the car in front.

'God, some people shouldn't be on the roads,' she says, turning to her radio, clicking through the stations until she finds what she wants. Not seeing the car coming towards us until it blasts its horn and swerves out of her way.

'That's better. What were we saying? Yes, I'm sure a few more sessions will help.'

By help, she means effect some miraculous transformation on me into super-daughter, with the incredible social life and the hordes of desirable, glamorous friends she thinks I ought to have — forgetting the more basic, fundamental things that are totally missing from my life. Noticeable only by their absence.

When I get home, I kick my shoes off and run, feeling the cool soft grass under my bare feet. I stretch out my arms, catching handfuls of air, relishing my freedom, wishing Theo was here under the low branches of the old cedar, a ray of sun lighting his face.

9

2016

Talking to Will unleashes a storm surge of memories. About him and about April too; about the last time I drove to Musgrove, for my mother's funeral, grieving and guilt-stricken that I hadn't been with her at the end; the feeling that I'd deserted her; that it took losing her to see how alike we'd been, both of us unhappy, lonely; not knowing until it was too late. About my childhood; a sense of dread I could never explain; the hollow feeling I could never fill.

It's early when I leave the house, the past still preoccupying me, its presence unwelcome, as I'm assailed by the kind of silent questions that can't be answered, that only belong to such an hour. As I drive, I'm wondering where it went wrong; why April fell out of love with me; where my mother's inherent sadness came from; why Will betrayed me. Unable to stop the most illogical of thoughts that, as the common denominator of them all, I'm somehow responsible, when I hear an echo of Clara's voice.

'You young people don't know how good you have it.'

It's almost as if she's here, beside me, in the car. Irritation rises in me at her all-knowingness. And in a sense, she's right, because I've never been homeless or starving, but even so. She has no idea. I've suffered, I know that. Maybe no less or no more than anyone else, but what happened all those years ago almost destroyed me.

I keep driving, barely noticing as the darkness lightens to a pale, pearlescent blue, breaking off just outside Portsmouth to take the familiar road that winds its way towards Musgrove.

The decision's impulsive, more out of curiosity than anything else. And in the time I've been away, it's sprouted shiny new housing developments which encroach across farmland towards the hills lying to the north; the vast school playing fields that I remember are pockmarked by a rash of Portakabins, yet the road where I grew up is strangely untouched. I pass my parents' old house, where an unexpected wave of déjà vu sweeps over me. It's smaller, more modest than I remember, with the ghosts of my mother cooking and cleaning inside, my father in his office in town. I feel a nostalgic pang for my childhood which is as suddenly gone.

The North Star is a couple of similarly untouched streets away. Apart from the police presence, the tape cordoning off the car park, the yellow notices by the roadside asking passers-by for any information, it's as I remember it, yet changed forever by the knowledge that a man died here, brutally. Today, for now, I keep going, through the town that's stirring into life, taking the narrow lane that twists away from it towards the hills.

Temporarily blinded as the low sun edges above the horizon, I pull up where the lane ends

74

and a stony path stretches across bare fields until it fades into Reynard's Woods.

It's a quiet, timeless landscape that, unlike the town, hasn't changed. As a teenager, I had felt miles away out here, removed from the world. It had been the place where we were free from the constraints of the adults in our lives — a forty-minute walk that had been irrelevant when I was with April, that's somehow diminished by the ten minutes it takes by car.

* * *

On the outskirts of Tonbridge I find a small barber's shop, uncomfortable that by the time he's finished, without the overgrowth of hair to hide behind, I feel as exposed as the white skin round my hairline. Catching sight of my reflection as I'm walking out, I realize I also need clothes. Chinos and a couple of shirts, bought in haste from the first shop I come to.

Yet again, as I walk back to my car, swept along by the flow of people who have both place and purpose, I'm besieged by doubts, questioning what good I can do; why I'm even here. April deserves a better lawyer than I am. Silently reminding myself that I'm here out of choice. No one forced me. That now I've driven all this way, I should at least go and see her.

But too easily, round the next corner I find a B&B, in a white-painted Victorian town house that's just a short drive from the hospital where April is. The street is quiet, the house imposing in stature yet reassuringly shabby, so that I hesitate only briefly before I pull over and park.

When she opens the door to me, the landlady looks me up and down, as if for some reason I'm not what she's expecting. Then while she takes down my details, a column in yesterday's paper that has been left folded open on a glass-covered coffee table, as if on purpose, instantly catches my eye.

While she continues writing, I pick it up, hoping it's not what I think it is — to no avail.

A man's body was found in the early hours of yesterday morning, in the town of Musgrove, north of Portsmouth. His body was discovered by the landlord, in a car parked behind a local pub. He's been identified as local man Bryan Norton.

It's started. I'm guessing that already the press has picked up that there's a story because not all murders reach the national papers. Tomorrow, or the day after or the day after that, if a journalist has contacts, or if someone can be persuaded with a surreptitious bribe to let it slip, they'll have April's name too. Just a matter of time before they start tunnelling relentlessly into the past.

10

St Antony's is big, light and suffocating, with chemical-laced air that sticks in my nostrils. I read the ludicrously themed ward names and look at the incongruous, contemporary prints hung on the walls as I make my way into its maze of corridors, then through the swing doors to ICU, which is, by contrast, dark and windowless. A place where every breath is counted and every heartbeat measured; where life holds on. Just.

It seems miraculous that nobody stops me. I pass one or two small rooms with slatted blinds in the windows before I see a nurse walking towards me.

'It's a little early for visiting, sir.'

I feel myself frown. I hadn't even considered visiting hours. If someone's unconscious, what does it matter?

She looks kindly at me. 'Who've you come to see?'

'I'm sorry. I didn't think. April Moon.'

The nurse looks puzzled. 'We've no one by that name here, I'm afraid. You could check with reception in case she's been moved. Here, I'll show you the quickest way.'

As she walks past me towards the swing doors, I glance wildly around because I can't leave without seeing April, catching sight of a whiteboard near the nurses' station. Amongst the scrawled list of names, I see *April Rousseau* written in uneven letters and take a shot in the dark.

'Hey, just a minute . . . ' I catch her up. 'I got that wrong. She kept the name Rousseau after her divorce. I was forgetting. I haven't seen her in a very long time.'

I'm bluffing. I've no idea where the Rousseau comes from, but I'm counting on the nurse not knowing any more than I do.

She looks at me doubtfully. 'I'm sorry, but in the circumstances, you should probably leave . . . Mr . . . '

'Calaway,' I tell her, wondering if there's a Mr Rousseau and, if so, whether he's here. Does he even know? 'Noah Calaway. I know what's happened to her. Will Farrington told me. I imagine he's been here?'

'No one's been here.' The nurse shakes her head. Then she looks at me with interest. 'You know Mr Farrington?'

'Yes. And I know how this looks, just turning up like this,' I say, more confidently. 'But I'm an old friend. And once she comes round, I'll be acting as her lawyer.'

The nurse looks uncertain. 'Do you have proof?'

I shake my head resignedly. 'A driving licence with my name on it.' Knowing how lame it sounds, then adding, 'You can call the firm I do some work for, if you like.' Rummaging in my pocket for one of Jed's cards, finding there isn't one.

From the way she looks at me, I know she's

not sure. That she should probably ask me to leave. But then she sighs. 'It's all right. I believe you. But you won't be able to go in, I'm afraid. The police have someone with her round the clock. But you'd know about that, wouldn't you? Being a lawyer?'

'Of course.' I nod, but it had completely slipped my mind. She's right, of course. With April a suspect, the police won't be leaving anything to chance.

Glancing around, the nurse lowers her voice. 'Just a suggestion, but if by any chance the sister comes round, tell her you're Mrs Rousseau's lawyer. It'll save a lot of trouble. She's along there — in bed seven.'

I nod gratefully. 'Thanks.'

Guessing that it's my connection to Will that's swung her decision in my favour, I walk in the direction she's pointed me in, until I reach a door on which there's a number seven. It's another tiny room with a slatted blind and, as I peer through, for a moment I think she's mistaken. The woman in the bed is tiny, fragile-looking, her skin like pale wax, her chest barely moving under the white sheet that's pulled up under her shoulders. Laid on top of it, one of her arms is threaded with lines that are plugged into the machines beside her.

Even through the window, I'm overwhelmed with the sense that she's not just unconscious. This woman's dying. Her heart might be beating and her lungs inflating, but she's too still, too empty of life.

A dulled shade of the glossy red I remember,

it's the hair that gives her away. I'm shocked as I take in the robust presence of the young PC sitting on a chair in the corner.

'It's a pity you can't go in and talk to her.' The same nurse, her voice quieter, comes from behind me. 'Even when patients don't respond, sometimes they can still hear. With people who've come round, some of them tell us that hearing voices is what they remember.'

'Has she opened her eyes at all?'

'Not yet.' The nurse's voice is gentle. 'She nearly didn't make it.'

I know she's telling me that even now, even though she's alive, April may not make it. It's in the spaces in between; what she doesn't say, the tone of her voice. Then I feel her hand, light on my shoulder, before she quietly turns and walks away. A memory comes back, a day I haven't thought of for many years, long enough ago that life was simple and untroubled, yet sharp as if it happened yesterday.

'*Do you remember that day?*' I ask her silently through the window, wondering if what the nurse said is true; if, from the distant place April's gone to, she can hear my voice, maybe she can hear my thoughts too.

'*On top of Reynard's Hill? I slipped. Nearly went over the edge. You saved me.*'

I pause, because I can still remember how the ground crumbled, falling away under my feet. '*Remember how we ran?*'

Ran until our legs gave way underneath us, tumbling us to the ground, where we laughed wildly, until our eyes locked and we fell into an

80

awed kind of silence.

That had been the thing about April. She'd had darker moments where, for a while, I'd lose her; but there'd been an overwhelming intensity about her, a desire to live each moment that doesn't tally with this frail woman who's taken an overdose.

As this and other thoughts race through my head, I'm still watching her for the faintest indication that she's sensed my presence, but she hasn't moved. There's not a flicker.

11

As I walk away, I'm caught, swinging between hope and despair, faith and cynicism, telling myself other people have come out of comas so there's no reason why April won't; yet convinced that whatever the nurse might think and wherever April is, she's too far away to hear me.

But on the drive back towards my B&B, my unease grows as I find myself going full circle. The North Star was hardly her local. April must have been in Musgrove for a reason.

To kill Norton? Before driving the hour or so home to take an overdose?

I push the thought from my mind, because there are people who can kill and people who can't — maybe a group in the middle who, if pushed, just might. Knowing that April isn't one of them and, when I least need it, hearing Clara's voice.

You could be wrong.

But she doesn't know April.

It's then I realize I can't leave her and my thoughts swiftly turn to what lies ahead: should I defend her? The painstaking research that's required; the in-depth scrutiny of April's life; the leaving-no-stone-unturned level of detail involved, in the pursuit of a single piece of information someone's deliberately hidden or forgotten about, that can make the difference between innocence and guilt, prison or freedom.

And it isn't obvious, whatever the police think, whatever Will says — not even with her phone and her glove found in Norton's car. Until they have fingerprints, a witness, a motive, nothing is certain.

*   *   *

Back in my room, my mind has already turned to the people in her life. Work colleagues, her friends, neighbours if there are any. Any family — and I need to find out about Norton, too, because there could be any number of innocent reasons behind their meeting that night. And just a twist of bad luck that the night they met up was the same night the murderer chose to strike.

I switch on my laptop and type April Rousseau, then Kent, into the search bar. It takes seconds to find two, one of whom I dismiss immediately, due to her age. I copy down the address of the other, then pause, because I'm acting for April, but without her consent and assuming that when she comes round she'd have no objection. Knowing I could just as easily be wrong; and that if I'm caught entering her house, it would entirely prejudice my case. Dismissing the thought just as quickly, knowing it's a chance I have to take.

*   *   *

That April is under police guard suggests her home may have been secured, but I at least have to check it out. With April's postcode typed into it, my satnav takes me a mile or so out of Tonbridge, along a meandering B-road and then into a quiet lane. As I turn into it, on either side are empty fields with just the occasional large house set in its own gardens, well spaced from its neighbours. I continue slowly along a stretch of a hundred yards or so, before coming to a sharp bend.

It's darker here, the lane narrowing to a single track under the cover of tall trees, their branches seeming to close overhead. Behind unkempt hedges, I glimpse one or two smaller houses before my satnav indicates that I've arrived.

Pulling over, I stop beside a narrow gate on which a sign says Holly Cottage. Then I hesitate, because this is where April lives and though at the moment it's quiet, the police will inevitably come and search here. I continue a few yards up the lane, where I pull onto the grass verge and turn the engine off. Then I wait, but not a car passes, nor is there a sign of anyone.

As I walk back down the lane and slip through the gate, I'm not sure what I'm expecting, but it's not this, a small stone cottage that looks as much a part of the landscape as the woods that surround it; its weathered, faded exterior the legacy of the elements, of time. Against the grey of the flint, the brickwork around the windows is an ugly red, the paint on the frames cracked and peeling to reveal the grain of the wood underneath, its appearance softened by the mass of sprawling borders, the pale green of newly unfurled leaves, the curved paths cut into unmown grass full of wild flowers.

The entire garden is edged by trees, and I look up, my eye drawn not only to their height, but to the gnarled spread of their branches. Then I notice more trees, only they're smaller, a whole new generation, still saplings, planted at intervals here and there. But it's the sound that gets to me. Surrounding me, it's stereophonic; the wind through the leaves and birdsong.

★   ★   ★

I'm still caught in its spell as I walk round to the back, checking for an unlocked door or unlatched window, when suddenly the back of my neck prickles. Slowly turning, I look around, seeing nothing, yet with an unmistakable sense that I'm being watched.

12

1999

After April went back to London early, I was numb. I'd been prepared to give up everything for her. Even move, just to be with her. Not only had I lost her, I'd lost a future that had so briefly, brightly presented itself. I felt let down — and cheated too. The 'sweet' in her letter was patronizing. Nor did I accept her allusions to a dark secret that would ultimately keep us apart. Of course there were things we didn't know about each other. In the few days we'd spent together, we'd just started. Now, we'd never have the chance.

The excitement of my plans to go to London became a distant memory. Forced to push all thoughts of April from my head, I ripped up the letter I'd written to my mother. Now, I couldn't leave for Bristol soon enough.

It took days rather than the weeks or months I'd believed it would, but immersed in student life, I discovered that the teenage heart was more resilient than I'd realized. I met other girls, though no one I felt the same way about, and after four years that flew past, I left there armed with my degree and a job in a London law firm.

To me, Flanagan's sounded more like an Irish bar than a law firm. It was certainly as noisy and frenetic. I worked hard and played hard, sharing an extortionately priced and cavernous Canary Wharf flat, now and then managing to catch up with Will, who was still a student and currently on an obstetrics rotation. Our meetings were characteristically brief, for two reasons.

'Please buy me dinner, mate. I'm so bloody poor, you wouldn't believe,' he bemoaned. 'Do you know how often I don't eat?'

I didn't believe a word of it. He looked far too healthy. 'Yeah, well, when you're a rich, privately practising doctor, I'll expect repayment. Two steak and chips,' I ordered from the waitress.

Will's face took on an expression of bliss.

'Both rare,' I added.

'Cheers,' he said happily, downing the beer I'd bought him. 'Hope they won't be long, only, well, I've a hot date.' He winked. 'Bloody stunning nurse called Karina. Mustn't be late.'

As ever, Will would eat and run. I thought nothing of it. It's how life was — fast and furious, meetings social and otherwise crammed in wherever we could fit them.

★   ★   ★

It was a couple of months before I saw him again. Another dinner that I paid for, regaled while we ate by Will's tales of life on the ward; only when I asked about Karina, he was oddly reticent.

'Who?' He blinked at me.

'The beautiful Karina. Bloody stunning nurse, I think your words were. You were dating. Surely you remember?'

But instead of the light-hearted response I was expecting, a condescending look crossed his face. 'Dating,' he mocked. 'Ever the romantic, aren't you, Noah? I was fucking her. And now I'm not.'

It wasn't his choice of words that surprised me. It was the callousness with which he spoke, how cold his eyes were as he looked at me. What had I missed?

The next thing he said, however, shocked me.

'Oh, but you'll never believe who I did run into. That girl from school that you were obsessed with.'

'Who do you mean?' I asked, overly casually, feeling a heat rise in me and glad of the darkness in the bar, because he could only be talking about one person.

'Remember April? She was stunning then, but now . . . '

I didn't like the look on his face, or the way he whistled. Trying to hide how I felt merely at the mention of her name, I was aware of his eyes boring into me. 'Where? How was she?'

Even now, I couldn't share the truth with him, that however much I told myself otherwise, I'd give my right arm to see her again.

'Some of us went into this bar in Soho. I was so rat-arsed I nearly didn't recognize her. Anyway, it was definitely her. Like I said, fucking stunning.'

'Which bar?' My heart was in my mouth as I waited for his reply.

Will threw his head back and laughed. 'God. You know, I really must have been pissed. Some place beginning with L, I think . . . Sorry, mate, I can't remember. Never mind.' He glanced at his watch. 'I think I've just about got time for another beer . . . '

That Will had run into April and hadn't thought to tell me until now should have set off warning bells, but then I'd never actually told him how I felt about her. He had no idea that it had ever been more than a crush.

★　★　★

It was no good. No matter how I tried to convince myself that she'd dumped me four years ago and I'd moved on, she was still the goddess — and I was the same love-struck teenager. Other girls didn't stand a chance. My obsession reignited, I couldn't get April out of my head. Far from getting over her, time had given me new hope that maybe now, both of us older, our lives more settled, we had a chance.

Soho was a part of the city I wasn't familiar with, though after a few weeks of exploring every street and checking out every bar with a name that began with the letter L, I soon was. But having failed to find her anywhere, I was close to giving up when I stumbled across Lola's.

If I'd blinked, I would have missed it. I'd been walking up a side street when I saw the dark doorway into a huge old town house. There was nothing obvious about it, just 'Lola's' in small neon-pink letters set to one side. And it was like none of the other bars or clubs I'd been into, but I had to try.

Over the traffic noise behind me, the swish of cars through the puddles, I could hear the dull bass thud from inside as I opened the door to the rest of my life.

★ ★ ★

Of course, I hadn't known at the time — it was much later when I looked back and thought of opening that door as a defining moment, in which I unsuspectingly chose the future that came after. What followed wasn't coincidence. There was no such thing. It was inevitable.

After handing over my money, I was shown down the stairs into a basement where the thumping got louder. At the bottom was a door into a large room crowded with bodies pressed close to each other, where dark corners were lit by vertical streams of coloured light. The music, of which I could only really make out the bass, felt vaguely sinister. I glanced around, out of place in my suit, but invisible to the people who stared at me, oblivious, from their vacant eyes on a chemical journey to someplace else.

I saw her almost immediately, behind the bar pouring a tray of shots, for a few seconds able to take in the tight dress she was wearing, the way her hair was swept up so that just a few strands of it escaped. I was still staring as she looked up and saw me.

I've wondered since if you can ever truly read a face. It's too easy to see what you so desperately want to see, even if it isn't there, I knew that. But as I walked towards her, I wasn't

90

mistaken. As her eyes met mine, they widened, before her face broke into a smile.

'Noah! What are you doing in here?' Ignoring the guy in the dress trying to order cocktails, looking at my open-necked shirt and dark suit, laughing at me.

I felt the smile stretch across my face as I shrugged. 'I felt like a beer.'

She shook her head, still smiling, clearly not believing me as she reached for a glass.

'Here.' She handed me the drink. 'Don't go away. I'll be right back.'

Still smiling, she turned to the cocktail guy and took his order. Taking a closer look at my surroundings, I decided that even after years at uni where I thought I'd seen it all, this was one weird place. I waited as she served more customers, then after a word with one of the other staff, she slipped out and joined me.

'I have ten minutes. My break. I took it early,' she explained, leading me through a door I hadn't noticed. She closed it, instantly muffling the noise, then turned to face me. 'I can't believe it! What are you doing here?'

It was dark in here too. I looked around at the black-painted walls of the small windowless room, then sat on one of the cushioned armchairs, watching her sit opposite. 'Ah. You see, I had dinner with Will.'

As I said Will's name, I saw her eyes flicker. 'He said he'd bumped into you — so I thought I'd come and see you. Interesting place . . . '

I didn't tell her that Will hadn't told me where; that I'd scoured all the clubs in Soho and that this was about the last one I'd try before I started all over again, because I'd been about to do that. Even I could see how stalkerish that might sound.

'He came in with some friends. I know, it looks weird in here,' she said. 'But it beats working in a straight bar — and the money's good. And also . . . '

The smile faded and she looked more serious. 'It gives me time. You'll be pleased, Noah. I had to stop for a while, but at long last, I'm actually studying.'

As she spoke, in some distant corner of my world I felt something slot into place. I listened as she told me about her course, which was the first stage of training to be a counsellor, and suddenly I could see it clearly. Life wasn't just about opportunity, it was about timing — not only for studying, for relationships too. But before I could say anything, she stood up again.

'I really should get back,' she said. 'It can be crazy out there. Look . . . Why don't we meet for brunch? On Sunday? There's a place on the King's Road called Alberto's. I could be there at eleven.'

I didn't know it, but I'd find it. I nodded. 'Great.'

She paused in the doorway. 'It's good to see you, Noah.'

I was silent, trying to summon the words. How to tell her that I'd only just figured it out, that our meeting up again right now was meant to be, but as she opened the door, the noise from the bar made it impossible.

'OK. Well . . . I'll see you? On Sunday?'

I nodded again, barely able to make out what she was saying. Her eyes looked intently at me, then she was gone.

As the door swung shut leaving me alone, a wave of euphoria washed over me. I knew this was no coincidence. Everything in my life, for as long as I could remember, had conspired to bring me to this moment. In a jubilant gesture, I punched the air.

13

As I wondered at how fate had once again brought us together, I didn't once consider that events, April herself even, had conspired equally as hard to keep us apart. For the rest of that week, I tried not to think about Sunday. Not to obsess, fantasize, read into it more than I should. It was just brunch, I told myself. I had no idea if she was with someone, yet imagined that since it was her idea that we meet again, she probably wasn't.

When I arrived at Alberto's, April was already there, at a table in a corner where the doors had been folded back and the cafe was open to the street. Engrossed in the book she was reading, she didn't look up and I had enough precious time to take in the faded blue dress scattered with flowers, the sun catching the side of her face; her hair, partly pinned up but mostly trailing gloriously down her back; her composure as she read. She was still reading as I walked over and pulled out the chair opposite her.

'Morning.'

She looked up. 'Noah! Hi! I was early . . . It's a good place to read.'

'Yeah.' I nodded, hating how self-conscious I suddenly felt. 'Shall I, er, order coffee?'

'They'll come over. Sit down.' Her eyes laughing at me as, still awkward, I did as she said.

'So what's the book?'

But she'd already closed it and slipped it into her bag. 'Coursework. I'll tell you about it some time. But tell me about you. I'm guessing you're a fully fledged force in the rage against injustice? With a big, swanky warehouse apartment overlooking the Thames?'

My grimace was involuntary. 'You're right about the flat. But the rest . . . It's not exactly like that.'

'Oh?' She leaned forward, her eyes bright as she rested her chin in her hands. 'So tell me. What is it like?'

'Oh, you'll wish you hadn't asked. Lots of paperwork, of the most laborious, tedious kind. Listening to your colleagues mouthing off about some or other deal they've pulled off or some or other colleague that's pissed them off or about their massive, er — converted warehouse flat — or new car . . . ' I stopped then, surprised by my own cynicism; realizing I was talking about myself and that my dream career wasn't quite how I'd hoped it would be.

'It's how people are, Noah.' April spoke softly. 'Are you surprised?'

I frowned. 'Yeah. When these guys boast about their deals, they're talking about people. Their future, their families' futures . . . And to some of the people I work with, it's like a game. With winners and losers, not always for the right reasons, either.' Was it naive to want more?

April shook her head. 'Same old Noah. But isn't that what life is? With winners and losers — a game?'

She said it light-heartedly, but a shadow crossed her face, as though she knew something I didn't. I opened my mouth to ask her more, but we were interrupted by the arrival of a waitress.

'So.' After we'd ordered, I sat back and looked at her. 'Tell me about your life, starting from when you left me that letter four years ago. What is it with you and letters?'

I was trying to make it sound humorous, but I saw a flush of pink tinge her cheeks.

'That was quite bad,' she said, looking embarrassed. 'I'm sorry. Just so you know, I did regret it. I should have met you, at least. Told you face to face.'

'It doesn't matter.' Under the table, I clasped my hands together. 'Sorry! I couldn't resist that. But where did you rush off to?'

She sighed. 'When I saw you that time, I'd just got a job, and moved into my own flat. I felt great about it. It was the first time I'd ever felt in control of my life. And then when we spent those days together . . . '

She glanced away as she remembered. 'It got complicated. I liked being with you, but I needed to feel in control of my life. So I ran.'

'Then what?'

She shrugged. 'I worked. Really hard. That was about it. I had bills to pay. I had to make it work.'

It was the first time I realized the magnitude of how important that was to her. The unspoken line — *so that she never had to go back.* Ever since she'd escaped from the family she didn't talk about, April had been fighting to keep hold of her own, very different kind of future, in the real world — while I was at uni, where I'd never been truly on my own.

'It must have been hard,' I said cautiously, struggling to imagine fending for myself at that point, remembering that if she hadn't left the letter and gone without me, it was exactly how it would have been for me too.

'Sometimes.' A shadow crossed her face. 'But it was OK.'

'You know, for a first date, this is one serious conversation,' I told her.

Her eyes widened and I saw uncertainty flicker in them. 'Is that what this is? A first date?'

I held my nerve, her gaze. 'I was hoping so.'

⋆ ⋆ ⋆

As it turned out, it was. For once, it seemed that I was right. Time was on our side. When April wasn't either working or studying, we went on more dates. Movies, crowded bars, cold, crisp nights when we walked and talked under the stars. There was no hurry, nothing to prove, just a blissful inevitability that this was right.

Then in November, for the first time in months, I met up with Will again.

'You've been bloody elusive, mate,' he joked over the rowdiness of the bar where he'd suggested we meet. 'It has to be a girl, right?'

I nodded, feeling something welling inside me that perhaps was pride. 'Not just any girl.'

Will looked at me with more interest. 'Who is

she? Come on, man. Spill.'

'You'll never believe this, but it's April.' I wasn't going to tell him how I'd trekked the streets of Soho, determined to find her.

I never fathomed the look that crossed his face. It was the only time I'd ever seen him lost for words. He just blinked. 'You're kidding me. I knew you had a crush on her. But that was kids' stuff. You've moved on, surely?'

'It's not like that,' I told him, my head nodding, feeling the smile plaster itself on my face. 'We're good friends. We see a lot of each other . . . that's all. It's great. How about you?'

'There are girls, plural,' he said shortly. 'That's what you should be doing, mate.'

But despite his best attempts to dissuade me, I knew I was happy as I was.

★   ★   ★

I learned things about April I hadn't known before. Her need to escape London for open fields and trees; that she had dark days that would come out of nowhere, sapping the joy from life, painting each day a noxious black — until they passed, leaving in their place a need that was almost desperate for beautiful things. But not for April the jewellery and clothes that other girls coveted. There was a black-and-white spotted feather, from a woodpecker, she told me; a small heart-shaped stone. A piece of bark covered with different shades of lichen. And poetry, in particular a tiny, leather-bound volume that had been her grandmother's, where she said the font was as beautiful as the words described on its pages.

There were other things, including letters, but she didn't share them, locking them away in a small battered chest, another thing of beauty in itself, because the aged wood was inlaid with brass and mother-of-pearl. I never knew exactly what she kept in there and saw nothing wrong with that. Even though I wanted to share my every thought, every dream with her, I didn't expect her to do the same.

Not long after we'd started seeing each other, April had the weekend off. We spent it mostly in her old brass bed under the sloping roof of her attic flat, rather than in the sparse expanse of mine, waking to watch the sun come up, wrapped in her bedcovers, the window thrown open on a soft-lit London I didn't recognize, with empty streets and majestic buildings and almost silence. Then at night, we'd gaze up at the darkness, watching the stars.

I could have stayed like that forever and that was when it crept up on me, quietly at first until I felt it in every fibre of my being. In the way even our thoughts seemed in tune. She was the woman I wanted to spend my life with.

Of course I was wary. Of moving too fast; of feeling too much too soon. I didn't want to lose her again. I didn't want to get hurt again either. But as we lay in bed, April must have been aware of it too. I awoke hours later to find the bed empty, the flat silent.

I got up to look for her, wandering out to her small sitting room, where she sat huddled on her sofa, a cardigan over her shoulders, staring into the darkness.

'April?' I spoke softly so as not to startle her. 'Are you OK, honey?'

When she didn't move, I sat on the edge of the sofa behind her, then put my arms round her, sensing the blackness that had her in its grip again.

'You're cold.' Pulling her against my own body, still warm from sleep.

For what felt like ages, we sat there, neither of us speaking, until eventually April spoke.

'Do you ever think . . . ' Her voice was a whisper. I felt her shudder against me. Then she added, 'That you can be too happy?'

'Nope.' Ignoring the shiver running down my own spine as I kissed her neck through her hair. 'Sorry. Not possible.'

But when she turned to face me, her eyes were troubled. 'I'm serious, Noah. Only it never lasts, does it? Happiness.'

Her words held the ghost of fear. I reached out, stroking the fall of hair off her face.

'Hey, what is this?' I said more gently, watching for a hint of a smile on her lips, wanting to reassure her. 'Nothing's going to happen, you know that. We're allowed to be happy.'

She didn't smile. Looking away from me, she shook her head. 'It isn't always that simple, is it?'

But it wasn't really a question. I held her against me, knowing her despondent mood would pass, until her voice came out of the darkness.

'Do you ever think, Noah? About life — and death? Because nothing's certain, is it?'

'Except love,' I said, pulling her closer, ignoring the flicker of disquiet I felt. Doing what I always did, believing what I wanted to believe. Turning from the shadow of the past.

14

Was April right? For a while, were we too happy?
A lifetime's worth of happiness condensed into a
few months, until its quota had been exhausted
so that after, there could only be discontent? It
was a cloud that hung not just over April. This
time I felt it too.

She spent a lot of time out walking, alone. But
then it passed, as it always did. Christmas came.
Apart from a brief visit to the care home that
these days my mother rarely left, we spent it
together. Laughing at the Christmas tree I'd
bought, which was only small yet dwarfed April's
flat and was ludicrously hung with the bling of
lights and shimmering baubles; opening the
many presents we'd bought each other; eating
and drinking far too much.

Even then, every so often it came back to me.
Was it possible to feel too much happiness? I
watched the fairy lights flicker, then spark
brightly again, as I thought of Will's last-minute
invitation for New Year's Eve, back in Musgrove
at his parents' house. It would be some party, I
knew that. I'd been to many over the years, all
with free-flowing champagne and mountains of
food. I pictured it — the grand, lavishly
decorated house with the enormous tree just
inside the front door, towering above the equally
glittering guests.

When I mentioned it to April, far from

enthusing as I'd thought she would, she hesitated. 'We could, if you want to — to be honest, I thought we were going to spend it here. Just the two of us.'

It was how we spent most of our time — just the two of us, in the moments we weren't working, of which there weren't enough, still caught in that blissful state that didn't need other people. Just like April, I was content to spend them with her.

When I awoke on Christmas morning, I lay there, listening to her quiet breathing beside me as a fleeting memory came to me, of the Christmas with my parents after I'd just met April in school. Their idea of Christmas was a quiet, traditional affair. In my wildest schoolboy dreams, I wouldn't have been able to imagine this. Yet just lying here, with April sleeping beside me, I was the happiest I'd been my entire life.

That word again. *Happy* . . . I'm not sure if it was the magic of Christmas, but this time, it didn't haunt me. All day, the rare sense of peace, of at last being where I was meant to be, stayed with me. The rest of the world barely existed, bar the muffled sounds from the flat above us, the distant strains of church bells, the rumble of a passing car far below.

Having already given April my presents, I felt in my pocket for the last one, which I'd thought so long and hard about but had yet to give her. It was quick, I knew that, but I couldn't see the point in putting off what I believed was inevitable and I was waiting for the right moment that never seemed to present itself.

I found it that evening, when she finished her phone call to her old friend Bea. Grabbing her hands and twirling her over to the sofa, where she sat down, I took a deep breath and fished in my pocket.

Her answer was in her eyes. Even before I went down on one knee in front of her and asked.

⋆ ⋆ ⋆

The ring was a perfect fit. I persuaded April we should go to Will's party — not least because I wanted to show her off and tell the whole world we were going to be married, already imagining a country-house wedding with April in a beautiful dress and all our friends crowded round us.

'We should check out some venues,' I told her. 'Places get booked up.'

'Hey! I've only just said yes!' She was laughing, but I could see the excitement in her eyes. 'We're young, Noah! We have our whole lives ahead of us! There's no hurry . . . '

'Oh, but there is . . . ' I was impatient, aware of the long years of waiting condensed into this one moment.

⋆ ⋆ ⋆

I'd called Will to tell him, expecting a cool reaction and a lecture about being too young to tie myself down, but to my surprise, I was wrong.

'Congratulations, mate. Happy for you —

both. Put her on, will you? So I can tell her myself?'

In my bubble I handed the phone to April. 'Here, honey ... It's Will. He wants to congratulate you.'

I saw her lips tighten as she took it. 'Thanks.'

Then she listened, in silence, before adding, 'I'm not sure.'

She turned away from me after that, so I couldn't clearly hear what she was saying, before hanging up a minute or so later.

'What aren't you sure about?' I said.

She looked blankly at me.

'You said something about not being sure,' I said, curious.

'Oh.' A frown flickered across her face as she glanced away. 'He said he's looking forward to seeing us. You know, on New Year's Eve. He was talking about announcing our engagement.'

'Wouldn't that be something! He's a good mate, isn't he?' I pulled her into my arms, thinking of Will's party again. How unexpectedly great life was. So much had changed this last year that I couldn't help but wonder what the next would bring.

Then I felt her sigh against me as her eyes sought mine.

'I'm so happy, Noah. But sometimes ... Don't you wish we could run away? From everything? Go somewhere it's just us ... '

Her voice was quiet — and wistful. I felt a sudden flash of disquiet.

Gently I pulled away from her, looking into her eyes. 'Hey, if that's what you want, we'll do

105

that. We can go away, get married on a beach somewhere. Anywhere. Just us.'

I meant every word. It could have been a small-town registry office for all I cared. I thought she was talking about our wedding, but she could equally have been talking about our future. And I'd have moved to the other side of the world with her. All that really mattered was being together.

⋆ ⋆ ⋆

Over the next few days we told our friends, then lightly sketched the outline of our wedding day, April at last conceding that a country wedding somewhere not too flash or ostentatious, now she'd thought about it, would be amazing.

Then early on New Year's Eve, before breakfast, she went out alone. 'I just need to get one or two things,' she said, reaching up to kiss me, pulling on her big coat and winding a scarf round her neck.

'I'll come with you. I could do with a walk.' I looked around for my jacket, then hesitated, remembering I'd promised to call my mother. 'I'll just make a quick call. Two minutes — OK?'

But she shook her head. 'It's OK. You stay here. I won't be long.'

Though she didn't say, I guessed it was one of those times she wanted to be alone. After calling my mother for the briefest of conversations, I switched on the television, picking up the end of an old film, then watching the one that followed, only at the end realizing April still wasn't back.

I was starting to get anxious when I heard her key in the door. When she came in, instead of being flushed from the cold, her face was pale.

'Hey, are you OK?'

Still in her coat, she came and sat on the sofa, staring at the carpet before pulling off her boots.

'Not really. I don't know. I was walking — I think I got cold.'

I took her hands in mine. They were like ice. 'You should have called me.'

She shook her head. 'It's my fault. I should have come back — but I went and sat in the park. I thought it would pass, but it hasn't. I just feel really sick, Noah. And I ache.'

'It sounds like flu.' I watched as she slipped her coat off and curled up on the sofa, then fetched a throw from her bed and gently covered her.

She didn't protest, just closed her eyes. A few minutes later, from the rhythmic sound of her breathing I guessed she was sleeping. After an hour, she still hadn't moved.

Much later, as it was getting dark, I gently woke her.

'You've been asleep for hours,' I told her softly. 'I don't think we're going to get to Will's.'

She lifted her head. 'Oh, Noah . . . ' Her head sank back onto the sofa. 'I'm so sorry. I know how much you wanted to go tonight.'

'It's okay. It doesn't matter. It's just a party.' I'd been looking forward to it, but it wasn't important. There would always be other parties. 'You should go. I'll be fine here on my own.'

'I'm hardly going without you,' I told her,

imagining walking into Will's alone. 'And we can see Will any time.'

It was true. I called him and explained. Then we saw the New Year in, just the two of us, April curled up against me, revived enough by midnight to share the champagne we'd been going to take to the party.

The next day, she felt better. In just a few days, she was herself again. And then the holiday was over and it was back to work.

15

As I stand at the back of April's cottage, nowhere is there any sign of forced entry. Had the door been open when the police found her that night? Then when they left, they'd have locked up and taken the key. But I'm wondering also if there's a spare key, hidden for whoever might need it, somewhere not too obvious. When I'd moved into my aunt's cottage, I'd found my own front-door key where I'd been told it would be, under the clichéd upturned flowerpot, cracked from frost. Mad, I'd thought at first, inviting just anyone into your home like that, until I'd seen the old windows and rusted, ill-fitting locks that wouldn't keep anyone out. That sanctuary was illusive.

Here, however, the windows are locked tight and there's no upturned flowerpot, just a flat, moss-covered stone placed deliberately near the door. When I lift it enough to feel underneath, I find what I'm looking for.

The key fits the back door and, as I push it open, the wind suddenly picks up. Then out of the corner of my eye I see a cat watching across the garden, before it streaks towards me and, without hesitation, vanishes inside.

I wasn't sentimental, but there was something poignant about walking in on April's life, frozen since the moment she left. Her coat thrown over a chair, the suede boots left underneath where she'd slipped them off, the heels of them worn down from wear; her keys on a worktop, as if she'd just come in from a walk.

In the middle of her kitchen table are unopened letters, next to a bowl of green apples and a pile of newly folded washing on which the scent still lingers; in a heavy jug on the windowsill are stems of lilac, cut, I'm guessing, from the bush I'd noticed in her garden.

As I explore, there are so many signs, small, but of disproportionate significance, that she hadn't planned to kill herself. From the seed packets, a neat bundle held by a rubber band waiting to be planted once the soil had warmed, to the page ripped out of a magazine advertising a weekend break in the French Riviera — in the autumn. A half-written shopping list, tickets for a theatre production in a month's time — all of it suggesting she was planning on being here.

The more I look around, the more I'm convinced I'm right. It's a home that's cared for, a refuge, that feels loved. Nowhere is there any indication of a disturbed mind. If she'd been in the grip of depression, there'd be no flowers, no bowl of apples, no neatly folded laundry, because such things are rendered invisible by it.

April would have tidied, too, I'm sure of it. Left things in order, hidden her most private self from the prying eyes she knew would come here afterwards. The police, her next of kin, even house clearance, all picking through the remnants of her life. It wasn't her way to leave herself on display to strangers.

Something must have happened between her and Norton that night — whether she killed him or not — that was so terrible, that sent her somewhere so dark, so hopeless, that ending her life was her only option.

I'm wondering what it could have been when my eye is drawn to a sudden movement in the doorway as the cat reappears, staring watchfully at me, before arching its back. I take a step towards it, stopping when it yowls ferociously. As the hairs on the back of my neck prickle, in a moment of absolute certainty, I know without any shadow of a doubt.

April wouldn't have abandoned a cat.

★   ★   ★

I ignore the cat as I explore further, through a door that leads into a small sitting room with pale, bare floorboards and soft-coloured furnishings, my conviction growing that it's as if April's just gone out — for a paper, maybe, or to call on a neighbour; that any minute, the back door will swing open and I'll hear her footsteps in the kitchen, the sound of her soft, clear voice.

As I skim a bookcase full of titles on various therapies, I take in the few photos, of April with groups of other nameless people; of someone I don't know holding a baby.

Another doorway leads down the single brick step that's worn smooth with age, into what appears to be her study. In a corner, there's a small desk, with two armchairs angled by the window. Possibly a consulting room — if she's still working as a counsellor, which, from the books she's collected, seems likely — and I picture her sitting there with her clients. Wonder how it is to inhabit someone else's world.

Nowhere is there evidence that anyone else lives here. For some unknown reason, I'm relieved to know that; assume she must have married and divorced, yet kept the name, Rousseau.

I'm halfway up the stairs when I pause, overwhelmed by the strangest sense that I'm not alone, startled by the faintest trace of footsteps treading the stairs just behind me; turning to find no one there. Frozen, imagining a ghostly hand brushing against my skin as I think of her unconscious body in the hospital, so lifeless, empty of the energy, the essence of what makes her April; as I consider also that maybe that part of her is still here.

Then an image comes to me, of that last night, of April coming up these stairs, for whatever unknown reason, with no choice, her despair so great it still echoes here. Feeling it crawl under my skin and become my own.

It's a picture that stays with me, grows more vivid, so that my heart is thudding as I enter her bedroom. The bedcovers are disturbed, and there's a tipped-over vodka bottle on the floor. An image of April swallowing pills and vodka flashes through my mind. It's followed by another of the police arriving, tracing her address as soon as they find her phone, the sound of them breaking in, then the urgency in their voices as they find her. Was she unconscious, already floating somewhere else, as they stretchered her body down the stairs?

My thoughts are broken by the cat, leaping on the bed, looking at me expectantly. This time, when I reach out my hand, it blinks back at me, as if reading my mind, then comes over and rubs its head against my hand.

'I know how you feel,' I tell it, listening to the throaty purr. 'Come on, buddy. Let's find you some food.'

★ ★ ★

I find a box of dry cat food down in the kitchen and tip it into an empty bowl, watching while the cat wolfs it down, then hear the phone ring in another room. After three rings, my ears prick up as it goes to voicemail.

'Hello, you've reached April Rousseau. Please leave your name and number and I'll call you back.'

It's unmistakably April's voice. There's a brief pause, before a woman speaks.

'Hello? April, it's Sadie Westwood. We had an appointment today ... I don't know what happened, but I was hoping you could fit me in, tonight — or maybe tomorrow, if it's easier ... Can you call me, please?'

The voice wavers, almost tearful, then leaves a number before the call ends. I frantically look around for a piece of paper, repeating the number to myself and jotting it down before I forget, guessing she's almost certainly a client but not wanting to play the message back, or leave any other trace of my presence for when the police come here.

Realizing there are likely to be more clients like Sadie Westwood, who have appointments, who ought to be told, I go back to April's study, where in one of the drawers of her desk I find folders containing client details. It's on impulse that I take them. Noticing her diary, I pick that up too. Then as I walk back through the sitting room, I find myself drawn again to the photos, picking them up in turn, curiously studying the faces as new questions come to me. Does she have a family? And if she has, do they know?

Outside again, I'm about to lock the door when a furious yowl alerts me to the fact that the cat is still inside. I open the door and it streaks out, vanishing into the trees. Locking up, in a moment of rashness I consider keeping the key, but decide against it, sliding it back under the stone.

Just moments later, I'm in my car pulling on my seat belt when, a few metres further down the lane, a police car pulls up. In my driving mirror I watch as two uniformed police cross the lane and go through April's gate. As one of them talks on their radio, I can't help but wonder. Coincidence? Or was I right?

Were they tipped off? Was I being watched?

★ ★ ★

Back in my room at the B&B, I eat the sandwich I bought earlier and pour myself a drink, then

114

another, enough to allow the tension to ebb away but not sufficient that when I sleep, I don't dream vividly. As my eyes close, I'm back in April's cottage. Long grass bleached to the colour of hay has grown up against the windows. I'm in her study, where the light casts shadows and twisting tendrils of plants creep silently through broken windows and cracks in the walls.

Around me, obscured by the softness of the leaves, the walls have vanished, then while I watch, flowers start to open, one by one, like stars appear as night falls, until there's a whole mass of them. It's eerily, surreally beautiful — but suddenly it changes. I hear the wind first, a distant howl that comes closer, sweeping past me, tearing at the leaves, and while I watch, the tendrils wilt and colours fade. The leaves start to drop, while the flowers wither, their petals falling in soft monochrome, carpeting the floor.

As the last of them fall like snowflakes, as the wind dies, I hear a cry and, looking down, see cushioned in their softness a baby.

ELLA

'It's only a cat.'

My father's words, the day a beautiful black-and-white cat streaked across the road and under his car. I felt the slight bump as he crushed it. Was haunted by its ghostly cry for weeks afterwards. Felt angry with him forever, because he had no right to say that.

'It's only a cat.'

No cat is just a cat. It's as alive, as deserving of life as he is, like the ants he boils alive in the cracks between his paving stones and the swatted butterflies that have lost their way and come inside. The rabbits gassed in the garden and the pheasants he raises, then shoots for sport. His decision if they live or die.

'Don't make such a fuss. They're just pheasants, Ella.' My mother's words.

Not thinking for one moment that it was the first time I'd seen them, strung up outside by their necks. Dead.

'Beautiful,' she adds, thinking of the meat which Gabriela will cook, after she's plucked and cleaned them, not their brilliant colours and iridescent feathers and staring, glassy eyes.

'You really should learn to shoot.'

Everything about her is in that one sentence. Daughters have obligations to fulfil, expectations to meet, should be seen with the right people in the right places. Take part in the obscenity of killing for the sake of killing.

'My daughter shoots.' She'd love to say that. How doesn't she get who I really am? How I think? What I care about?

I open my mouth to tell her that no way, not ever, in my whole life, will I kill a living creature just for sport, when Gabriela catches my eye.

Gabriela's the housekeeper, PA and multipurpose filler-in-the-cracks in my family. We are the family she always wanted, she tells me proudly. 'Your father — so handsome, so successful! And your mother who is so very beautiful . . . But you, little Ella, will discover your own talents . . . '

'Rock music,' I tell her pointedly. Unlike my mother, Gabriela already knows about the pink electric guitar at the back of my wardrobe.

But she shakes her head. 'You are different, little one,' she says, her eyes wide, this intense expression on her face. 'You don't always have to listen to them.' She means my parents.

'It's like they don't know me,' I try to tell her. 'You've heard them . . . '

But Gabriela's loyal, won't hear a word against the beautiful singer and the successful surgeon. She holds a finger to my lips.

'No more,' she says quietly. 'You'll find your way. It won't always be like this.'

16

That I have April's notes in my possession poses a dilemma that's twofold, not only because they're confidential, between April and her clients, but it's likely, also, that the police will want them.

I'm trying to prove April's innocence, but I'm guilty of breaking into her cottage and potentially withholding information from the police; of blatantly flouting the law. But it's a risk I'm prepared to take. I'm here not only as a lawyer. I'm here because I knew her.

In my room at my B&B, brushing aside my misgivings, I make a call I know can't wait.

It's answered almost immediately, by a woman who sounds young, which for no logical reason throws me.

'May I speak to Sadie Westwood?'

'This is Sadie.'

'Ms Westwood? My name's Noah Calaway. I'm a friend of April Rousseau's . . . I'm sorry, but I have some rather worrying news . . . ' I pause, aware of how fragile this woman sounded when she left her message on April's phone. 'She's had an accident.' Pausing, giving her time to take it in, before adding, 'I'm afraid she's in hospital.'

She gasps. '*Oh* . . . my goodness, that's terrible. Oh, poor April. Is she all right?'

'It's a little soon to say,' I tell her gently, then

take a deep breath. 'I was wondering — would you mind if we talked about her? Only I think she might be in trouble.'

'Oh! Of course. Anything — if it would help. Oh, poor April . . . What kind of trouble?' She sounds nervous, jittery, clearly shocked.

'I think she's been framed for something she didn't do.' I give her a few seconds to take it in.

'Oh . . . That's terrible.' She hesitates. 'Are you another therapist?'

'No. I'm her lawyer.'

At the word lawyer, there's another gasp. I'm not sure what emotional landscape Sadie Westwood occupies, but I'd hazard a guess it's an unstable one — which presumably is why she needs April.

'Oh. Oh, dear. Yes.' She sounds confused. 'Of course. If it will help her. But she's always so calm — and such a happy person. She never has any problems, you know. She's just one of those incredible people — who copes.'

'I'm sure she is. Did you ever discuss her personal life with her?'

'Not really, I'm afraid. You see, I haven't been well — she was helping me . . . It sounds so selfish, doesn't it, when you put it like that?' Her anxiety obvious.

'No. Not at all.' Telling her what she wants to hear, because even if April had confided in her, I'm not sure Sadie Westwood would have noticed.

'Look, could I leave you my number? If you think of anything, can you call me?'

I recite the number twice because she gets it

119

wrong, then end the call, irritated. Not just by Sadie Westwood's assumptions that April's life was easy and that April somehow mysteriously 'coped' — but because she dimly reminds me of a small part of myself. A part of which I'm not proud.

★ ★ ★

The presence of April's client notes continues to make me uncomfortable. They're deeply private and confidential, yet with nothing else to go on and carefully avoiding more personal information, I know also that I need to go through them.

After making a list of names, I speak to six clients initially, half of whom used to see her once or more weekly, though none of them recently, and learn nothing that seems significant.

The next morning, I return to the hospital. But as I go through the swing doors into ICU, as I approach April's room, I hear raised voices from inside, so that my heart twists in hope. Has she come round? Is a doctor with her? As I reach the door, I see it is a doctor, one I'd hoped I wouldn't see.

He looks up just as he falls silent, arms folded as he stands over her. There's a WPC there today, awkward as she looks uncertainly at him.

He's still lean, his red hair prematurely grey, dressed for work in a suit, the ID that's slung round his neck gaining him entrance where I was refused. I look for a flicker of surprise, but Will's

120

face is blank as he walks out and closes the door behind him.

'Noah . . . ' He pauses. 'I wondered if I'd see you.' His air one of indifference as he appraises me. 'I had a patient to check on. I thought I'd call in — see how she is.'

This — after so many years, so many wrongs. As though nothing has happened. Minimizing, trivializing the part he played in it. As he stands in front of me, my searing hate is reflexive.

'Any change?' Not trusting myself to say more, because I have no more to say to him, and from his most expansive bedside manner, in the way I curl up inside, I know one thing with certainty: *you can never truly forget the past.*

He shakes his head. 'Not so far. They're running tests — as yet, they don't know what damage was done to her internal organs. One thing is pretty clear, though. She didn't intend on being found.'

I'm silent.

'Well, you've got to admit, it doesn't look good,' he adds.

'Maybe not,' I tell him. 'But the truth will come out. It usually does.'

His eyes narrow, just slightly, at the corners. His voice is deceptively light. 'You still believe she's innocent?'

I hold his gaze. 'Until proven otherwise . . . I do.' Watching his split-second hesitation before he glances at his watch.

'I have to go.' He reaches into his pocket. 'If you feel like a drink some time, give me a call.'

I stare at the card he's holding, then curiosity

gets the better of me. 'Just one question. Why did you call?'

If I've caught him off guard, he hides it well.

He passes me the card. 'I thought you should know.'

Which tells me nothing, as he turns and strides away, his footsteps fading down the corridor. I already know I won't call him. Then pushing thoughts of Will from my head, I turn back to look through the slatted blind at April, because this isn't about him. It never was.

She looks the same as yesterday, just as small and lifeless, her existence simply a trace on the monitor she's wired up to, her only movement the slight rise and fall of her chest in time with the machine that's breathing for her.

'Hey,' I say silently through the glass, like the last time. 'It's good to see you.'

I hold my breath, waiting for a sign that she's heard me; wishing she'd turn her head towards me and open her eyes, so that I could watch them widen with disbelief.

Then I'm chastising myself for my choice of words. It isn't good to see her, not like this. And what had Will been thinking — if not exactly shouting, then talking so angrily to her? Why didn't that WPC stop him? In my pocket, my fingers find his card.

As I read it, a faint echo comes to me of April's voice, warning me not to trust him. Clear enough that it startles me, so that I look towards her face as another memory comes back from a long time ago.

17

'I thought I'd ask Will to be my best man,' I told April happily. 'I mean, he's my oldest friend. And you've known him just as long. He'll make a great speech.' He would, too, with just the right blend of warmth and wit, laced with irreverence — just enough but not too much. 'He's the obvious choice.'

April seemed less enthusiastic than I was. 'You think?'

'Of course. Why? Don't you agree?'

She was silent, measuring her words. When she looked up, her face was serious. 'Be careful of Will. I know you think he's a good friend, but — ' She broke off.

'But what?' I persisted, surprised by her reluctance, adding, 'Come on . . . Tell me!'

'Just . . . there's another side to him, that's all. A selfish one. He has a ruthless streak.'

Half jokingly, and because none of us is perfect, I defended my oldest friend. 'He's single-minded and determined . . . He's always been like that.' Then as I looked at her, an unwanted sense of unease came over me. 'Has something happened between you?'

Again, she hesitated before saying, 'No. Nothing like that. It's just a feeling I have.' Then her voice changed as though she'd had a change of heart, but her smile was forced. 'You know what I'm like! Anyway, you know him far better than I do. Honestly, forget I said anything.'

I let it go, when I should have pushed her. But I was too happy, too swept along by our wedding plans, eager to only see the best in Will and everyone else, and I let it pass.

★ ★ ★

I was foolish enough to believe that such happiness was my due. That I actually deserved it, giving it no further thought as I rode the wave that just kept on going. Believing this was how my life was now, never for one moment stopping to consider that from such a height, the only way was down.

The weeks had gathered momentum, and with just days to go, I was flying. How many people had ever felt like I did at that moment? I was in our South London flat, having taken leave from the high-profile law firm I'd joined a few months earlier, two days from marrying the woman of my dreams in the most romantic country-house setting I'd ever seen. Even the weather was on our side. It was June, high pressure established over the country meaning we were guaranteed sun. It didn't get better than that.

It had already been quite a year. Moving into the home we were still renovating, our spare time filled with wedding planning, tasting menus and wines, making decisions and then changing our minds again, making last-minute changes to the seating plan as the number of guests oscillated. I was secretly looking forward to it all being over, to the process of actually being married and away on our honeymoon, then starting out on the rest of our lives.

'Hey! We've had more cards. Want to open them?' April's voice drifted through to the kitchen, where I was deep in thought.

She appeared, framed for a moment in the doorway, her eyes bright, her long hair untidily caught up, before coming over to kiss me briefly on the cheek and depositing the mail on top of my paper.

'There was a call from the hotel this morning. I said you'd call back,' I told her, starting on the cards.

'Oh? Did they say what about?'

I shook my head. 'I would have asked, only it was that bossy woman who doesn't like me. I thought I'd leave it to you.'

It had made sense to leave the finer details to April. Once we'd booked the venue, she'd become absorbed in planning the place settings and the flowers. I knew it was going to look beautiful.

'Noah! Emma's not bossy. She's just organized — which seeing as you're not, is just as well.'

Feeling slightly guilty, I put the cards down and got up, walking over and getting out a couple of mugs. 'I did book the honeymoon, remember? It's just that you have such impeccable taste, I think it's far better if you make these decisions. I trust you. Completely.' Wondering if she knew I was talking about far more than the wedding.

'Really . . . ' Arching an eyebrow at me as I put my arms round her, pulling her close, breathing in the scent of her as I kissed the slender line of her neck.

'Noah . . . ' She tried to wriggle out of my arms. 'I have to go out again. In ten minutes.'

'You said you were here this afternoon. And I thought everything was done.'

'It is. Almost. Just one or two last-minute . . . small things. That's all. OK? Now quickly, coffee or tea?'

'I'll make coffee. Anything I can do?'

She shook her head. 'Really. It's nothing. And I shouldn't be long.'

I'd let my arms fall away. There were aspects of our wedding day that were out of bounds to me, at least until the big day itself. And it didn't matter. After Saturday, with the wedding over, we'd only have the rest of our lives.

She drank half her mug before picking up her keys and dashing out. I called my mother's care home to confirm the transport we'd booked to the wedding for her and one of the carers, who was coming along to look after her. That done, after tidying the kitchen I was restless, eventually pulling out a file I'd brought back from the office about a domestic-abuse case I was working on, a case that interested me on several levels. The wife was a smart, educated, accomplished woman. I couldn't understand how someone like her had married such a violent man. Had he hidden it from her all that time? Or had love blinded her to the truth?

Engrossed, I didn't notice the time passing. Only after the sun slipped behind the rooftops and I was straining my eyes to read the text, did I register how late it was.

April had said she wouldn't be long. Hours ago. Suddenly I was filled with unease, followed by guilt that I hadn't noticed. Finding the phone, I called her mobile. There was no reply.

A train of startling thoughts rushed through my head, of worst-case scenarios, imagining her hit by a car and taken to hospital — or worse — as I hunted around for Bea's number. If she was anywhere else, Bea's place was most likely where she'd go.

'Hello, darling.' After leaving school, Bea had gone to college and reinvented herself. Effortlessly glamorous, these days she called everyone darling.

'Bea. Have you seen April? This afternoon? Only she told me she was going out — ages ago. She's not back.'

I broke off, suddenly paralysed by fear. What if she'd had second thoughts? *What if she wasn't coming back?*

'We spoke earlier.' My fears escalating as Bea hesitated. 'Lunchtime. She told me she was on her way home. Noah, look, you know I adore both of you. And it's not really any of my business, but . . .'

But I wasn't listening — I didn't want to, not to the seriousness in her voice, the unspoken suggestion that something was wrong. Hearing keys in the front door, I cut her short.

'It's OK! She's just walked in! Cheers, Bea. See you on the big day!'

I went to meet April, filled with relief that my fears had been for nothing, pausing to watch her pull off her jacket and hang it up just inside the front door, before draping her scarf over the top. Feeling so much love for her, I thought she must be able to feel it even from there.

'Did you get it done? Your mystery deed?'

Her head down as she slipped her shoes off, she said nothing. Then she stood up, turning so that I saw her face. As I looked at her, I felt my blood run colder than ice.

There was a terrifying sadness in her eyes, worse than any blackness I'd ever seen there. Fear struck me again, only far harder this time. Before I knew it, I was beside her, my arms tightly round her.

'April? Honey ... What's wrong? What's happened?'

As she slumped against me, suddenly, I knew I wasn't ready. I never would be. Whatever was so bad, so close to our wedding, I didn't want to hear it.

As if she knew, she lifted her head, for a moment looking into my eyes as if searching for something.

'I'm sorry,' she said, glancing momentarily away. Managing a glimmer of a smile. 'It's just wedding nerves catching up with me.'

'Where were you today? I was worried,' I said quietly. 'I thought for a minute there you'd changed your mind.'

128

The smallest sigh came from her. 'I would never, never do that,' she said. 'Look at me, Noah. Believe me. I want to be with you, more than anything in the world.'

I looked into her eyes, knowing I believed her, fighting an irrational desire to keep my arms round her, terrified that if I didn't, I'd lose her.

★   ★   ★

I knew something was wrong, but no matter how many times I asked, she wouldn't tell me. Not even much later, when we were in bed and she couldn't sleep and simply lay there, staring up at the ceiling.

'You do love me, Noah? No matter what?'

It was what we always said to each other. *No matter what.*

'Hmmm.' I pulled her closer, my earlier unease dissipating slightly.

'You know I love you too? No matter what?' I thought I heard her say, but much later, when I tried to remember, I was never sure. I should have stayed awake that night, kept my arms tight round her, got her to talk to me, told her that whatever was wrong, we were strong. We'd survive. But instead, I slept, waking the next morning to find her sitting on the bed.

I pulled myself up against the pillows. 'Hey . . . '

She had her back to me. Still drowsy, I reached for her, wanting to feel her warmth against me. Suddenly alert as I noticed she was dressed.

'April? Honey? Are you all right?'

She didn't reply at first, then as she turned, the look on her face chilled me.

18

Afterwards, when I played her words back in my head, I told myself there'd been a mistake. A misunderstanding. It couldn't have happened. We were getting married. My denial replaced by shock, remembering her face, ashen, as she'd told me.

'This is the hardest thing I've ever had to do.'

As she spoke, her words had stopped my heart; a numbness started in my brain, flowing through my body.

'Something's happened, Noah.'

Her voice had been quiet, full of sadness as she went on.

'I can't marry you.'

Trying to make sense of what she was saying, my brain had been unable to take it in. We were getting married. Tomorrow. The hotel was booked, the guests had accepted. We couldn't cancel. Not now.

'I wouldn't make you happy, Noah. Not if you knew.'

Her voice had been full of regret — but resolute. I'd begged her to stop. It didn't matter what had happened, or what she'd done, I'd told her. I loved her enough to forgive her anything. But before she could reply, the doorbell had rung and she went to answer it. Pulling on pyjamas as fast as I could, I'd rushed after her. But by the time I got there, she'd gone.

131

She'd obviously packed before I'd woken and called a taxi. Now, in a state of shock, I was overwhelmed with the need to find her. I fumbled with my phone, frantically calling her, forced to listen as each time it went to voicemail.

My voice was shaking as I poured my heart into a string of desperate messages, telling April it didn't matter what she'd done, it was past, behind us, and there was nothing that would stop me loving her. Until there was no more space, by which time I'd run out of words.

I remember little after that, just that I sat, unable to move, unaware of time passing. I never asked who told him. Where he got a key. Later I'd assumed it was April — or maybe Bea — but I was still sitting in the same place, staring at the table, when Will quietly let himself in.

I felt his hand on my shoulder, then heard him pull out the chair opposite. For once, he didn't talk, just sat in silence with me while I held the phone as though my life depended on it.

I don't remember how long we stayed like that, neither of us moving, just that it was Will who eventually spoke.

'Noah? Mate, I know this is hard. But we need to call the hotel.'

It was as if my insides were gripped by a giant hand. 'I can't . . . ' The hand twisted. 'Not without talking to her. I need to find her, Will. You have to help me.'

He glanced at the phone I was still clutching tightly.

'She doesn't mean it.' My face was wet with tears, but I didn't care. 'She can't. This is a terrible mistake — but that's all it is. If I talk to her, she'll see that. I know she will . . . '

Across the table from me, Will rested his head in his hands. Then he told me she'd asked him to come here. It was over. She wasn't coming back.

Spoken out loud, there was a finality in his words that in my shocked state I didn't question.

'I'm sorry, mate. Very sorry. Look, I know this isn't what you want to hear, but you need to let the hotel know.'

I never asked him why. I thought of the day April and I had planned so carefully, looked forward to for so long. Getting up, pacing over to the window, looking out on yet another perfect summer's morning, I was still unable to take it in.

Will must have realized. 'I'll do it for you — if you like.'

Leaving the phone on the table, I'd gone outside at that point. To hear him tell them the wedding was cancelled was more than I could cope with. I heard him call my mother's care home, and Bea. Then between them they'd begun the onerous task of calling our guests.

★   ★   ★

I remember little about the days that followed. In a word, my world had imploded. Nothing existed outside my grief. I had no plan, no solution and, I believed, no future, because April had taken it with her. It was as my mind comprehended this that I gave up. From the moment I woke, I drank, until my vision blurred and my pain dulled, until I collapsed into unconsciousness. Anaesthetizing my mind, every cell in my body, day in and day out, until one morning when I wasn't expecting him, Will came round.

'If you carry on like this, you'll fucking kill yourself,' he told me. 'It's ten o'clock in the morning, man — and you're plastered.'

'You have no idea,' I'd thrown back at him, taking another slug of whisky, not caring. 'You have no idea how this feels.'

'Yeah. Right.'

'You're fucking single, Will.' Taking another swig, completely missing his sarcasm. 'You screw a different girl every week. That's nothing like me and April.' Just saying her name sent another stab of pain through me.

My glass empty again, I reached for the bottle. But this time, Will was quicker than me, grabbing it, across the room in seconds and pouring it down the sink.

'Don't be so sure.' His eyes narrowed. 'You've been so caught up in your perfect little world, mate, you don't know the half of it.'

Just like with Bea, I wasn't listening. Not to his allusion to what were possibly his own problems, nor that somewhere along the line maybe I'd missed something. This was my tragedy — not Will's.

'Do you know how many times I've lost her, Will? And every time, she came back? This time, she won't, though. I know she won't.' My voice choked, my body shaking with unsuppressed emotion.

'Poor Noah,' Will had mocked. 'Welcome to

the real world. She was keeping something from you. Anyway, didn't you ever ask her where she went?'

In my alcoholic haze, I missed it — that he knew how April would disappear.

'We knew everything about each other,' I hurled at him, my pain translated into anger. 'Everything that counted. You don't understand because you've never had a relationship like that. Most people haven't.'

Will shook his head. 'You're completely deluded. You have no idea, do you?' His words loaded with cynicism.

I'd stared at him. 'What do you mean?'

'Oh, man. You need to wake up to yourself. You want the truth?'

As he spoke, I heard his condescension, felt his coldness, dimly registering that Will didn't care about me. Not really. I didn't even know why he was here. I felt a wave of hatred for him. But he went on, oblivious.

'She was with other blokes. The whole time. You didn't know that, did you? Your perfect little April's nothing but a cheap slut. Think yourself lucky you found out now . . . '

I was drunk, but I felt each word tear deeper into me, until I couldn't take any more. He hadn't finished his sentence when I got to my feet and took a swing at him, punching him as hard as I could in the mouth.

'*Fuck* . . . ' Will bent over, his face white, his hands splattered with blood that was dripping onto the kitchen floor. 'You're a bastard, Noah.'

'Get out,' I told him, suddenly sober. 'Or I'll fucking kill you.' My body was tense, my fists clenched involuntarily. I meant every word.

' . . . bathroom,' Will muttered, ignoring me as he staggered towards it.

But I blocked the way. 'Just get the fuck out.'

He stood, still holding his jaw, as if weighing up whether I meant it, before picking up his keys and walking out.

Once he'd gone, I sat there, hearing his words over and over, fury raging through me. Will was wrong. He had to be. Hearing what I'd missed the first time round, gripped by an icy chill. Who was he to know where April went? How would he know? But it was all lies, I tried to convince myself; my trust pitted by silent doubts.

I poured myself a drink, then another, remembering the day before she left. The look in her eyes as she told me she wanted to be with me more than anything. How I'd believed her. Those long walks she used to take, preferring to be alone . . . It had never entered my mind that she might be meeting someone. In my naivety, I'd believed everything she told me.

Hurling my glass at the wall, suddenly I was out of control, throwing everything within reach, the sound of shattering glass and china fuelling me on. Whatever had happened to make her leave, April had loved me. There was a reason she'd left like this. There had to be. When I found her — and I would find her — she'd explain, I knew she would. I loved her. I could forgive her anything. Will had always been jealous, I could see that now. He couldn't bear the existence of my happiness.

If it was just that, I could have forgiven him too. But I couldn't. After the way he'd spoken about April, I never would.

19

The wave had broken, hurling me into seething, boiling depths through which I plummeted to the bottom. Indeterminate days passed, during which I wallowed, wanting to drown, imagining a release from misery. But it was a lowest point from which I had found myself slowly, unwillingly, inevitably drifting upwards.

When I sobered up and confronted what I'd done to the flat, I realized also, much as I hated admitting it, that Will had been right — but about one thing only. I didn't know April as well as I thought. If I had, she wouldn't have gone.

I'd been aware of the shadow that followed her; but I'd been too happy, on the crest of my wave, hadn't questioned once — *why*. But it was love that had done that to me. Love, its palette of warmth and colour and light, reaching rosy-tinted brushstrokes into every corner of my life; that was now buried under the ugly shade of bitterness. I'd made a mistake. I'd trusted April. It was a mistake I wouldn't make twice.

After clearing up the flat, remorselessly mopping up Will's blood from where it had congealed on the kitchen floor, I threw out the empty bottles, returned wedding gifts and discovered how expensive cancelling a wedding was. I made no attempt to contact Will. Bea came round once or twice — sweet Bea, who was always April's friend and oddly awkward now that she'd gone. I always suspected it was Bea who let herself in when I wasn't there and packed a few more of April's things. But whatever she knew, she remained fiercely loyal and wouldn't be drawn.

'I know it probably doesn't feel like it, but perhaps it wasn't meant to be,' she said quietly, sipping tea from a cup and saucer she'd found in the kitchen that I didn't recognize. Maybe an unreturned wedding gift, something else I hadn't known about.

Even if she was right, it was too soon to hear her say that. 'But I keep thinking of before, Bea. We broke up, you know that, but I've always believed we were meant to be together.'

I was still hanging on, desperate for her to offer even the smallest shred of hope.

'Oh, Noah. Darling . . . ' Putting down her cup, Bea sighed. 'I do know she loved you. Really loved you — in her way. For what it's worth.'

'She should have talked to me, Bea. We could have worked out whatever was troubling her. I know we could.'

Bea shook her head unhappily. 'Do you know what I think? You loved each other. But sometimes, love isn't enough. Isn't that desperately sad?'

'No,' I said, stung. 'You're wrong. Love, real love, like April and I had, can conquer anything.' Even now, I still believed that. Then I looked at her.

'Is that what she thought? She told you, didn't she, Bea? *Why?*'

She shook her head again. 'Don't, Noah. She's my friend.'

'If she did, you have to tell me. Please.'

Hearing the note of desperation in my voice, and sensing my rising panic, she glanced at her watch. 'Oh, my, is that the time?'

Bea reached for her handbag. But as she got up to go, I was across the room, beside her, grasping her arms.

'Bea . . . I'm asking you . . . Begging you . . . *Please tell me* . . .'

'Noah! Please. You're hurting me.' She pulled away from me, a look of fear crossing her face.

Ashamed, I released her, stepping back. 'Sorry . . . Sorry, Bea. I don't know what came over me.'

But already pulling on her jacket, she headed for the door.

'Bea . . . Please. Wait . . .' I called after her.

Her hand on the latch, she paused, her voice shaky as she composed herself. 'Let her go, Noah. Move on. Now I must be off, darling, I'm so sorry.'

★ ★ ★

In the aftermath, I oscillated between reluctant acceptance and devastation, battling through long days at work, only to come home to a flat that resounded with loneliness, where every mug and every cushion was a reminder of what I'd lost, where my escape was to drink. It was only time — long, lonely months — that forced me to accept the truth I denied for so long. April

140

wasn't coming back.

There were to be no letters or calls, no messages — inferred or otherwise — to be delivered by Bea or Will or anyone else, not that either of them was speaking to me. Nor was there any sense in trying to find her. No one nearby had heard from her and, after the wedding was called off, mutual friends had drifted away on the tide of my embarrassment.

I was alone.

ELLA

'Hi, Ella. How are you?'

'Hi. I'm good.' *Slipping into the chair opposite the ugly painting, which has become less ugly and more funny now I've seen it a few times.*

'Did your mother bring you today?' *Julia flicks through some papers on her desk before coming to sit with me.*

'No. She's away. Italy, I think.' *I screw up my face because I've lost track of where she is — Dubrovnik, Paris, Florence all merged into a month-long euro-blur.*

'Gabriela did.' *Slipping up. She didn't ask.*

Her lips twitch slightly. Ha. I always knew it was a game. Then she sits back and crosses her ankles. I find myself staring at the small crescent moon tattooed on one of them.

Sensing my gaze, she uncrosses them. 'I know. It's bad for my circulation. So what would you like to talk about?'

That's a new one. What does she want me to say?

I shrug. 'Don't know. Whatever.' *It's her show, not mine.*

She's quiet for a moment. Then she says quite quietly, 'Can I level with you? Only I'm puzzled. You're smart, Ella. You seem incredibly perceptive. I don't buy it — that you don't get on with your mother. Not per se. You might

142

have your differences, about who you should hang out with and how she thinks you should spend your time . . . '

Her silence tells me she's worked it out. My heart a little bird trapped in a cage as I sit there.

'Only I'm wondering if, maybe, there's something else.'

'You're forgetting one thing,' I tell her, slumping in my chair, folding my arms tight round me, because it's a step too far and she's forgetting the rules. I came here for a reason — my mother's reason. She can't make me talk about anything else. 'It wasn't my idea to come here.'

She nods. 'I know. But you could have wriggled out of it by now — if you really wanted to. You've just told me your mother's away — how would she know if you skipped a week? I might be wrong . . . But I'm guessing you have your own reason for coming here. A really good one.'

OK. She's challenging me. But as she speaks, I hear something unfamiliar in her voice, feeling surprise, then something stronger that gives me goosebumps as I realize.

She cares.

She actually cares. I don't know how to feel, just stare at my hands in my lap where I'm picking at one of my fingernails, feeling the lump in my throat, shocked to find my eyes full of tears.

Swallowing as she says, gently, 'Am I right?'

I don't meet her eyes. Feel my head nod, once, on its own.

143

She doesn't do anything. Just lets me sit, blinking away tears. Why did she have to do this? When everything is already complicated.

It's my own fault. I shouldn't have looked. But I had to.

And I wish I hadn't, but I can't tell her.

Because if I do, then everyone will know.

20

2016

In the hospital I watch April through the blinds, still caught in the past, the shadow of which lingers beside me, as heavy footsteps get louder and then come to a stop and I'm jolted back to the present.

'Excuse me, sir?'

It's a man's voice and I turn to look at him. He's stocky, in an ill-fitting suit and open-necked shirt. 'Detective Sergeant Ryder.' He lifts his ID. 'Could I have a word?'

I take an instant dislike to him. He's too loud, too substantial for this place of frail, damaged bodies and shattered lives.

I follow him anyway, back along the corridor and into a small room where so many have sat before; where their desperation and hope still hang in the air, cling to the papered walls. Closing the door, he gestures to me to sit in one of the upright plastic chairs, then gets straight to the point.

'I understand from one of the nurses that you're a friend of Ms Rousseau's?'

'That's right.' I send silent thanks to the friendly, brown-haired nurse for not telling him I'm her lawyer. Until I find out where he's coming from; for leaving that pleasure to me.

'In that case, sir, I'd like to ask you a few

questions. Could I take your name?'

'Noah Calaway.'

He writes it down, as he does my home address and phone number, adding that of the B&B where I'm staying, before he goes on to ask about my occupation.

'Writer,' I tell him.

'You got anything published?' He stares, clearly curious.

'A couple of books.' I shrug.

'Should I have heard of you?' His gaze unflinching.

'Possibly.' I hold his gaze. 'I write under my own name, Detective Sergeant. If you'd read one of my books, I imagine you'd have remembered.'

A frown flickers briefly on his face but then, his interest short-lived, he goes on. 'Have you had any contact with Ms Rousseau in recent weeks?'

'To be honest, not for some time. A mutual acquaintance called me and told me what had happened. That's why I'm here.'

'Can I ask where you were the night of the murder, sir?'

'At home. Alone,' I tell him bluntly, because he'll ask.

Ryder pauses. 'In Devon.'

'Yes.'

Frowning at me, he puts down his pen. 'Long way to come just to see an old friend you haven't seen for — how long?'

'About sixteen years.' I hold his gaze for a moment. 'Our mutual acquaintance seemed to think she's the only suspect. That her phone was in the car and presumably fibres from her gloves all over the murder weapon.'

I can see his discomfiture — that this writer he hasn't heard of has the balls not to be intimidated by him; even worse, stands his ground.

'Look.' He shuffles his pages slightly. 'All I can say is that so far, with the evidence we have, we're not looking for anyone else.'

'So everyone tells me.' I already know this from Will. Folding my arms, heartened, because whatever he says, it's not as conclusive as he wants it to be. Anyone can wear gloves.

'You must be considering the possibility?'

Ryder looks up sharply.

'But if you don't find anything, I guess the trial will be straightforward,' I add, not letting on that I know more about the legal process than he thinks.

Leaning back in his chair, Ryder actually smirks. 'Assuming there is one.'

I know what he's saying. *Assuming she comes round.* I like him even less.

'What do you write?' Hostile words, because he's not asking out of pure interest.

'Crime.' I watch him digest this, the cynical curl of his lips, as if it explains everything.

'Right.' He smirks. 'Fancy yourself a bit of an expert, I suppose.'

'I have my own opinion. That's not a crime, though, is it, Detective Sergeant?' Keeping my voice intentionally light, by now not caring if I rile him.

He pauses before saying nastily, 'It's horse shit.'

'Excuse me?' I stare at his narrowed eyes.

'What those nurses always tell you — you know, about how they can hear.' He says it coldly, and as he watches me for a response, I see it for what it is. The ugliest, clumsiest of tactics — Ryder's been in his job too long.

'Unless you know otherwise?' Casually, like an afterthought.

When he already knows I haven't been allowed into April's room. I've no time for this, nothing more to say to him. Getting to my feet, I speak through gritted teeth. 'If you have everything you need from me, Detective Sergeant, I'll be on my way. Now, if you'll excuse me . . . '

'Care to tell me what you know?' he calls after me as I turn my back on him and walk out. 'We're all busy, Calaway. Don't waste everyone's time . . . ' His voice fading as the swing doors close behind me.

★   ★   ★

The same dubious moral compass of creeps like Ryder that influenced my departure from the legal world strengthens my resolve to prove him wrong. It's Ryder I'm thinking about as I drive the couple of hours it takes to get to Musgrove. He was right about one thing, though. A phone, April's glove and the murder weapon hadn't got into that car on their own.

The next place I needed to call was the North Star, just reopening after the conclusion of the police investigation there. Where the price of information is alcohol; where it seems also that

148

I'm remembered. I push the familiar door open and wander over to the bar, catapulted back to my teenage years until I see John Slater, the landlord. That he has aged so markedly somehow shocks me.

'Well, I never . . . You youngsters don't half make me feel old,' he says, dimly recognizing me, but then people — and beer — have been John's trade for most of his life. 'What are you having?'

'Hello, John. Beer. I don't mind which,' I add, resisting the allure of the line of spirit bottles, as he nods towards the names I don't recognize.

Slowly he pulls me a pint, which seems to take immense effort, while I look around, taking in how little has changed.

'It's the same old place.' He grunts. 'People are always telling me what fancy nonsense I should do with it. Can't see the point in changing it when it works just fine the way it is. Anyway, truth is, I won't be here much longer. I'm selling up.'

I thrust a ten-pound note at him but he waves it away.

'On the house. So what brings you here?'

'Work,' I tell him. 'The murder the other night. I wanted to talk to you — about the victim.'

His face folding into wrinkles as he frowns at me. 'Never had you down as a copper.'

'I'm not. I'm a writer — but I used to be a lawyer.'

He nods, as if somehow seeing that suits me better, pouring himself a half then indicating towards a table in the corner. 'Shall we?'

He's slow on his feet as we cross the room, where he pulls out a chair and, with a sigh, sinks into it.

'I'm trying to remember who your mates were. My memory isn't what it used to be.'

'There were a few of us, but usually I was with Will Farrington.' Nodding as I watch him place me, recognition dawning on his face.

'I always knew the pair of you were underage, you know.'

'You did?' Even now, slightly wrong-footed by the nerve of my seventeen-year-old self.

'Oh, everyone tried it on in those days! Mind you, if you'd misbehaved, you'd have been out of here faster than you liked. Done well, hasn't he? Your mate.'

'Will? I suppose he has.' I'm amazed that John remembers both Will and me, but in his next breath I discover why.

'No suppose about it.' John looks more serious. 'Has a magic touch, that bloke. Happens he's a bit of an expert on this heart condition my young grandson has. If you ask me, it was him that single-handedly saved him.'

Will, I'm thinking, yet again, his presence everywhere I turn.

'To be honest, we're not in touch.'

John raises his eyebrows.

'We fell out. Years ago. History,' I add dismissively.

'Well, he did all this surgery,' John says. 'Touch and go it was, for a while, but it's done the trick. My grandson's like any other lad now. He really is.'

150

'That's good news,' I say politely, imagining Will glorying in the adulation of the families he helps, all of them oblivious to his ruthless, selfish streak.

'He's a bloody miracle worker,' John says. A shadow crosses his face. 'Not all the kids are so lucky. He comes in now and then — Mr Farrington. Seems to work in hospitals all over the country.'

Since when did John call him *Mr Farrington*? But I haven't come here to talk about Will.

'That night, John . . . ' I pause. 'Did you see — or hear — anything unusual?'

'Not particularly. Norton came in. He wasn't a regular, but he'd show up, from time to time. He sat over there.' Pointing to a table near the door. 'He wasn't looking so good, but then he never did. Always thought there was something shifty about him . . . Anyway, then this woman came in — attractive, she was. Younger than him, with long red hair. They talked. Thought she looked upset at one point.' He frowns. 'In fact, I nearly went over. He was a strange bloke. I didn't think any more of it, until late that night when I was locking up. There was this car out there. I'm used to that, people leaving their cars when they drink too much . . . Only the thing was, there was someone in it. Thought it was just a bloke sleeping it off, but when I got closer . . . ' Slowly shaking his head, he grimaces. 'Won't forget that in a hurry.'

He falls silent. I give him a minute to clear the image of Norton's bloodied body from his head.

'The red-haired woman — did you recognize

151

her? She came in here, once or twice, with me and Will — but it was a long time ago.'

John frowns. 'I thought I might have, but to be honest, I couldn't say for sure. Sorry,' he adds. 'I remember you two well enough, but back in those days you were always in here, weren't you?'

I suppose, thinking back, we probably had been, though it hadn't seemed like that at the time. 'Do you remember seeing either of them leave?'

'I remember her leaving. She looked terrible. After, he came over to the bar and had a couple more drinks. I remember seeing his keys on the bar and thinking he shouldn't be driving. But that was about it.'

'Any idea what the time was?'

He nods slowly. 'Must have been tennish when she left — maybe a bit later. Norton was in here till closing.'

I frown. 'Do you know anything about him?'

John looks blank. 'Not really. Last I heard, Norton was living with Fiona Draper. Nice lady by all accounts. But then I can't say I really knew the bloke.'

'What about CCTV footage? I saw you have a camera outside.'

He shakes his head unhappily. 'The police are looking at what there is. Only some young bugger cut the cables a couple of weeks back. One of those hoodlums from across town, I wouldn't mind betting. I had to throw a few of them out a while back. Their idea of revenge, I don't doubt. I hadn't got round to fixing it.'

I try to push him further, but apart from

giving me an address for Fiona Draper, there's nothing he can tell me. After thanking him for the beer, I leave my number, asking him to call me if he remembers anything else.

As I get in my car, I'm thinking about what John told me, which isn't as much as I'd hoped. I know that April and Norton were in the pub that night, at the same table, that she left before he did and whatever they talked about upset her. At the moment, much though I don't like it, the likelihood is that their meeting was prearranged. Even to me, it would have to be some coincidence that brought her all the way from Kent the same night he was killed.

And there's the CCTV. It's not impossible that whoever killed Norton disabled that too, in advance — perhaps the only indication of premeditation, rather than an act in the heat of the moment.

*   *   *

But whatever Norton said to her, however upset she was, even though there's been a murder and an attempted suicide, linked by a phone and a single glove, I'm unable to see April with a knife in her hand, stabbing him.

As I drive away from the North Star, recognizing Will's old road, impulsively I turn into it, taking in the huge, elegantly proportioned houses, mostly Georgian, positioned at the ends of smart drives and indicative of their owners' wealth. Then I pass the house his parents used to own — may still own, for all I know — for the

153

first time acknowledging the difference in our backgrounds that was always there, but that I'd never seen.

Was it here where his arrogance and conceit had taken root? I hadn't seen it in his parents just as I hadn't seen it in him, missing it, as I'd missed so much. Then curiosity takes me further, across to the other side of town, which spreads untidily westwards. Where it's shabby, the houses smaller, uniformly reproduced in matching narrow streets, turning into Magnolia Way, now wearing the cheap gaudy clothes of someone who's trying too hard. The new playground and incongruous flower beds, a too-thin layer of gloss through which I glimpse the same surly mouths and lines of discontent.

⋆   ⋆   ⋆

Back at the B&B, I get out the file I took from April's cottage, pulling out the list of clients I made yesterday, then reaching for my phone. The first three numbers I try don't answer and a couple hang up on me. I'm rapidly losing heart, until I come to a Nina Hendry who, fortunately, is prepared to talk.

'I was given her number by my GP,' Nina tells me. 'I'd lost two babies — it wasn't a good time. April helped me through it.'

'When was the last time you saw her?' I ask.

'It was about two years ago. After my baby was born, but I never forgot her. I don't think I'd have got this far without her.'

From what she tells me, I assume that once

her baby was born, Nina no longer needed April. That this is the nature of the relationship between client and therapist; the entrusting of your most intimate fears to a stranger; that's transient.

* * *

The next two clients I speak to say much the same about April. How she helped them; how indebted to her they felt. And the more I hear, the more it confirms the profile of the compassionate, caring woman I remember her as.

I've deliberately avoided reading the more detailed notes April's made, not wanting to pry into the privacy of her clients. But in the absence of any other source, I've no choice but to look more deeply. The date of each appointment and April's observations are carefully recorded, but it soon becomes apparent that not one of them has seen her in the last year.

It fits with her diary, where more names are listed — names I don't have notes for. Which means there must be another file.

21

I wait for the cover that near-dusk affords me, when there's still enough natural light for me to search the cottage. But as I draw closer, I see the police have now secured it. There's a police car parked outside, and tape across the entrance to April's garden. I drive past, waiting until I'm round the corner and out of sight before pulling up at the side of the lane.

As I search for another way in, further up the lane I find a gate into a field. Climbing over it, I head in what I hope is the right direction. Like last time, I feel myself seduced by the silence. Apart from the sun, the degree lower which it slips just perceptible behind the trees, nothing moves. Not the air, heavy with the sweet scent of a honeysuckle falling through an overhanging branch; not a leaf. As I take it all in, the effect is hypnotic. As if, for a moment, the world is still.

A blackbird's cry breaks the spell. I carry on walking through the damp grass, noticing that the soft down of the same willow seed that plagued me in Devon has reached here too, in the stillness settling like the lightest of snowfalls.

Following the hedge line, I reach the back of April's garden and then, seeing a light on inside the cottage, I pause, hidden among the trees, until it's switched off and two policemen emerge. As they make their way down the path, I wait for the gate to click shut followed by the closing of car doors.

Hoping they won't be coming back, at least until the morning, and seizing my chance, I climb over the hedge and head straight for April's back door. The key is where I left it, under the stone. Quickly I let myself in, closing the door behind me, not daring to turn the light on but, even without it, the mark of police disrespect is obvious everywhere I look. Some kind of search has been carried out, drawers left callously open, papers rifled through and left scattered, the contents of cupboards spilling out. I feel a flicker of anger, wondering why they have to leave it like this, as I hurry through to the sitting room, where it's the same. April's furniture has been moved, her books disturbed, and I go to her study with the sinking feeling that whatever was here to find, it's most likely the police will have taken it.

I try to think. Could April have had something to hide?

Trying to remember all those years back, her small attic flat. The old bedstead that came with it; the small kitchen table and two chairs she got rid of when we moved, because she said that furniture should be either beautiful or loved, and these were neither.

April had been adept at hiding secrets from me. So adept that I still don't know what they were. And with the perspective that comes only from time, at last I understand that, no matter how much I'd loved her, it hadn't been enough; that she'd done the right thing leaving me all those years ago. That my own blinkered naivety had been bad enough, but unspoken secrets are worse.

Looking around the room, I frown. If the police haven't found them, somewhere here are more client notes. If they're hidden, they're most likely important. And knowing April, it'll be an obscure place that she knew for certain would never be found. With the help of the torch from my phone, carefully I go through the room again, but find nothing.

Deciding I need to search upstairs, as I pass the bookcase something grates. At the same time familiar yet out of place, I recognize one of my old law books, a large, hefty tome I hadn't missed, that doesn't belong here. Sliding it out, as I turn its yellowing pages I know I've found something.

Inside the book is what I've been looking for. April's notes, loosely slotted between its pages. It's a genius hiding place. I run my eye briefly over the first three or four, checking the dates before safely placing them back inside.

The book held tightly, knowing I have what I came for, I hesitate in the doorway, not wanting to leave such a loved house so untidy; then, at the back of the bookcase, I catch sight of a notebook.

Curious, I slide it out, flicking quickly through its pages with building interest before slipping it in my pocket. As I pick up my old law book, I notice that the framed photos I saw last time have been taken, most likely by the police — all bar one that they've missed, that's been knocked off the bookshelf onto the floor.

It's a photo of a woman holding a baby and I pick it up, this time looking more closely at the woman's face, too shadowed to make out her features as she looks down at the baby. April's face? Strange, irrational recognition flickers, just for a second, before it's gone.

I lay it on top of the law book, feeling my skin prickle, but it's not with cold. It's the chill of unease, aware the police could come back at any moment. Then as I'm walking out to the kitchen, something else sends a shiver down my spine.

While I've been searching the study, someone's been into the kitchen and fed the cat.

*   *   *

I tell myself I'm mistaken, that there'd been food in the bowl when I came in and I hadn't noticed. There's probably a good neighbour, who'd maybe noticed April's absence. Or maybe the police filled it before they left — unlikely but not impossible. But unease follows me as, in a hurry, I lock the door, hide the key and cross the garden, wondering if I've been seen, feeling the air seeming to stir into life, the stillness of earlier gone.

With a new sense of urgency I cross the garden, clambering over the hedge, and in my haste get caught up on brambles, relaxing slightly only once I'm in the field, away from the cottage and making my way back to the lane. But as I climb over the gate and walk down the lane towards my car, I hear another car in the distance, drawing closer before it slows down behind me. Tense, I force myself to just keep walking, trying not to run, not wanting to draw attention to myself, aware of how isolated I am and discovering a new, paranoid fear.

But this time the car passes, my heart slowing as I realize no one's after me. Back in my car, I lock the doors and glance in my driver's mirror. See nothing, rationalizing with myself as I drive away. Telling myself I've nothing anyone could want. All I have is a set of client notes that no one other than April knows about. I'm of no interest to anyone.

It's only in the safety of my room, after a shower and a glass of whisky warm my blood, the curtains drawn against the darkness, that as I study the pages of April's notes I see the faintest, breath-on-glass trace of a pattern.

As I read more, suddenly my mind is razor sharp, so that I skim through them at speed, making my own separate rough notes as the pattern grows clearer and, at last, I have something.

All the women in this group of clients were in the later stages of pregnancy when they met April; and in the most chilling of coincidences, each woman's baby had a life-threatening illness.

Putting the notes down, I can only guess at the significance of this, unsure whether it's by coincidence or design. I try to imagine what it's like, at what for most parents is a time filled with hope, expectations, joy, instead to be agonizing over a future that might not happen, about the medical interventions that may or may not help them.

In the midst of the hardest time these women had ever known, April was the person to whom they turned. Most likely still is — when I check the dates of the appointments, some are recent. Opening her diary, I find the same names pencilled in over the coming days.

Slowly I put the diary down. I need to talk to all of them, for no other reason than if they don't know what's happened to April, they should be told.

⋆　⋆　⋆

I'm up early the next morning, after a cold shower cuts through the bleariness of my hangover and brings faint colour to my cheeks, pulling on jeans and trainers as I go out, just to walk. It's by chance I pass a newsagent. As I glance towards it, the headline screams out at me.

WOMAN SUSPECTED OF MURDER — BRYAN NORTON KNEW HIS KILLER

Underneath, there's a photograph of a man. Picking up the paper, I study it more closely, feeling my skin crawl as a host of ugly, unwanted memories spiral to the forefront of my mind.

It's a face I saw just once, a long time ago; that I'll never forget. Age has blurred his sharp features, the cruelty in his hooded eyes, but nausea rises in my throat. If what Will's told me is true, that this man is April's stepfather, it changes everything.

22

The longer April was absent from school, the more I convinced myself my concern for her was genuine. April was clever. She deserved good grades but if she wasn't careful, this close to the exams, she'd stuff it up big time. And no one seemed to care except me. There was absolutely no self-interest involved in what I was doing, I decided. If she'd moved away, then I'd just have to live with it, but if she was ill, then I could help her.

Not sure where to start, I gathered together all my courage and tracked down Emily, one of April's friends, who during one of her rare appearances at school was having a surreptitious smoke behind the bike sheds.

'Excuse me,' I said tentatively as I crept up behind her.

She leaped up and threw the cigarette on the ground, then stood on it. 'Fuck it, you made me jump.' She shook her head in disgust. 'What d'you want, Noah? I just wasted a perfectly good fag.'

Up close, her lashes were clogged with mascara. She glared at me and I noticed how dull her hair was, unlike April's which always shone as though she polished it.

'Sorry. Only, I was wondering . . . I haven't seen April . . . '

'What's it to you?' said Emily suspiciously, picking up her fag and lighting it again.

'She's in some of my classes. And she's missing all this revision and practice papers for the exams . . . I was just worried. That's all.'

Emily inhaled deeply.

'I haven't a frigging clue. We had this row and I haven't spoken to her since.'

'Well, can't you find out?' I persisted. 'You're her friend, aren't you?'

She exhaled a long breath. I watched in fascination as the coils of smoke slowly rotated in the air.

'Not really. And I won't be seeing her again,' she said finally. 'My mum won't let me, anyway.'

'Why?' I was curious. I couldn't imagine anyone telling Emily what to do.

'Her brother's a shit,' said Emily shortly. 'Like, he really is. And her stepfather's done time.'

'Just tell me where she lives,' I said stubbornly. 'And I won't tell anyone you told. I promise.'

'You really that fussed?' She frowned at me. 'Can't imagine why. She's with that Pete bloke — you know that, don't you?' She looked at her watch. 'Shit, I should be in English.'

She took another drag, examining her nails as I stood there, refusing to budge.

'Eighty-three Magnolia Way,' she said eventually, without looking up. 'Down the north end of town. Don't fucking say I told you.'

She threw her fag into a patch of grass where it smouldered until she stepped back and ground it out with her heel.

* ★ *

There was no time to waste, not with this new piece of knowledge burned into my brain. With my school bag stuffed with revision notes for April, as soon as lessons were over I set off.

83 Magnolia Way sounded pretty, I thought, in my naivety picturing a street similar to ours, homely and friendly with neat front gardens, because that was all I really knew.

Vaguely heading towards what I thought was the north end of Musgrove, it was a different route from the one I usually took. I was half hoping that fate would take a hand and I'd just stumble across Magnolia Way but of course it didn't work like that. Just as I was despairing of ever finding it, I came to a corner shop with crates and newspapers stacked high outside. As I hesitated, wondering whether to go in and ask, a woman came out.

'Excuse me.' The words were out before I could stop them. 'Only, I'm looking for Magnolia Way. Is it near here, d'you know?'

She paused, not looking at me. 'I'll say. Everyone round here knows Magnolia Way.' Only I didn't like the way she said it.

'Could you give me directions, please?'

This time she properly looked at me. 'What's a boy like you going there for? Or need I ask . . . ' She laughed, a harsh, hollow sound. 'If you've any sense, you'll turn round and go back to where you've come from. That's all I've got to say. Now if you don't mind . . . '

She started to walk away.

'Wait!' I called after her, but she shook her head and hurried down the street.

I stood there watching her scurry away, still muttering to herself, when a voice spoke from behind me.

'Down the end, turn left, first right. That's Magnolia Way.'

I turned round. A young man, unshaven and in ripped jeans, leaned against a lamp post, grinning crookedly. Then he took a swig from the bottle he was holding. 'Who are you looking for?'

'Thanks,' I said hastily and started walking.

'*Hey! Not so fast . . .* '

I could hear him lurching along behind me and, praying he was too drunk to keep up, I broke into a jog, reaching the end, turning left and then right. And as my heart sank, I wished I hadn't.

★ ★ ★

There was nothing remotely pretty about Magnolia Way. In fact it was the most dismal place I'd ever seen. For the first time in my fifteen years, dimly I registered how privileged I was. As I ventured tentatively along the street, reading house numbers, I noticed piles of stinking rubbish littering the tired, pissed-on patches of grass outside front doors, more of it discarded carelessly everywhere I looked. Someone's skinny cat yowled as it fled from under a car and only now and then was the grimness broken by a tidy patch of garden or freshly painted window.

It seemed the cruellest twist of the fates that someone as beautiful as April had been born into the midst of such squalor. Either that, or a celestial mistake. Suddenly my heart leaped as I considered that Emily had given me the wrong address, her idea of a sick joke. But I didn't know for sure. What if April was here and I'd walked away?

Feeling less and less safe the further I went, I kept going, telling myself April did this every day and that if she could do that, I most certainly could do it once.

I'd got as far as number 79 when I heard it. It was a horrible, high-pitched wailing that broke off for a few seconds, then started again. As I walked, I listened, sickened, as it got louder, fighting the urge to turn and run for my life. But I kept walking, unable to tell which house it came from.

Then behind me, I heard footsteps and turned to see a man. Rough and dishevelled, he was ugly in every sense of the word, in the sharpness of his face, how his eyes were lit like burning coals as he glanced up and down the street, in his manner as he shoved past a woman pushing a pushchair as he came towards me.

I walked faster, wanting to get away from him, checking the numbers on the houses as the awful wailing grew quieter, until I reached number 83. Realized the noise was coming from inside.

Looking over my shoulder, I saw the man leaning against a lamp post. Though he didn't move, just his presence was menacing, his eyes narrowed as he watched me.

Filled with trepidation as I pushed the door open, I took a final glance at him just as he spat onto the pavement and turned to stride away in the opposite direction. Then, my heart still pounding, I stepped inside.

'Hello?' I called out, noticing the bolts were bent and the locks broken. *'Hello? April? Are you there?'*

I took another tentative step, then froze, as from somewhere close by I heard a dog bark. The faint wailing noise stopped.

Venturing further in, the first thing I noticed was the stink. Of cigarettes, left where they'd been ground into the worn carpet; of old food and rubbish. Trying not to gag, I went into what appeared to be a sitting room, where it got no better. I just stared, horrified that people could even live here, least of all April. This was no place for a goddess. The wallpaper was ripped in places, the carpet dirty, and everywhere I looked there was stuff: takeaway boxes, beer bottles, piles of clothes, all of it strewn without a thought.

'What . . . are you doing here?'

The whisper was so faint, for a moment I thought I'd imagined it. I spun round.

Huddled on the floor against the wall, she was slumped over, her arms clasped round her knees. She looked terrible, her beautiful hair lank and her face bleached of colour, as though the blood had been drained out of her.

'I was worried. You haven't been in school . . . Are you OK? What's happened? What's wrong?'

But I knew she wasn't OK. I started to panic.

'What's happened? You're hurt . . . ' I was out of my depth, but I stepped towards her, desperate to help while having no idea what to do.

'Go away,' she muttered, closing her eyes against what looked like a wave of pain.

'There was a man,' I said suddenly. 'He was watching me. Did he hurt you?'

She shook her head, mumbling something I couldn't make out, and as I watched with horror, she started to shake. Then her eyes seemed to roll up and disappear into her head, as she slumped even further forwards.

23

Of course, there was no telephone. After I'd tried several times to stir her, I took off my jacket with trembling hands, carefully spreading it over her, before running up the street in search of a phone box. The first one I came to had been vandalized, the handset ripped out leaving a mess of frayed wires. I couldn't see another. Desperate, I ran back to the corner shop I'd passed earlier, where I burst in and pleaded with the owner.

'Please, sir, can I use your phone? Only a friend of mine's been hurt, really hurt. She needs help, sir. *Please . . .* '

I don't know if he'd ever been called 'sir' before, but something in my rushed, heartfelt plea convinced him and his look of hostility gave way to one of mistrust.

'In here.' He beckoned me into a small, gloomy office. 'Be quick. And don't go trying no funny stuff.'

'I won't, I swear on my life,' I told him, having no idea what he meant and using words I'd never used before, but then this was like nothing I'd ever done before.

My hands shaking, I dialled before he could change his mind.

★　★　★

I waited with April for what felt like hours, but in reality could have been no more than fifteen minutes, crouched on the floor beside her while she drifted in and out of consciousness. Each time she came to, murmuring words I couldn't make out before lapsing into silence again, I'd panic, desperately searching for signs of life, from the slightest flutter of her eyelashes to the pulse in her neck, overwhelmed with relief when I found it.

As the distant sound of a siren reached me, I leaned towards her. 'It's okay,' I told her quietly. 'Help is coming, I promise. You'll be OK . . . '

Her eyelids fluttered open as another wave of pain racked her face. 'You shouldn't be here, Noah . . . ' Her voice was so quiet I could barely hear her. 'It isn't safe . . . '

In spite of everything, I felt my heart swell. She cared. In spite of her pain, she was concerned for me. But before I could reply, there was a knock on the door, followed by a voice.

'Hello? Anyone there?'

I was already on my feet, then in the hallway, filled with relief. 'Quick. She's in here.'

★   ★   ★

I stood back after that while they carefully checked April over, then very gently lifted her onto a stretcher and took her out to the ambulance. Then they drove away, leaving me there alone.

Now that April was on her way to hospital, I couldn't get out of there fast enough, running

170

until I couldn't breathe, then slowing to a walk, feeling a mixture of emotions engulf me. Elation that I'd helped her, but mostly horror at how much pain she'd been in, no closer to knowing what had happened to her. But I'd gathered one important, precious piece of information from the ambulance driver. I knew which hospital they'd taken her to.

The next day at school, I made a point of finding Emily.

'You what?' she said, when I told her what had happened. Instead of being worried, as I'd thought she'd look, she seemed vaguely impressed.

'She's in the new hospital, the one that's just opened.' I didn't tell her I was planning to visit April. I didn't tell anyone, just watched the clock on the wall slowly tick, wondering why today was the longest day ever.

★ ★ ★

I'd been to hospitals before, when my mother was ill. But it had been years earlier and my hazy recollections didn't prepare me for the countless busy corridors and several floors of exotically named wards, like Alaska and Costa Brava, which did nothing to take away from the bleakness.

After asking several nurses, eventually I found her, pausing in the door of the ward, staring at the bed at the end by the window, shocked at how small and young she looked. Having come all this way, as I looked at the families flocking round the other beds, I hesitated, suddenly not sure I should be here. But then April turned her head towards me and her eyes lit up.

With each step as I walked towards her, my awkwardness was back. By the time I reached her bed, it had practically paralysed me.

'Sorry.' I'd noticed the bedsides of the other patients, laden with cards, grapes, flowers. April's was pitifully empty. I looked at the starched white sheets covering her. 'I should have brought you something.'

'It's OK. Thank you, Noah — for coming here. And for . . . '

April looked away and a tear rolled down her cheek. Suddenly less awkward, noticing a chair against the wall, I pulled it over to her bedside.

'Are you OK?'

She looked back at me, blinking away tears, nodding just once. 'I will be. When I'm out of here.'

The glimmer of her old spirit satisfied me. It wouldn't be long before she'd be back in school — and in my life.

'Before . . . ' I hesitated, not sure how to ask. 'Why did you miss so much school?'

But she didn't answer, just stared towards the window.

'Will you have to go back there?' I couldn't keep the horror out of my voice at the thought of her going back, near that man whose evil face still haunted me, but the alternative, of her going away, was even worse.

'I don't know yet.' Her voice was achingly empty. Then she sighed. 'They've said I can't.

172

They're talking about a place I can stay. Just until I'm better.'

'What . . . Like a hotel?' Even in my naivety, I knew it was a stupid thing to say, but I couldn't imagine what else she meant. 'Nearby though, so you can finish school?'

April looked away. 'Maybe. They haven't said.'

I didn't understand. Not who *they* were, or why April couldn't carry on at school, stay with friends nearby — like Emily or Bea — or something. Just for a few weeks and pass her exams with flying colours, as I knew she would.

'But it's important, April.' Feeling myself blush at the sound of her name on my lips, but meaning every word. 'You're really clever. Even when you miss school, your grades are still good. You can't give up.'

But she just looked away from me. 'You don't know what it's like.'

The full force of her sadness hit me. 'Then tell me,' I said, desperately. 'Tell me all of it, because I want to know.'

In that moment, I thought at last, she was going to let me into her world, but then a nurse came over and I was asked to leave.

★　★　★

I returned the next day, and the one after that, noticing the colour creeping into April's cheeks and movement into her limbs; as the trauma she'd been through brought us closer. But on the fourth day, just as I was setting off, my mother stopped me.

173

'You're out so much at the moment, Noah. With your exams coming up, your father and I would rather you stayed at home.'

I stared at her in horror. 'I have to go . . . It's arranged.'

But she shook her head, turning back to the kitchen. 'I'm sorry, but that's enough, Noah. It can wait until your exams are over.'

This was how it was. My parents would issue orders I was expected to obey unquestioningly. Well, not this time. I felt an explosion of heat inside me. April was waiting for me. No way was I staying at home.

'I have to meet a friend. From school,' I called after her. 'They're really ill, in hospital. I said I'd visit and you can't stop me.'

I liked how I sounded wild, reckless even. I wasn't a kid. Whatever my mother said, I was going.

'You'll do as you're told.' But the anger in her voice was half-hearted enough not to stop me.

It was the first time I'd openly defied my mother. It's perhaps why, as I reached to open the front door, I heard her voice behind me.

'Just this once I'll drive you, Noah. As long as when you get back, you work.' As I listened to how tired she sounded, I knew I'd found her Achilles heel; that it was easier for her to take me herself than try to stop me.

We drove in a silence that bordered on glacial. My mother was clearly unhappy about what we were doing, yet unable to reason with me. As we parked, she unfastened her seat belt to get out.

I shook my head at her, because this wasn't part of the deal. Nurses were one thing, but my friendship with April was far too young and fragile for interlopers like my mother to come blundering between us.

'There's no point in you coming,' I told her abruptly. 'It's no one you know.'

'I'm coming in with you,' she said firmly, locking the car.

Her presence beside me filled me with resentment, dampening my excitement at the thought of seeing April. When we reached April's floor, I had to get away from her.

I was in too much of a hurry to see the fear that flickered in her eyes, racing along the familiar corridor to the end and through double swing doors into the ward.

Only when I checked my watch and saw it was way before visiting time did I hesitate.

'It's lucky you're early today!' It was one of the nurses, clearly recognizing me.

'I just realized. Is that OK?' Her comment puzzled me.

She winked. 'Just this once. As long as you're quiet.'

At first, I didn't see what she meant. At the far end of the ward, April was standing by her bed, her back to me. Then as I got closer, I saw she was fully dressed with a bag on the floor by her feet.

Suddenly I realized what the nurse had been telling me. 'You're leaving . . . '

Hearing my footsteps, she turned. 'Noah! You're early.'

'You're going,' I repeated.

My words were accusing, held the selfishness of my youth, I knew that, but I couldn't help it. Then I saw the worry in her eyes.

'It's good! It means I'm better! And I'm glad you're here. I wanted to tell you in person.'

'You're going back to that house?' Hating the thought of her being there, yet hating the thought of her going somewhere unknown, maybe further away, even more.

'It's not up to me, Noah. I'm underage. I just have to do what they say. But we've got a few minutes — they're not here yet.'

'Who's they?' I asked her, not understanding. 'And you'll be at school, won't you? When you're really better?'

I waited for her to smile, to tell me that she'd need to rest a bit longer, but yes, she'd be back at school — and everything would return to normal. But her silence told me that wasn't going to happen.

'The thing is,' she said slowly, 'I'm going away.'

As her words sank in, it was my worst nightmare. I felt my mouth open in protest. Then her hand touched my arm.

'Listen, Noah. It's for the best. It gets me away from . . . ' She stopped. I waited, knowing she was going to say something terrible. But all she said was ' . . . horrible people. And a load of stuff.'

I gazed into her eyes, hungry for a glimpse of whatever it was as she blinked at me.

'Oh, Noah, you don't want to know.'

'I do,' I said stubbornly. 'I've already told you that.'

She sighed, then I felt her hand reach for mine. 'You were right — what you said, about exams being important. They are, to you. You'll get good grades and be a doctor or a politician and you'll be someone, Noah. I know you will.'

For the second time that afternoon, I felt powerless. There were so many people intent on controlling our lives. Being a teenager sucked. I looked at April, following her gaze out of the window onto the rooftops, turning to face her.

'So will you,' I told her, biting back my frustration. 'Be someone, I mean. You know you can. You can do anything you set your mind to.'

But she shook her head. 'I'm not like you. I won't be doing my exams. I've missed too much school, anyway.' She said it in a quiet, resigned way that told me she'd decided.

I couldn't bear it. I got up, pulling my hand from hers, wanting to shout and rage about how unfair this was. How whoever was behind this should seriously think what was best for April, because one thing I did know was that taking her away from school, and from her friends, wasn't it.

'Noah?'

I didn't want to believe that there was another world, one I didn't understand. Nor was I giving up. Not yet. I couldn't. I was about to tell her what a big mistake this was, but it wasn't to be.

'April? Your car's here. Are you ready?' It was the same nurse I'd seen on my way in.

Turning my back on her, I walked over to the

window, unable to believe this was happening, feeling my fists clenched in my pockets, my entire body rigid. She couldn't go. Not now. Not like this.

As I stared into the distance, I felt her standing beside me.

'Please, Noah . . . Try and understand. It's for the best.'

I was convinced she was wrong. Then I got my first glimpse of how breathtakingly cruel life can be as, in what was simultaneously the most brilliant and most wretched moment of my life, she reached up and kissed my cheek.

★   ★   ★

I don't remember exactly what happened next. I was too consumed with my own pain to notice how she walked out of the ward and disappeared from sight. Nor, to start with, did I see my mother, standing at the nurses' station, a look of horror on her face.

★   ★   ★

Somehow I dragged myself out of there along the same corridors I'd just flown in on. Just ten minutes later, I was back in the car with my mother. Ten minutes during which I replayed my fantasies for the last time, of April staying, metamorphosing back into the goddess she really was; of her finally being a part of my real life.

As the fantasies faded, I tried to tell myself that it was for the good — for April at least. That people would look after her and that she wouldn't have to go back to that awful house. But it was not knowing when I'd see her again. The pain I felt, so awful and so real, so deep in my chest, I actually believed was from my heart.

It didn't help that I knew my parents wouldn't let this go. I could just tell, but I'd no idea how serious it was until it turned into a full-blown family summit at the dining table, my father, stern, at the head, my mother opposite me.

I sat down, my heart heavy as lead as my father started, stark disapproval in his voice.

'Noah, your mother's been telling me what happened. How well do you know this — April?'

Instantly I felt myself tense. Her name on his lips was wrong. 'She started school when I did. I don't know her that well, really, I mean, I like her, a lot as it happens, but we don't talk that much.'

Even though I didn't want to be here, talking about her, with *them*, I prided myself on the honesty of my reply, regretful that I couldn't tell them differently and that actually we'd become really, *really* close friends. I missed the glances they gave each other.

'We've been to see Mrs Jones.'

Suddenly I was crippled with embarrassment. Mrs Jones was my class teacher.

'Why?' I cried out. 'It's got nothing to do with her.'

'That's enough.' My father's voice was sharp.

'So you'd been to her house before?' My mother's face unfamiliarly shocked.

'No! I'd no idea where she lived. Emily

179

. . . Someone at school told me.'

'I'm not sure I understand,' said my father slowly, 'why you've been visiting her in hospital. And if you were friends, as you say, why you didn't tell us?'

I didn't like the accusing note in his voice. I'd done nothing wrong. What was he getting at?

'She'd been off school. I was worried she'd mess up her exams. She's really clever, only she'd missed too many lessons. I was taking her some revision notes when I found her, that was all. Then I called an ambulance.'

For reasons I didn't understand, this was turning into some kind of a moral inquisition. Instead of them telling me *well done*, and how I'd done exactly the right thing, I watched anxious, uncertain glances float between them.

'I don't understand why you're being like this,' I cried, pushing the chair back. 'She was hurt, I tried to help her, only I couldn't. It's obvious you don't trust me, either.' I glanced at my mother.

My father frowned. 'Don't speak to your mother like that.'

'This is ridiculous. I can't tell you what actually happened, because I don't know. I just know April's better — and that's all that matters,' I told them angrily.

'She didn't tell you?' My mother seemed relieved. 'I was talking to one of the nurses. Apparently a man hit her. In the stomach,' she added.

'*He hit her?*' I felt horrified, sick at the thought of anyone intentionally hurting her and thinking

180

of that horrible, ugly man who'd followed me. Could it have been him? I remember how he'd watched me about to go inside.

'The nurse said she'll be fine . . . But I don't think she'll be going back to school, Noah. In fact, I don't think you'll be seeing April again.'

I already knew that, from April, but the relief in my mother's words and the worry that was now smoothed from her rippled brow made it all the more real. As I sat there, trapped between them, I felt the bottom fall out of my world, leaving a whirling, empty void from which I couldn't escape.

But somehow I pulled myself away. Running from the room, I slammed the door behind me, ignored the roar of my father's voice, demanding I come back there, *right now*. What was wrong with them? This was so utterly unfair. Not only did they not understand, but my parents sucked. My life sucked. This shouldn't happen. Everything was going wrong. I was the person who'd gone to rescue April and now she'd left me.

ELLA

Everyone I know has a secret. Sophie's is her crush on Mr McKenzie, our art teacher. Kat's is that even though everyone thinks she wants to be a Hollywood star, in her dreams she wants to be a surfer. But there's that thing with secrets too, how they take over your head, feeding on your every thought, growing bigger all the time until the day comes they're so heavy you can't walk.

'Oh, Ella — are you hurt?'

I hobble over to my usual chair and stare at the ugly painting. 'Not really. Just ache a bit.'

My therapist looks sympathetic. 'You look really sore. Maybe your mum should take you to see someone?'

Oh, Jeez, please not more strangers sticking their noses in my life. Anyway, my mother's still away.

'I guess my back hurts a bit.' *So does my brain and my heart, in a sad, stabbing kind of way.*

'You've probably pulled a muscle.'

'Yeah,' *I say, in a way that even to me sounds like 'no'.*

She frowns.

'It's OK. Really,' *I tell her, meaning it this time, because it's no big deal and I hate being pitied. And it's not the first time I've felt like this.*

Her face softens. 'Oh, Ella . . . '

Two gentle words that stab me, a knife in my heart.

' . . . what's wrong?'

I can't even look at her. I bend my head to pick at an invisible spot on my jeans for what feels like ages. Then hear myself sigh, as I realize that now she knows that there really is something, if I don't tell her, it'll be the next time — or the one after. But can I trust her?

Then because I can't bear this any longer, and because the air is so thick that I'm suffocating, I break the rule.

'It's my brother.' As I speak, my jaw clenches.

Then I make myself look up to watch her face, because words hide things but faces don't, and because you can't trust even the most likely people.

'I didn't know you had a brother!' Which is what she was always going to say — but from the way her eyes startle, her involuntary surprise, I want to believe her.

'No one does. He's twenty.' I shrug, swallowing the lump in my throat, watching a puzzled look cross her face as she takes in what I've said.

'How come you've never mentioned him before?'

I shrug.

'Is he in trouble?'

I hesitate. 'I don't think so. I don't know. He doesn't come to our house.'

'Oh? Did something happen?'

I hold her gaze. Now for the million-dollar question. Do I really trust her?

'I think so . . . ' I'm stalling. Then I take a deep breath that sticks in my lungs, because even the air is heavy. 'I'm really scared to tell you.'

She doesn't speak for a moment. 'You don't have to tell me anything, Ella. But think of it like this. What's the worst that can happen if you do?'

I feel the millions of little capillaries inside my chest tighten. The answer to that depends on whether she can keep a secret. What's the worst that can happen if she can't? 'Can you open the window, please?'

I watch her get up and go over to the window, throwing it open, feeling relief as cooler air reaches me. Buying time — for both of us. I mean, it's some bombshell, telling her I have a brother no one knows about.

When she sits back down, neither of us moves. And suddenly I know that whatever comes next, I have to tell someone. That if I don't, it's going to crush me. Nice choice you have here, Ella. Death by crushing or death by telling the truth.

'My mother isn't his mother.' It comes out in a rush, even before I've decided I'm doing this. 'In fact . . . ' I hesitate, because what I'm about to say sounds unbelievable. 'I'm not sure she even knows about him.'

She looks shocked. 'But if you know about him . . . Surely your father wouldn't keep something like that from her?'

'You won't say anything, will you?' I'm holding my breath. I mean, she must know I'd sue her or report her if she did, but it's really important. I need to make sure.

She waits. She does that a lot. Waits. Therapists' code again, meaning 'tell me more'.

'Look,' I start, trying to sound casual, even though my heart is thudding and my head feels light, because she needs some perspective. 'Most families are weird. You're a therapist — you must see it all the time. They all have stuff they don't want people to know about. Like Sophie's mother's having an affair. It's like really, really obvious — but no one talks about it.' I shrug. 'Theo's kind of a secret, that's all. It's not a big deal.'

Just big enough that some days it paralyses me. I read upside down as she writes 'Theo', then adds a question mark, before looking up again, puzzled.

I say it again. 'You won't mention him to my mother, will you? Please?'

She hesitates. 'Not if you don't want me to. Patient confidentiality applies to therapists, as well as doctors, as I'm sure you know. But . . . '

I follow her glance towards the clock, where the minute hand creeps towards the hour, as I hear the next question forming, the one I've already decided not to answer.

Where is he . . . ?

Knowing there's still time.

But she doesn't ask.

24

What disturbs me most about the photo in the paper is that I hadn't known — and I should have — that the man who attacked April all that time ago was her stepfather. Not even when we were about to be married, when I should have been the person she most trusted. Perhaps fear had prevented her from naming him, or she just wanted to forget. But if that was the case, how come, after all this time, she'd arranged to meet him?

As I wrestle with the facts, I'm thinking of a teenage girl, terrified into silence; how it might be, not to be able to share the horror and the pain; in doing so unloading some of it, but not knowing if others would believe you. How it might be easier always to keep it to yourself.

I can see, too, how an outsider would view his murder as revenge for what Norton did to her all those years ago. But there's another question, an important one, because apart from me, does anyone else even know about him?

If someone does, if April is charged with Norton's murder, it gives her a motive. But it still doesn't make her guilty, I remind myself. There could be any number of people who wished him dead.

So far, I don't have the answers. Turning to

the back of April's diary where a few phone numbers are listed, I search for familiar names, hoping to find Bea's, not even knowing if they're still in touch. But it isn't there.

I spend the rest of the morning trying to get a sense of April's life. Making more lists, of her regular clients, the odd ones that stop by now and then; the clinic where she works one day a week, mapping as far as I can the last few months. By late afternoon, my floor is spread with pages from her folders and notes of my own.

Then as I get up, I manage to clumsily knock over the photo I took from her cottage, of the woman and the baby, cursing that I've broken the frame. I remove the photo from the shattered glass and see what's written on the back.

With Theo.

I feel myself frown as I stare at the name, but before I can give it more thought, my phone vibrates in my pocket. I pull it out, noting an unfamiliar number.

'Hello?'

Wishing I hadn't. Realizing, as soon as he speaks, it's Will.

25

I accept Will's invitation to lunch at his home the following day, because so far, all I've drawn is a blank, and because also, I'm curious. About his family and about his home, too, because Will's one of those rare people who seems to have it all.

I gather up more of April's notes and continue reading, learning more about territory that's unfamiliar to me. The stories of parents in emotional turmoil, families in crisis, facing the unimaginable as their baby hovers between life and death; all of them linked by the common thread of sadness.

And the more I read, the more I understand that for this most awful part of their lives, April was a lifeline, offering support, sharing the load of their pain. Typically, she gives little away about herself, but what she writes indicates that she has more than just an idea of what they're suffering.

I pause at that point, wondering what's happened to her since we parted. Then in another sentence, she writes about miracles, about hope and how fragile life is. How there are no guarantees, but there is always now.

I stop reading at that point because it's how she used to make me feel.

In the moment.

★　★　★

The next morning I make a fleeting visit to the hospital, where I'm now a familiar enough face that the nurses don't question my presence as I take my usual place at the window looking into her room, silently projecting my thoughts.

I hope you don't mind my being here. I won't stay long. I just wanted to say that I'll do everything I can to help you.

Then I add, *Believe it or not, I'm having lunch with Will. Am I stupid or what?*

It's intended humorously and I try to imagine what she'd say, half waiting for a reply, straining my ears for a whispered word, my eyes for a butterfly flutter of lashes on her cheek.

'I sometimes question their reasons for keeping visitors away.' The voice comes from behind me.

'Sorry?' I turn to see one of the nurses.

'Well, when someone's been on life support as long as Ms Rousseau has, you'd think the police would try anything and everything to bring her round.' Like me, she's gazing through the window at April.

'It's procedure.' I pause. 'I might lean too close to her, she might whisper something no one else can hear. But I agree with you.'

I don't stay long. There seems no point in holding imaginary conversations with someone who isn't there. I walk out of the hospital, no more convinced that she'll wake up than I was yesterday, almost at my car when my mobile rings. This time I recognize the number.

'Will.'

'Hi. Sorry, Noah . . . There was an emergency

and I got called in this morning, which means I won't be home after all. But we could still meet, if you like. There's this pub up the road from you — the White Horse, on the Edenbridge road — don't know if you know it?' Like me, he's brusque, businesslike; establishing ground rules.

'I'm sure I'll find it.'

'Good. I should be able to make it for one thirty.'

*   *   *

I find the pub easily, so that I'm early enough to buy a pint and find a table next to a sash window that looks onto a neat, ordered garden.

Will is minutes behind me and, in the couple of seconds before he sees me, I watch him, confident and self-assured in an expensive suit and open-necked white shirt. With the same charisma he's always had, only honed and polished by years of professional acclaim.

He strides over, holding out his hand. 'Good to see you, Noah. Sorry about the change of plan.'

'It's fine. Nice pub.'

'Another drink?'

I shake my head, picking up the glass I long to drink but have barely touched, because I need a clear head, still watching as he walks over to the bar, chatting to the staff. It seems here, like everywhere else, Will is known.

'I was quite surprised to hear from you,' I say carefully, when he comes back and sits down opposite me. 'And I'm still curious, about why you called.'

Will raises his eyebrows, then lifting his glass, briefly glances away. 'You're a difficult man to track down, Noah. And Devon of all places . . . What is it you find to do down there?'

The gloves surreptitiously slipped off, his voice light with an undercurrent of sarcasm. I feel myself stiffen. 'I'm a writer.'

I don't tell him that I'm moderately successful but I've yet to write a bestseller.

'My turn to be surprised,' he says smoothly. 'I had you down as a career lawyer.'

I know the kind he means, who spend their working lives in small offices dealing with equally small, menial, unexciting cases for moderate fees. Like my father.

'I still work now and then. I guess I got sidetracked,' I tell him by way of explanation, then stop, folding my arms and then unfolding them again, aware of the spectre of awkward silence that's settled between us.

'Look, I'm not going to apologize,' Will says eventually. 'It was a mess. But it's history. We should clear the air. April was the screwed-up one. We both know that. Though, when you think about her background, it's hardly surprising.'

I'm silent, because it's not how I remember it, and whatever April had or hadn't done, it was Will who was guilty as hell of fucking my life up. Sitting back, I look straight at him. 'And you've kept in touch with her?'

Will shrugs. 'For professional reasons. It just

so happened that her name turned up on a register we use. She's quite a highly regarded bereavement counsellor and so it's useful if I need to refer anyone. It doesn't happen often, but sadly, not all my patients make it.'

His reference to death is matter of fact. By contrast, I think of April's notes, full of compassion; of her gentleness with wounded creatures when I first knew her, suddenly remembering the bird she rescued.

'Do you see her much?' Recalling how gently she'd picked it up and carried it to the woods.

'Hardly ever,' Will says. 'Look, are you seriously considering representing her? Only, is that wise? I've already spoken to a chap I know — he says he'll fit her in. If you've any doubts . . . '

That he's curt, rather than kind and concerned, tells me how little he cares.

'I'm sure.'

'Even after what she did to you?'

He's mocking me. I fight an urge to get up and walk out, but I need information from Will. It takes every last shred of self-control to stay put. I manage a shrug.

'It's in the past. Like you said earlier. It's history. I've moved on. But there's one thing I'm interested to know. And that's why.' Sitting back, I fix my gaze on him. 'Why you're so sure she's guilty.'

'I'd say it's obvious.' For a moment, Will's eyes shift sideways. 'Firstly, there's the evidence. The murder weapon. And her phone . . . And, of course, there's what that bastard Norton did to her all those years ago. I mean, what sort of guy rapes his fifteen-year-old stepdaughter?'

As he speaks, I'm hiding my shock, my churning stomach, because this is the first I've heard about a rape. I'd called the ambulance for April, visited her in the hospital — yet I still hadn't known. And she'd never told me, in all the time we were together.

'But of course, you'd know all about that,' he says lightly, still watching me.

I'm completely thrown, yet in the midst of my turbulent emotions, I'm determined to give nothing away, because we're sparring partners, Will and I. In combat. Our relationship reduced to winning and losing.

I nod the lie.

'You've got to admit — it all points to her being guilty,' he says.

'You're forgetting one thing.' Holding myself together, I lean forward, meeting his eyes, clutching at the first thing that comes to me. 'If it was revenge she wanted, why leave it so long?'

It's clear he isn't expecting that. I watch as his jaw clenches. 'I don't know. Maybe she ran into him and just lost it. Shall we order?'

⋆ ⋆ ⋆

After that, I'm only half listening as Will tells me about his incredibly talented wife and beautiful daughter, about the house on the South Downs, my ears pricking up when he mentions tours and concert halls.

'You've probably heard of Rebecca Masters?'

His face smug, enjoying my reaction which makes it clear I have. It had been impossible to miss their wedding, splashed across the papers, a lavish affair between the world-famous singer and the dashing surgeon. 'You really must come to the house — for dinner. We'll fix a date.'

I nod. 'Great.'

It's not a world I'm familiar with, but even so, I've seen Rebecca perform on television, at the most prestigious venues round the world with the most famous orchestras. And suddenly I don't need to see the house to know it's spectacular, a mansion set amongst landscaped gardens, immaculately maintained. Then my thoughts turn to their daughter, wondering how it is to be the child of such legendary parents; if there's any corner in Will's life for the ordinary.

26

2000

After the wedding was called off, after I got over the initial shock enough to stay sober, I began to look for April. It was reflexive, just as I couldn't help reliving our past, holding on to the pain that was my only link to her, as I trudged around the places we used to go.

I didn't so much as catch a glimpse of her hair or a turn of her cheek. It was as though she'd vanished. I gave up in every sense of the word. It wasn't long afterwards that I felt myself shut down. By locking away my most painful emotions, I was able to face the next stage, as I thought of it. I moved out of the flat — which, at the time, symbolically meant moving on. Closing the door on our old home, oblivious to the knowledge that what was in my head would be harder to shift.

My new flat was a studio, its minimalist interior entirely different from the home April and I had shared, which at the same time both soothed and troubled me, its emptiness a statement only of how little I cared.

In a life that was barely recognizable, I focused on work, putting in progressively longer hours as casework filled my head and took over my life. Even walking along the street, my mind would be on the latest case I was working on, to the extent that I'd reach my destination without any memory of how I got there. Days that blurred into each other while alcohol blurred my nights.

It was six months later, on one such mindless walk late at night, that I stumbled, literally, into Bea.

'Watch out . . . ' A woman's voice jolted me from my thoughts. Then she looked up. '*Noah!* How are you, darling!' Her annoyance gone as she reached up and kissed me on both cheeks.

'Hello, Bea.' Catching a faint whiff of something I thought was brandy on her breath, I was relieved that after my outburst the last time I saw her, she appeared to hold no grudges. 'You look fantastic.'

She did. Her fair hair elegantly swept up, she wore a print dress nipped in at the waist and matching red heels.

'Thank you.' She smiled, her eyes lighting at the compliment.

'You've obviously been to quite a party.'

I was dusting off social skills that, these days, I had little use for. But as I spoke, I watched her smile vanish and a look of pure shock replace it. She stared at me, and I knew that whatever she was going to say, it wasn't good.

I heard it under the gloom of a street lamp, to a soundtrack of passing cars, as Bea took one of my hands. 'Oh, Noah . . . What I have to tell you isn't going to be easy.'

'It can't be worse than the last few months,' I joked feebly, hoping I was right. 'I imagine it's something to do with April.'

Bea nodded, then looked away, and in those few seconds I realized I'd far from given up on April, feeling a cataclysmic sense of the earth shifting under my feet. Then she turned back, meeting my gaze.

'Noah, you should know, she's with someone.' Even as I glanced around at the passing cars, I could feel her eyes on me.

I shrugged. 'It was inevitable. Sooner or later.' I'd hoped just not sooner — or for a long time. Preferably never.

'Are you OK?'

I shrugged again. 'Of course. It's over between us. I know that.'

She hesitated. 'The thing is, it's a bit more than just *with someone*.' Her eyes darting anxiously. 'They're engaged. That's where I've been tonight — to their engagement party. Well, not really a party. It was small — just a few of us. For drinks — and dinner.'

'Great,' I nodded, feigning enthusiasm, determined not to show the truth, that I was still heartbroken and that this news, drip-fed, piece by agonizing piece, was just as devastating now, several months later.

'Oh, Noah.' Bea looked desolate. 'You wouldn't say that if you knew. It isn't great. She says it's what she wants, but I don't see how it can be . . . '

I felt myself shiver, but I had to know.

'Who is it?' I demanded. 'Who's she marrying?'

I didn't need to hear her whispered answer. Bea's stricken face said it all.

I don't know how many miles I walked that night in total darkness, oblivious to every face and building I passed, seeing only April with Will, imagining them together; searching for elusive answers to impossible questions. I couldn't understand how she could even consider it. Then I thought of Will's effortless charm, and the way so many girls seemed to fall for it. Had they been having an affair all along? Had April ever truly loved me? Feeling an unsurpassed hatred towards Will, who I'd believed for so long was my friend, who'd told me April was a whore, then proposed to her.

He'd broken all the rules, intent on getting only what he wanted — no matter who was in his way. Good old Will, who was everybody's friend, all the time playing me for a fool.

It was as the last vestige of my love for April was snuffed out that a new understanding dawned on me. Life wasn't fair or caring or just, nor did the good guy get the girl — that was a myth too. Life was a bastard. As for the girl, she belonged to the double-crossing, lying, cheating weasels of the world — like Will — and always would.

ELLA

In between our appointments, I decide I trust Julia. I like how she doesn't tell me what to do or anything. No 'strategies' or 'exercises' like the others tried to give me, which is kind of cool. And telling her about Theo helped, kind of. After I told her, I felt the wave of her shock, then watched her file it away with everything else she knows about me. But it's still a game. With rules. Next time I see her, I already know what's coming.

'I've been thinking a lot about what you told me last time. About Theo.'

I pause, in one of those expensive silences when she waits for me to break, looking at the tiny plait in the side of her hair that's threaded into her ponytail. She always has cool hair.

Eventually, when I don't respond, she continues. 'Only I was wondering. If your parents don't talk about Theo, and you don't think your mother even knows about him, I was wondering how you do?'

There it is. Well, she'd better listen up, because this is where it starts to get complicated.

'First, I'll ask you a question.' I wait again, to check she's really listening. 'Only, if you had a letter that you really, and I mean really, didn't want people to ever read, like if you'd done something bad that you didn't want anyone to know about, you'd rip it up or burn it — or

199

something — wouldn't you?'

'Yes. Probably.' She looks puzzled. 'I suppose you might have a reason to keep it. But then you'd hide it away, really well.'

'Right. But you agree? As long as the letter exists, you know there's a risk — or a possibility — of it being found. It's the potential effect of its existence.'

I pause as she looks blankly at me. But I've given this a lot of thought.

'Things mostly happen because of cause and effect, don't they?' I continue. 'Even people. For example, I am an effect caused by the sexual union of my parents.' Which is something I'd rather not think about. 'Everything about me — my hair colour, the blue of my eyes, how tall I am, how quickly my brain works, comes from my genes, comes from them.'

She frowns. 'I'm familiar with the principles of cause and effect — but I'm not sure what you're getting at.'

I try again. 'OK. Here's another example. In theory, you could say the first two years of my life are missing. I don't remember them — I was too young. And there are no photos. They got lost when we moved.'

She looks stricken. 'That's terrible.'

I nod. 'It's annoying. But the effect is that the world has been spared another set of cutesy baby photos, because of the useless removal firm. Agreed?'

It sounds flippant and I'm not. Some days it makes me really sad, but there's nothing I can do. The photos have gone. Her eyes follow mine.

'OK. Look at it this way. If you hadn't done something bad, you wouldn't have written the letter about it in the first place. So you wouldn't have to hide it.'

I wait to check she's got it.

'The letter is caused by the bad thing you did,' I say slowly, watching her. 'And then the letter becomes the cause of being found, because it exists.'

She shakes her head. 'I've no idea what you're telling me here.'

I give up, then it all comes out in a rush. 'OK. Where I'm going is, I found something.'

Then I feel the flush of guilt in my cheeks. Neither of us breathes. If you had a pin and dropped it, you'd hear the high-pitched ting of metal hitting the wood floor as it bounces, then rolls.

I wonder if I've told her enough. But not too much.

She holds the kaleidoscope of my thoughts. Twists it. 'Somewhere you shouldn't have been looking?'

I meet her eyes.

27

2016

I hadn't known that Will's betrayal had cut far deeper than April's. That I'd forgiven her, but not him. That not only do I dislike Will, I don't trust him.

And for as long as April's in a coma, for as long as he's voicing his opinions of her, because he's a famous surgeon and because status is power, people will listen to him.

Back in my room, I try to ignore the whisky bottle, putting the kettle on instead, wishing I had access to April's mobile, which there's no chance of, because as I already know from Will, the police have it.

Then, drinking my tea, I pick up her diary once more, starting all over again at the beginning of January. By the time I reach the end of March, a routine's emerging, with the same names cropping up each week at their usual appointment time. For example, Daisy Rubinstein favours Thursday mornings and Caitlin Merrow does every Friday at midday without exception. Sadie Westwood's name is there, more often than not crossed out and pencilled in again, which after I've spoken to her, doesn't surprise me at all.

Every fortnight or so, usually on a Tuesday, she's written '*clinic*'. There are other, more random entries related to dental appointments, or reminders to herself. Then two weeks ago, an entry that's simply the letter '*B*', written beside '*The North Star*'.

I stare at it; feel myself frown. My first thought is of Norton. *Bryan* Norton. Could she have seen him more than once? Or had she gone there for some other reason? Could the B stand for Beatrice? Are they still in touch? Even occasionally, maybe, because they'd been close for so long. If they are, Bea might know something.

Not for the first time, I wish I had April's phone. But with most of the world connected by the Internet, as I've found out it's not easy to disappear. When it comes to social networking, I'm not a natural but for the first time in about three years, wondering why I hadn't thought of it before, I click on to Facebook — and I'm in luck. When I search for her name, I find April uses it too. In just seconds, I'm looking at a list of her friends.

As I scroll down the brief list, the only Beatrice is a Beatrice Fairchild. I don't recall Bea's surname, but I recognize her face. Like us all, older, but when I click on it, still the same glamorous Bea I remember.

From the looks of it, Bea isn't someone who splashes her life across the Internet either. Her profile is private, which seems somewhat out of character for the Bea I remember, highly sociable, with a flamboyant, devil-may-care streak. But, as I know too well, things happen. People don't stay the same.

Curious to know more, I google her, but the

only B. Fairchild is ex-directory and without more to go on, such as a place or occupation, she remains unremarkably, obstinately invisible.

But at least, with Facebook, I can ask.

Hello Bea, I hope this reaches you. I'm not sure if you're still in touch with April but there was an accident and she's unconscious in hospital — St Antony's, in Tonbridge. There's more, though. She's in trouble, which is why I'm hoping you might be able to help.

I hesitate, add my mobile number — I'd rather a verbal conversation than a digital one — then hit send.

★　★　★

Out of the rest of April's Facebook friends, I recognize no one, but I figure it would be more surprising if I did. I turn my attention to her clients again, but when I continue making calls down the list, it's clear the relationship April has with them is professional only. Everyone I speak to knows little of her personal life.

But later that afternoon, when I call Daisy Rubinstein, April's regular Thursday-morning appointment, she invites me over to talk to her.

April clearly had a following — the Rubinsteins' house is twenty miles away, which strikes me as a long way to drive just to talk. It's a modest house in a quiet neighbourhood. Ordinary. But as she shows me in, I start to see she's anything but.

'I don't know April well, but if there's anything I can do to help?' Daisy has long straight hair and, even with the huge dark circles under her eyes that tell their own story, she's pretty.

'Before — I didn't tell you everything. April's on life support. She took an overdose. The police suspect she may have killed someone, then tried to kill herself, only they broke in before the pills had taken effect.'

'God.' Daisy looks shocked. 'So, what does this have to do with you?'

'We were friends,' I tell her briefly. 'A long time ago. And I'm — well, I was — a lawyer. I knew her very well.' I hesitate, wondering how much to tell her. 'Would you agree that there are some people who are incapable of harming others? I believe April's one of them, but I need to prove that.'

'I see.' I watch her twist and turn the facts I've given her, trying to make them fit with the April she knows. Then she frowns. 'Excuse me, but I'm having trouble with this.'

'So am I. I suppose what I'm asking for is any insight you might have, as her client — professionally or personally.'

Daisy frowns. 'I can tell you how I met her. It was my GP who suggested contacting April. He said she might help a little — that she was a good counsellor. Anyway, when I met her, I was seven months pregnant. My unborn baby had been diagnosed with an incurable condition.' Her voice is low and accented, and suddenly she looks tired beyond belief.

'It's a long story — but my baby had an infantile form of Tay–Sachs disease. You may have heard of it . . . ' She glances at me.

I shake my head.

'No,' she says, as if to herself, then looks at me. 'Don't worry. A lot of people haven't. Basically, it's a progressive disease of the nervous system. And incurable. To begin with, you can't tell. Even when you know it's there, it's invisible when they're born. And so you wait, watching, knowing that over the course of just a few months, it will slowly and cruelly take your child's life. Just as they're getting to know your face, they lose their sight. You want to talk to them, reassure them, and then you realize they can't hear you.' Her voice falters. 'Their taste goes, then they can't feel when you touch them. Eventually they become paralyzed.' She breaks off, looking at me, stricken. 'That's when you know you don't have long.'

I'm shocked, trying to imagine how it must be to be presented with such a diagnosis. To have a sick child you can't comfort. To always know the torment that lies ahead. For a moment, neither of us speaks.

She goes on. 'There is no treatment and I was faced with the remaining two months of my pregnancy, carrying my baby, knowing he would suffer, then die — or having a termination.'

'I'm so sorry,' I say humbly. 'I can't imagine.'

'You can't. I couldn't. Not until it was happening to me. I would go and see April. Do you know her house? Only we'd sit in those chairs in her study, by the window that looks out

206

onto her beautiful garden. I'd scream and cry, and she'd just sit there. I swear . . . ' She pauses again. 'I knew nothing would change, and I can't explain it, but she knew, deep inside, how I felt. Not just that, though. It was like she took some of the weight of my hideous burden. God. I've often wondered how many burdens she must have carried, because not many people could do that.'

I know nothing about parenthood, but I know about loss. Even so, I can only glimpse the hell Daisy has suffered. Is still suffering, for all I know. But it's only a glimpse, unlike April, who would have witnessed Daisy's pain first-hand. And Daisy hasn't told me if her pregnancy went to term; if her baby is still alive. Then in her next breath she answers both of my questions.

'Losing a child changes you forever.'

The silence is broken when she gets up.

'I'm sorry,' she says suddenly. 'I'm not sure why I'm telling you all this. I didn't mean to burden you. I think I can only tell you that April's extraordinary. There isn't a name for what she does, but I truly believe she shared my pain and, in doing so, made it more bearable. Will you let me know? How she's doing?'

Feeling her eyes on me, I find myself nodding. 'Of course. And thank you — for talking to me.'

Outside in my car, I sit for ages in silence, thinking firstly of April, then Daisy, humbled by such honesty, thinking about how impossible her choices were, how cruel the reality for her and her child. How fine the line between life and death.

28

The next morning, there's still no response from Beatrice. Planning to visit the hospital, I get up later than I'd intended, shower, then head to the dining room for breakfast, pouring a cup of coffee and picking up a couple of the papers lying on the side.

Knowing exactly what I'm looking for, but not happy when, four pages in, I find it.

MURDER SUSPECT IN ATTEMPTED SUICIDE

An unnamed woman is suspected of murdering Bryan Norton, before attempting to take her own life. Police were unable to give her name, but said that they were not looking for anyone else in connection with the case. Norton, 76, was found stabbed in his car late last Monday night outside the North Star pub.

It's mentioned in the other paper too. God knows how they got hold of this. So now the speculation will start. Someone will find April's name and her relationship to Norton. The whole matter of the past she'd left behind catching up with the life she's built for herself; the people who hold her in such esteem. Who rely on her, trust her. What impact will it have on them?

What little appetite I had gone, I get up and

208

drop the papers in the bin. Then I head for the hospital, my head full of thoughts about the unfairness of what's happening. How, whether she's guilty or not, the world will know what April tried so hard to keep hidden.

As soon as I enter ICU, I see the familiar face of one of the nurses.

'Morning, Mr Calaway.'

'Good morning. How is April?'

'She's doing OK.' Quiet, guarded words that don't raise my hopes, that tell me she's no worse, nor is she better.

It's not a surprise. I nod my thanks, continuing along the corridor towards April's room.

'You've just missed another visitor,' the nurse calls after me.

I turn round. 'Who was that?'

The nurse shakes her head. 'She didn't say who she was. She had fair hair. A little shorter than I am — she was here for some time. I think they must be friends — she seemed quite upset.'

Bea. She'd read my Facebook message. It must have been her.

'How long ago?' I ask the nurse, my hopes rising.

'She only left a few minutes ago. I'm surprised you didn't pass her on your way in.'

'Thanks. I think I know who she was. I might just see if I can catch her,' I call over my shoulder, already jogging down the corridor because there are many ways in and out of here, a three-dimensional maze of stairs, lifts, corridors. Through the swing doors I break into a run, taking the stairs, then at the bottom glance left and right, desperately searching for a glimpse of her.

There's no sign. I gamble then, going for the left corridor — what I now know to be the most direct way to the car park — breaking into a run, apologizing to the tide of people sweeping towards me, until I'm outside. But as I jog up and down the parking lanes, scanning the cars, there's no sign of her.

★　★　★

'Did you find her?' When I get back, the same nurse is waiting for me.

I shake my head. 'She must have gone. Was it the first time you'd seen her here?'

The nurse nods. 'Apart from you, and that lady today, there've been no other visitors — not while I've been here — that's if you don't count Mr Farrington. Such a wonderful man. She's lucky to have him looking after her.'

Will, again. I'm struck with irritation that everywhere I go, his glittering presence is inescapable.

Pushing him from my mind, I continue along the corridor to April's room, noticing straight away that it's different in there. In spite of the rules, there are flowers.

ELLA

It's 2014. Wednesday 16th July. A day I'll never forget, of powder-puff clouds and crystal rain. I'm excited, looking for my passport, because I'm going to Tuscany to stay with Kat.

'It's in your father's office.' My mother's voice floats down from upstairs where her hair is being curled and pinned and sprayed ready for a dinner party.

'The top drawer of his desk.'

I'm skipping down the long hallway, the tiles cool under my bare feet. Round the corner to the quietest part of the house, the hem of my dress swinging, thinking about this other world I need to pack for. About pale sand and turquoise water; pasta dinners and how it won't rain even once and the Italian boys Kat talks about; about the midsummer sun and the haze of heat over the hills.

I'm back in the cool damp of an English summer, pausing outside my father's office. It's habit. I'm not supposed to go in here, but it's OK today because my mother told me to. Opening the door, breathing leather and furniture polish and silence.

Walking across the thick carpet. Perching on the edge of his chair, spinning, just halfway round, then back again. Sliding open the top drawer, finding my passport just as my mother said. My eyes pulled to the one below, that has a key. Wondering what he locks away. Idly trying the drawer, expecting it to be locked shut. Surprised when it opens.

Not meaning to pry, as I leaf through what's there. Pick up the letter. Only as I read it, realizing what it is. A moment when time freezes, burned forever on my retina. I'm halfway through reading the second time, the names sinking in, when I hear footsteps. Folding the letter hastily. Laying it where I found it, closing the drawer just as the door handle turns. Getting to my feet as the door opens and my mother comes in.

Only half her hair pinned up.

Holding up the passport for her to see, turning away from her. Checking out of the corner of my eye that the drawer is closed.

'I was calling you. Didn't you hear me? Come and let Celia do your hair.'

Silencing a hundred questions I can never ask as I follow her. Electric shock tangled with guilt. Excitement banished. Happiness gone.

Does she know my father's secret? Am I the only person who doesn't know?

Wednesday 16th July 2014. The same day as five minutes ago. Time resumed, forever changed.

29

Having looked up the clinic where April works part-time, I find it's in Guildford. It seems a long way from where she lives when there are other clinics much closer, but maybe she had an expertise they felt was needed there.

The roads are clear and the drive doesn't take long. It's midday when I pull up outside the large, converted town house, realizing too late, as I go inside, that any clinic that's any good is likely to be busy and that I haven't exactly thought this through.

'Do you have an appointment, sir?' The receptionist looks up from her desk.

'I don't. Actually, I'm here about one of your therapists. April Rousseau.'

'Oh? One moment.' She glances down and quickly finishes typing something. I notice that the gold-edged name badge pinned on the cerise cardigan she's wearing says 'Elizabeth'.

'What about her?' She looks up again.

'I'm a friend. I'm also her lawyer.'

Elizabeth glances behind her, then leans towards me. 'I don't know what's happened, but there's enough gossip about that poor woman. She left a voicemail, explaining she didn't know when she'd next be in, so to please fit her clients in with other therapists.'

I frown. 'When was this?'

'Some time the other night. Late. I picked it

up the next morning. She sounded terribly upset. I tried to call her back, of course, but she didn't answer. Has something happened?'

'Yes.' I glance around, wondering if there's a manager I should talk to. Judging Elizabeth to be trustworthy, I need as much help as I can get. 'Look, it's important — is there somewhere we can talk?'

'I don't know.' She looks doubtful. 'I'm on my own just now.'

But I look past her as one of her colleagues walks in.

'If you wait a moment, I'll see what I can do.'

It's a busy practice, the phone constantly ringing and being answered in hushed tones, clients wandering in and out to and from appointments. I glance at a board that lists the names of the therapists who work here, then at the young woman who comes over and sits down next to where Elizabeth was. Then Elizabeth comes back and I follow her into a small room.

'I'm Elizabeth Coleman,' she says. 'I've worked here for fifteen years, so there's not too much I don't know. Please tell me. What's happened?'

Sensing genuine concern in her voice, I tell her.

'It explains why the police were here,' she says quietly.

'When?' My ears prick up.

'Yesterday. Two of them came to see the practice manager. She's called a meeting later today.'

'About April?'

214

Elizabeth nods. 'I suppose it must be. I'm sorry, but I just don't believe it. Not April, of all people. She's gentle, compassionate . . . She's a therapist.' She looks completely flummoxed.

'If it's any help, neither do I,' I tell her. 'Can you tell me anything — related to her personal life — that might be helpful?'

Elizabeth shakes her head. 'April kept herself to herself. She's an excellent therapist. And enormously popular. It makes no sense. I suppose we'll have to tell her clients.'

I pause, because this is tricky. 'I know that many, if not all, of her private clients had difficult pregnancies. Some knew they were likely to lose their babies. I know it's confidential, but do you happen to know what kind of issues she dealt with here?'

Elizabeth clams up. 'I'm sorry, but I don't know anything about her clients — and even if I did, I wouldn't be able to discuss them with you. We deal with a whole spectrum of problems here, in confidence as I'm sure you must appreciate, Mr . . . '

'Calaway,' I say quickly. 'Noah Calaway.'

'Mr Calaway. I'd like to help, but you do understand, don't you?'

'Of course. I shouldn't have asked.' In a professionally run practice such as this, it's what I'd expect.

'It's fine.' Elizabeth gets up. 'I'll tell you what I can do. She used to have lunch with one or two of the girls. I could ask them for you — maybe if they know anything, they could give you a call?'

'Thank you.' I'm nodding but I'm not hopeful.

'I'll leave you my phone number. Er, do you have some paper?'

Cursing that I don't have a business card to give her, I realize how unprofessional it makes me look. She looks at me suspiciously. 'Come over to the desk and I'll make a note of it.'

★ ★ ★

After I leave there, I walk around Guildford until I find a small stationery shop that for an inflated price promises to have a hundred business cards printed in two hours' time. Then, hungry, I find a pub by the canal where I order a pint and a sandwich, sitting outside, wondering whether Elizabeth will do as she promised.

I'm halfway through my pint when a number flashes up on my mobile. Hopeful that it's one of April's therapist friends, I answer it.

'Noah Calaway.'

'Mr Calaway?' My heart sinks as I recognize the voice instantly. 'Detective Sergeant Ryder here. Do you have a moment?'

'Of course, Detective Sergeant. What can I do for you?'

'Just one or two questions, sir. About Ms Rousseau.'

'OK.'

'Well, we've been analyzing calls to and from her phone. The day before the murder took place, she called your home number in Devon. Three times, to be precise. Would you care to explain why you didn't tell me?'

I'm completely astounded. April called me?

How did she have my number? And why? 'I didn't know. Are you sure?'

'We have the times, sir. Five thirty p.m. Again at five thirty-five and then ten minutes later at five forty-five.'

'I have absolutely no idea. I work from home. It's rare for me to go out except maybe to get some food — it could have been around that time. I don't remember. Even if I'm there, I don't always hear the phone. In fact, I don't use it.'

'Is there anyone who may have seen you to confirm your whereabouts?'

'No. Unless maybe my neighbour saw me? Clara Hayward — she lives next door. She notices most things.'

'Thank you, sir. Just one other thing. Am I right in saying also that, some years ago, you and Ms Rousseau were engaged to be married?'

He sounds almost unbearably smug, as though he's enjoying the chance to catch me out.

'That's right. We were. She broke it off.'

'So I heard. But she must have told you, surely, that she'd been raped?'

Anger twists inside me that even he knows about this, that he's been digging into the fine print of April's life.

'Or weren't you aware of that?'

Making it obvious, from the edge in his voice, the exaggerated fake surprise twisted with delight as he hits a nerve, that he's enjoying this.

'She didn't tell me. I never found out why.' I try to keep the irritation out of my voice. 'She never explained. If you must know, I heard only very recently, from someone else.'

At the other end, Ryder coughs. 'You expect me to believe, sir, that the woman you were about to marry didn't confide in you? Strange, wouldn't you say? Or maybe she didn't trust you. Thought you might do something rash . . . '

'We talked about most things. Just not this.' Defensive against his barbed words and sharp tone. 'It was her choice — she must have had her reasons. It wouldn't be that surprising, surely, to want to forget?'

'You tell me . . . ' I know from his voice that Ryder's smirking. 'Anyway. That will be all for now. Sir,' he adds mockingly. 'No doubt someone will be in touch.'

After he's gone, I drain the rest of my pint, slamming the empty glass down on the table before hurling my sandwich into the canal, where a flurry of ducks fight over it before it sinks. Online or otherwise, I'm not an easy person to find. And again I'm thinking, where had April got my number? And why?

Then I'm remembering finding out about the rape, from Will in the pub. How I had been too fraught with horror at the picture my mind had painted, too shocked to know if he'd seen it, written on my face, that I hadn't known.

Ryder would undoubtedly have questioned Will. But also, if he was any good, he would have checked April's medical notes. Presumably it's all there, from her time in the hospital.

Back in my room, I get out the little notebook I found hidden at the back of April's bookcase, which previously I've only glanced at. Trying to decipher the scrawl of names, I recognize some from her client notes. Again, there are dates, but also what appear to be names of hospitals. Effingham Wood, Croydon Central and St Richard's being the ones I recognize. Then next to some of them, two initials.

The 'WF' catches my eye. Will Farrington? He told me he referred patients to her. Perhaps she was tracking where most of her clients came from.

Out of curiosity, I google Will and start to understand why people are in awe of him. According to the articles I find, he's involved in ground-breaking surgery in newborns with heart defects. This must have been what John at the North Star had been talking about.

The more I read on, the more I realize just how highly he's regarded. It explains his association with April, too, because surgery on a newborn carries a far higher than average risk. As Will told me himself, not all his patients make it. Some of their stories are there too — stories like Daisy Rubinstein's and stories where Will's or someone else's skill changed the course of a baby's life.

Even so, I've an inescapable sense that I'm missing something. There's no arguing with the cold, hard facts — the motive, the evidence, the murder victim, an unconscious murder suspect — but it's too neat, too obvious. Too perfect. Then there's the broken CCTV. The police may be mistaken, because there's another possibility they can't rule out. That all along, this was planned by someone.

That April was set up.

30

The possibility that April was set up haunts me but leaves me none the wiser, as the day of Norton's funeral arrives, dull and overcast. I park in the crematorium car park, knowing I have no place here, but curious to see who comes.

I walk up the path, seeing the police officer standing slightly apart from the people gathered outside one of the chapels, suggesting that this must be Norton's; then as I draw closer, notice his name displayed beside the door. As I scan the tight faces and hooded eyes that show nothing, the creased suits and dark coats brought out for the occasion, the small crowd contains no young people, nor is there anyone I know.

There's something odd about the mood, a lack of emotion of any kind, which means I'm somehow surprised that when the hearse pulls up, when life and death are briefly room-mates in the small square outside the crematorium, the woman who steps forward to follow the coffin looks so normal.

I'm last through the door into the chapel, sliding into the row of seats at the back, next to a thin woman in a skirt flecked with dust who smells of cheap scent. The police officer remains outside. The service that follows is one-size-fits-all — unremarkable, impersonal — yet somehow evoking emotions in me that don't belong here, that come from when my father died. Not just a sense of loss, but the reminder that for none of us can life be certain.

Anywhere else, for anyone else, the lack of a eulogy, the smallest personal touch, would have saddened me, but the man inside that wooden box raped his stepdaughter. There can be no rejoicing in his life.

It's a service in which no thought has been invested, just the briefest of brief words, the cheapest of gaudy funeral flowers, the only music a few piped bars as the curtain closes on Norton for the last time.

★　★　★

Afterwards, there is no invitation to a wake, which makes me think that perhaps there isn't one. I hang back, but everyone drifts away quite quickly and as I walk back to my car, suddenly I'm irritated — with the time I've wasted, that I've learned nothing. Away from the crematorium, I drive too fast, heading out of Musgrove until I miss the turn-off to the motorway and find myself caught in a one-way system. Narrowly missing the car that pulls out of nowhere just in front of me, my irritation peaks.

The driver sticks his finger up at me and my hand uncharacteristically connects with the horn, as I'm unable to contain my frustration at everything that suddenly seems set against me. Then recognizing the road to the North Star, on impulse I turn down it.

Leaving my jacket in the car, I pull off my tie

before wandering into the bar. There's no sign of John today and I wonder if he's taken a day off. I order a pint and, as I do so, out of the corner of my eye notice the funeral party come in.

I watch them emerge, butterfly-like, from their dark coats, shedding their silence, splashing noise and brashness across the room. Lively talk and shrill laughter have replaced earlier indifference, as they order drinks and make jokes before tucking into the platters of sandwiches that are brought out from the kitchen.

I feel myself frown, because this is definitely a wake of sorts, with the venue planned and the food ordered, though not open to just anyone. The ranks of Norton's followers-on are clearly closed.

But it's a strange send-off. My own default respect would find gravity more appropriate, no matter what Norton has done — or perhaps nothing at all, rather than this fairground-ride jollity. I continue to watch, their demeanour making me increasingly uncomfortable. And why come back to where Norton was killed? I flit between whether it's right or wrong, settling in the end on a need for closure. Until suddenly it comes to me, from their raised glasses and flushed faces, that it isn't Norton's life they're celebrating.

It's his death.

⋆ ⋆ ⋆

My uncomfortable feeling stays with me, such that I don't notice my neighbour from the funeral service weaving her way towards me, clearly the worse for wear, until she lurches into me.

'What are you doing over here?' Waving her empty glass around, clearly recognizing me. Under thick pancake make-up, her cheeks are reddened and her eyes too bright for only the one glass.

'I just got here.' I hold out my hand. 'Noah. Forgive me — you are?'

'Lena.' She winks a heavily shadowed eyelid. 'How did you know the old bastard, then?'

'We go back,' I say briefly. 'I happened to be in the area. But I didn't know him well.'

She steps closer, lowering her voice slightly. 'If you knew him at all, you'll know we're better off without him. Especially Fiona, the poor love.'

I frown. 'They weren't happy?'

Lena tips her head back and laughs, a horrible guttural sound. 'Happy? I should say not.'

'Why did she stay with him?' Shaking my head in disbelief, because I don't believe in sitting out the worst kind of relationship and because Norton deserved nothing.

But Lena's face takes on a look of suspicion. 'Didn't really know him at all, didya? Here, come over and talk to the others.' She's still talking to me as she turns and waves across the room. 'Someone will remember you — like Don. DON? Donny?'

Her shrill voice cutting through the hum of voices. Forgetting her empty glass, she starts weaving her way back towards them. I consider following her, but when I glance again towards the funeral party, some of them are already staring at me, their hostility undisguised. It's not the time to do this. She turns to see if I'm behind her, but I'm already out of there.

★ ★ ★

There's a sense of my world shifting, of the slashing of moral codes and social conventions; of solid ground under my feet turning to quicksand. Of too many people who live by their own rules; I can't help wondering, too, if I'm one of them. I contemplate calling Will. Trading my principles for his familiar smooth arrogance across a table, for an hour or two of inflammatory conversation and a few beers. I even pull over to call him, but before I've switched off the engine, my mobile buzzes and the screen lights up with an unknown number.

★ ★ ★

'Hello? Is that Mr Calaway?' It's a husky, slightly hesitant voice — a woman's.

'Hello. Yes, hold on a moment . . . ' Turning off the engine, I close the window against the traffic noise.

'Hello. How can I help you?'

'We haven't spoken before. Daisy gave me your number. Daisy Rubinstein?'

'Of course, I remember Daisy. Are you another of April's clients?'

'You could call me that . . . ' She hesitates. 'My name is Lara, Mr Calaway. Lara Collins.

224

Daisy said you were looking for information about April. Anyway, if you still are, I think I can help.'

'Actually, if there's anything at all you can tell me, it would be great. It really would.' After the grotesque charade of Norton's funeral, Lara Collins is salve on my anger. I feel myself breathe out my tension, suddenly hopeful. 'I can talk now, if you like.'

She hesitates. 'Or maybe we can meet? Would that be better?'

I understand — she wants to gauge the measure of me, decide whether or not she trusts me.

'Where do you live?'

Her voice is light. 'Oh. Of course, you wouldn't know, would you? I'm April's neighbour.'

I try to think where the nearest house to April's is, failing. 'I'm sorry. I'm not sure where you mean.'

'You can't see it from the road. But if you pass April's on your left, there's a drive a quarter of a mile further on. You're probably busy — ' She breaks off. 'But if you'd like to, you could come over now.'

'I could be with you in about an hour.' Adding hastily, 'And it's Noah.'

'Hi, Noah. See you in an hour.'

★ ★ ★

Lara Collins looks as delicate as she sounded when she called. Slight, with long, light brown hair in a ponytail, her faded ripped jeans are loose fitting. She shows me into a small, cosy kitchen that's dwarfed by an ancient Aga.

'Please sit down. Would you like coffee?'

I nod gratefully. 'Please — if it's no trouble.' As I sit down, my head starts to clear.

'Daisy told me what you said — about April,' she tells me as she fills the kettle. The softness of her voice belying what's only faintly visible underneath. Steel. 'I know it's impossible to truly know someone's heart, but I don't believe she did it.'

'Nor do I. Thank you.' I take the mug she hands me, staring at the familiar blue-and-white design of Spode's Willow Pattern, the only design I can put a name to, because April had loved it.

'April gave them to me.'

I look up, startled.

'The mugs. I saw you looking.' Lara slips into the chair opposite, pushing an escaped lock of hair behind an ear, stirring her mug thoughtfully.

'Since I saw Daisy, I have been trying to decide whether to tell you this. What I'm about to tell you, even Mark — he's my husband — doesn't know.' She hesitates. 'The question I have is, can I trust you?'

I'm not sure how you measure trust, whether in the honesty of a face, the directness of eye contact. Or deeper, whether it comes down to instinct.

Lara takes a deep breath. 'I think I'm telling you because April's a good person. She helped me, but also, we were friends. And I imagine there are things only a few people know about her.'

My mouth opens to tell her she's wrong. That you can truly know a person's heart. That I know April, probably better than anyone, because there are relationships where time is immaterial, because no matter how long since you've seen each other, whether two weeks or twenty years, it makes no difference.

'Something happened to April.' Lara speaks quietly. 'In the past. She never said what. But I know it was big.'

I frown. 'What makes you say that?'

'You can see it in her.' Lara's eyes are wide. 'You know, how there are people who have no time for small things? Pettiness, I mean. In the way they let things go — because whatever huge, life-changing thing happened to them, it gave them a perspective most of us can't ever have.'

She pauses for a moment, looking directly at me.

'April has no agenda.' Lara is resolute. 'No ego. No awards she's chasing. No.'

She sits back in her chair and frowns.

'What April does have is a gift.'

ELLA

As we sit under the ugly painting, I try to explain to her about how a sheltered childhood doesn't do you any favours.

'Everyone has to grow up,' I tell her. 'The more that's hidden from you, the harder it is.'

'That's one way of looking at it.' Julia's face is sad. 'I prefer to think of a carefree childhood as a gift. In an ideal world, children should feel safe — and free — at the same time.'

'Yeah. Right.' It comes out automatically.

She looks surprised. 'I think it's instinct. To protect your child — well, for most people.'

'Even from the truth?'

She frowns. 'This isn't really about childhood, is it? We're talking about Theo, right?'

I nod.

'I don't believe in lies, Ella. But don't you think there has to be a reason?'

Maybe she's right. But what about the bigger picture? Because when honesty and trust have gone, they're gone for good.

I sigh. 'Well, imagine you're me. You get to thirteen years old and, out of the blue, you discover a brother no one ever talks about.'

She shakes her head. 'Maybe his mother cut ties with your father for a reason. I know it's sad — but it happens. Or maybe your father is in touch with him — in secret — only the longer it goes on, the harder it is for him to explain to you

228

and your mother . . . But I don't know any more than you, Ella. I'm guessing. The only way to find out would be to try and talk to your father.'

'No way.' I blurt it out, then put my hand over my mouth while I think. 'It just doesn't make sense. I know I have a nice home and everything. So why isn't he part of it too?'

'I know it's hard,' she says quietly. 'When you discover your parents are not perfect. They get things wrong.' Then she frowns. 'You've known since you were thirteen?'

I nod.

'You've told no one?'

I stare at the floor. 'There wasn't any point.'

'It's a long time to keep a secret.' She pauses and I'm thinking WTF because I've done it again. She's going to squeeze out of me more than I want to tell her.

'I have a question,' she says carefully as I feel my eyes roll all on their own. 'When you've kept it to yourself all this time, why are you telling me now?'

Oh. She has no freaking idea, because I don't even want to think about the rest. The overheard phone calls, the dreams. The skeleton-leaf memories that don't belong to me. It's already a huge deal that she's the first person I actually trust enough to share just a tiny part of this.

Even if it helps, I can't tell her. I can't tell anyone. That when I went back and found the desk unlocked again, there was more.

31

As Lara tells me April has a gift, my head is reeling again, remembering the dream I had.

'Noah? Are you all right?'

Around me, the room starts to spin as Lara's disembodied voice comes to me. I lean forward, resting my head in my hands, because it's a day of crumbling bricks and steel girders that melt like butter. I'm thinking of the dream I had, the night before I left home, of the burning woman holding something out to me; her words, '*This is my gift.*'

For a brief moment, I stare into the glittering eyes of madness, before somehow pulling back. Telling myself that wherever it is they come from, dreams are just that. Dreams. Flimsy creations of the imagination — not real.

'Noah?' There's concern in Lara's voice.

'I remembered something, that's all.' My head in my hands, I'm silent. Eventually I look up at her.

'I'm reading too much into things. It's been one of those days.' I try to remember what she was saying. 'You were about to tell me, about April having a gift.'

'Yes.' Lara gets up and walks over to the window. 'She's an incredible counsellor. But she's also a healer.'

A wave of disappointment washes over me, because I was hoping for proof of April's innocence rather than the revelation that she's some kind of crackpot.

Sensing my response, Lara closes up. 'Maybe I shouldn't have told you.' She turns her back on me and gazes outside. 'Not everyone understands.'

Suddenly I'm light-headed again, then to my embarrassment overcome by nausea.

'Sorry, need to use your bathroom,' I mumble, getting up.

'Through there, on the right.' Turning to point the way, Lara watches me sharply.

* * *

When I come back in a while later, Lara throws the kitchen window open, then lets me drink the sweet tea she's made while she sits and watches me.

'Have you thought maybe you should see a doctor?'

It's a statement rather than a suggestion and it takes me aback.

I look at her, startled. 'There's nothing wrong with me. I'm fine.'

'Can I be honest?' Her eyes are unblinking. 'Only you really don't look well.'

'I'm all right, really,' I say feebly, aware of my clammy skin and the nausea, more distant but still there. 'It's been a long day.'

Knowing as well as Lara does, that's not why.

'My father was an alcoholic.' She says it quietly, without looking at me.

My hands are shaking and my throat parched.

But she's got this wrong. 'I like a drink as much as anyone, but I'm not an alcoholic.'

She doesn't reply, but her silence, the slump of her shoulders, send a ripple of alarm through me.

'Can I ask you something?' Deflecting the conversation away from myself; both of us aware of my inability to be honest even with myself, my classic denial.

'Of course.'

'Have you been feeding April's cat?'

'Yes.' She looks cautious.

'Great. I was there and I was quite sure that when I left, there was more food in the cat's bowl than when I'd arrived.'

'That was you? I'm so sorry. I wasn't sure who it was. I thought I'd forgotten to lock the door when I came in the last time. When I heard footsteps, I just left some food and went home. Silly, really. I should have checked. If I'd known . . . ' A frown flickers across her face. 'Why were you there?'

'I haven't explained. April and I were friends a long time ago. More than friends. Actually . . . ' Then because the entire day has felt off track, and because it can't become any stranger, I decide to tell her. 'April and I were going to be married.'

I know from Lara's silence that April hasn't told her. 'Anyway, like I said, it was a long time ago. I was — am — a lawyer. Like you, I think she's innocent. But I also think she may have been framed.'

Lara's face is grave. 'And you're trying to find proof.'

I nod. 'At the moment, I'm just trying to talk to people who know her. So far, I've drawn a blank, but I'm working on the assumption that someone, somewhere, must know something.'

Which is why I'm here. 'I suppose I'm wondering why you called.'

By the window, Lara hesitates as if undecided, then comes back over and sits down again.

'Before I tell you,' she says, 'I'm not someone who thinks they can talk flowers into blooming early or that vegetables scream when you pick them. OK?' She says it fiercely, needing me to understand.

'About a year ago, we'd been trying to start a family, but nothing had happened. It had got to the point where we were considering IVF. Anyway, then I fell pregnant. At last we were going to be the family we wanted. We were making plans. Imagining holidays, birthdays, Christmas — all those times that have so much more meaning when there are children . . . We were over the moon.' She sounds anything but, as she pauses, remembering.

'I went for a twelve-week scan. I'll never forget . . . ' She pauses again. 'Do you have children, Noah?'

I shake my head.

'Well. The scan is a big deal. You see your baby for the first time. I'll never forget it — only for all the wrong reasons.' There's pain in her eyes. 'Instead of telling us to listen to the heart or to look at our baby kicking, the nurse said nothing. Then she asked us to wait while she went to fetch someone. That was when we knew.'

Lara clasps her hands on the table. 'I won't bore you with all the details, but what followed was every parent's worst nightmare. There were more scans while they established there was a problem with the baby's heart. Then we were sent to a consultant. He told us there was nothing he could do. He offered us a choice, as he called it. Shall I tell you what our choice was?' She pauses, continuing more slowly. 'We could terminate, or go to term in the knowledge that our baby, if it wasn't stillborn, would die within days.'

She takes a breath. 'We saw a different consultant who said the same. That was in May last year. My baby was due in October. We'd wanted this baby so much, we couldn't terminate. Then I met April.

'I would go into her study and she would let me talk or cry, whatever I needed. You see, I was already grieving. For the baby I was carrying — the future Mark and I had planned for us all. Then one evening, she called me out of the blue. If I wasn't doing anything, would I like to come over. Mark wasn't back from work. I went.'

She pauses. 'That time, we sat outside. There's a corner of her garden where if you sit for long enough you can see the movement of the moon behind the trees. I didn't know you could do that — watch the moon move. It was incredibly still. And so peaceful. In between, we talked a little, and then I realized I was crying. I couldn't work out why, but I felt her touch my arm. Then she told me none of this was my fault. She told me life can be cruel, but extraordinary things can happen. That I shouldn't give up.'

The expression in Lara's eyes changes. 'It was all she said. But something changed and suddenly, inside, I felt calm. So calm — and warm. Hours had passed without me noticing. It was dark and I knew Mark would be wondering where I was. As I walked home, I remember looking up and thinking I'd never seen so many stars. You'll probably think it's silly.' She glances at me. 'But it was as though April had taken my memories and my pain for safekeeping. I've always wondered what it cost her to do that.'

I wait for her to continue.

'We became close. I'd bared my soul, I suppose you could say, but I felt safe with her.' Lara frowned slightly. 'Once I asked her how she was able to listen to so many clients, day in, day out, in so much pain. I remember exactly what she said.' Lara looks at me. 'She said she thought of them as being in freefall, only somehow, through no fault of their own, their parachutes had got tangled. She was their safety net.' She looks puzzled. 'After that, I sensed she was about to tell me something else, only she stopped herself.'

Lara swallows. Then her eyes glitter with tears. 'Our baby was stillborn. It was — is — so very hard. I would see other mothers and I couldn't help thinking, why me? Why us? But extraordinary things do happen. I'm pregnant again.'

As she holds her hands protectively over her belly, I see a barely perceptible roundness.

'We tried for years before,' she says softly. 'I'm not a religious person, but sometimes I wonder if our baby has found his way back.'

As she talks, her honesty, her portrayal of naked emotion, cracks a layer of ice on my frozen heart as I'm reminded that, even after the worst heartbreak and pain, it is still possible to be generous. To love.

Then she looks straight at me. 'Tell me, why am I opening my heart to you?'

I manage a glimmer of a smile, just as she says, 'April. What can I say? She's extraordinary.'

Then she frowns. 'You know, something might not have been right. Just lately. She didn't say, but I felt it. She wasn't as present, I think you could say. Normally, with April, she's so focused. She was, just not as fully. I think there was something on her mind.'

'You've no idea what?'

Lara shakes her head.

The day has been exhausting, extraordinary. Thanking Lara for her time, I leave her, deeply tired but calm, taking something with me from what she's shared.

But the day isn't over, the feeling doesn't last.

32

When I pull up and park outside the B&B, I'm barely out of my car before Ryder shatters my calm.

'I don't have all day,' he says nastily.

I feel myself tense, because a confrontation with him is the last thing I need tonight. 'Excuse me, Detective Sergeant, but it's been a long day. Couldn't this wait until tomorrow?'

His face reddens. 'You should try answering your phone.'

'Usually I would,' I tell him. 'Only it just so happens it needs charging.' I fish in my pocket, holding it up so that he can see the screen is dead. 'See? I'm not lying.'

Usually I'd bite my tongue, hide my irritation behind polite blankness, but after the day I've had, his vulgarity incenses me.

'Can we get on with this? I'd really like to go inside.'

He glowers. 'A question.' He makes no pretence of any courtesy. 'Only we tried to track down your neighbour — Mrs Clara Hayward.'

Anxiety curls inside me at the tone of his voice, because he thinks he's found something.

'Doesn't like you much, does she?'

He doesn't elaborate, just goes on.

'Then there are the three phone calls Ms Rousseau made to your home, phone calls you deny all knowledge of. Is there no one who might have seen you that day?'

'I live in the middle of nowhere.' My voice steely. 'Sometimes I don't see anyone for an entire week.'

Ryder's grin is a rictus smile. 'We'll get to the bottom of it, make no mistake. We've been on to the local station and they'll be sending someone round to see your neighbour. Sir.'

The 'sir' is mocking. I stare at him. 'Like I said, she may not have seen me.' Then I remember. 'Actually, there is someone who saw me. I took my car to be serviced.'

'How convenient.' Ryder stares at me. 'You have the name and number of the garage, I take it.'

'The mechanic's a chap called Sam. He rents an old barn at Lower Holdsworthy. That's about all I can tell you.'

'So you'll have a number for him.' Getting out a notepad and pen.

'All in here.' Waving my dead phone at him. 'Sorry.'

★   ★   ★

Eventually he leaves and I let myself into the house, where the landlady looks at me suspiciously.

'Everything all right?'

'Yes. Thank you.' I'm too bone weary to care that she's been watching from behind twitching curtains.

'That man you were talking to . . . ' She pauses. 'Was he police?'

'Detective Sergeant Ryder.' Starting up the stairs.

'There hasn't been any trouble, has there?'

'No. No trouble.'

Aware of her eyes following me, her obvious anxiety. Walking until I reach my room, when I lock the door and throw the window open, pouring myself a drink which I down in one before I pour another, plugging in my phone and deleting three messages without listening to them, all from Ryder. Then lying back on my bed, staring at the ceiling as the familiar warmth circulates in my veins.

Whatever he's thinking, I can prove to Ryder I've no part in this. There'll be evidence, somewhere. I just have to find it. Then the chilling thought strikes me — because I'm starting to suspect that April's been framed — what if I'm being set up too?

I pour another drink, then read for a couple of hours, dozing off before I go to bed so that I'm half-asleep when my mobile rings.

'Noah Calaway.'

'Hello? Noah? I'm sorry it's so late. It's Beatrice.'

33

Through its whisky-haze, my brain is slow to focus. 'Bea! You got my message!'

'I did. I almost didn't call you, Noah. I'm not sure I can help — I haven't seen April for such a long time. Only when I saw Norton's photo in the paper . . . Well, when your message said April was in trouble, I put two and two together. You'd better fill me in.'

'You won't believe it,' I tell her. 'Her phone and glove were found in Norton's car, with the murder weapon. The police picked them up and went straight to her home to arrest her. She'd taken an overdose. She didn't intend anyone to find her, Bea.'

'God.' Bea sounds shocked. 'I can't believe April would do that.'

'Did you know what Norton did to her?'

Bea sighs. 'I knew he abused her. She spared me the details, just said he was a complete bastard. He probably deserved what was coming to him.'

'Look, I should tell you — I'm here as her lawyer rather than a friend. The police think she's guilty and I'm equally sure she's not. I don't know how busy you are, but could we meet up? Talk about this properly. Maybe for lunch?'

She hesitates. 'I'm not sure. Noah, I'm in the middle of a pretty hideous divorce. I'm lying low.' She laughs hollowly. 'God, James would

240

love to catch me with someone.'

I try to reassure her. 'I don't mind where we meet. And I can assure you, no one knows me here, Bea — apart from my landlady and Will.'

'Oh.' She sounds unsure. 'I suppose a coffee wouldn't do any harm. How about tomorrow? I could do late morning — I live in Cheltenham, though.'

She sounds doubtful again. But distance is the least of my worries. 'It's not a problem. I'll come to you.'

'Actually, I know just the place!' Sounding more like the Bea I remember. 'The most dull, nondescript cafe there is — at Tambridge Services. Miles from my home and it'll save you having to drive all the way here. It's perfect, Noah. Anonymous and absolutely ghastly. No one ever hangs about there.'

★ ★ ★

When I get there, early, I see what Bea meant. Tambridge Services is indeed dismal. Inside are brown tables and chairs, and my nose wrinkles at the odour that lingers, of stale deep-fried food and cheap coffee. I buy a black tea, finding a quiet corner away from everyone else, where I wait.

Keeping half an eye on the door for Bea, I watch the random assortment of people wander in and out, then to my annoyance, someone comes and puts their bag on the table right opposite me. Just as I'm about to get up and walk away, she pulls off her hat and grins.

241

'Bea!' I get up and kiss the cheek she offers. 'You haven't changed — except, well, maybe that hat.'

She may be going through a divorce, but the years have been kind to her. There are a few faint laughter lines, but her hair is still honey blonde, her eyes bright.

'My clever disguise.' She hugs me, then holds me at arm's length, her eyes twinkling. 'You're a gorgeous man, Noah Calaway!' she says, sitting down, looking around. 'I'd forgotten quite what a dive this is.'

I wonder what kind of a man she's married to, who warrants such subterfuge. 'Yeah. It is, as you said — perfect. Can I get you a cup of tea? I thought it was the safest bet. I mean, a teabag and hot water . . . '

'Thank you, but I'll pass.' She glances at my cup with distrust.

'How are you? And I'm sorry — about . . . ' I'm talking about her divorce.

'About James? Don't be. He's a shit. I can't believe I stayed married for so long. It'll be over soon, and I can move on.' Her voice is bright enough, but in the faint shadows under her eyes I can see the weariness she tries to hide, its toll on her.

'What happened?' I start to ask, but she shakes her head.

'Honestly. Let's not go there. Tell me about April. If you ask me, Norton had it coming to him.' She glances around guiltily, then lowers her voice. 'I really shouldn't say things like that.'

'Actually, it happens I agree with you. What do

you know about him?'

Bea sighs. 'I met him once. And by met, I mean that I was at April's house, after school one day. Though I have to admit I completely asked for it.'

'What do you mean?' My ears prick up.

Bea shrugs. 'As you know, April and I used to hang out after school and she'd come back to mine. Quite often, as it happened. But when it came to inviting me to her own home, she was always reticent. Secretive. Of course, now I understand why. But then . . . '

She looks at me, her blue eyes honest and tinged with regret. 'I was a bitch, if you want the truth. I knew there was something she was keeping from me, but I'd no idea what it was. I told her that if she didn't take me back to hers, I wouldn't be her friend.'

Bea shakes her head. 'I don't know who I thought I was, giving her an ultimatum like that. Anyway, I remember walking down that street she lived on, thinking she was deliberately taking me to the wrong place. I'd never seen anywhere like it. Magnolia Drive, I think it was called.'

'It was.' It was how I'd felt.

'Of course, you went there. You probably remember that the house was just as grim. If I hadn't seen it for myself, I never could have believed April lived there. There was always something extraordinary about her, I always thought . . . Anyway, there we were in the kitchen, with April standing over at the sink, making us glasses of orange squash, when Norton came in. Straight away, he stood too

243

close to her. I remember staring at them, horrified, because she was so beautiful and he was this vile creep who was trying to touch her. That was when she turned and pushed him away. Then she told him to fuck right off. I'd never heard her speak like that — in jest maybe, at one of the idiots at school, but not meaning it. He started walking away — well, stumbling really. He was that drunk. Then he came over to me. I'll never forget how his eyes wandered up and down me, as though he could see through my clothes. He was repulsive.' Bea shudders.

'When he'd gone out of the room, I asked April if he was always like that. She nodded, then said she didn't want to talk about it. Shortly after that, her mother came in, then a man arrived. I heard their voices as they went upstairs.' She shakes her head as if trying to shake the memory. 'I don't think April could bear me being there. She told me I had to go, that it was a mistake asking me there.'

Bea's eyes fill with tears. 'I knew she was strong. She told me she used to fight to keep him away. But she didn't always win. I kept away from her after that.' Bea's voice wavered. 'Wasn't that awful? Of course, what I should have done was help her. Told one of our teachers or something. She hated it there. It was awful. And she had nowhere else to go.'

Until it got so bad that the authorities intervened, when Norton raped her.

Bea goes on. 'The worst of it was her family. She had an older brother. Jason, his name was. He was a nasty piece of work. He was killed a few years later — in a car accident, so the story went. Rumour had it he was into drugs. Anyway, back then, he and his friends . . . Well, you know how pretty April was. I never knew for sure, but I suspected he was taking their money in return for her . . . favours, let's call them.'

Suddenly I feel sick. 'Did she tell you that?'

Bea shakes her head. 'Not in so many words. But looking back, knowing what I know now, all the signs were there. And remember how she'd be off school for a few days, then she'd come back, a bit pale, perhaps? But other than that, you'd never have guessed.'

'I remember. She missed so much school,' I tell her.

'Dear Noah. Yes, I'm sure you do.' She hesitates. 'I was never sure if you knew why. I knew about one abortion, but there may have been more.'

'I had no idea.' I stare at the table. 'She never talked about any of it. Was it really as bad as you remember?' I was looking for another explanation, anything other than the sickening truth.

Bea looks sad. 'I don't think I'll ever forget. But is it really that much of a surprise? Her father wasn't around. Her mother was an alcoholic — and a prostitute. God only knows what went on in that house.'

It's too late, I know that. Even so, I'm flooded with guilt, because I should have known.

Bea reaches into her pocket for a tissue. 'Can you imagine how awful it is, growing up somewhere any spare money goes on cheap booze, where sex is cheap — but it's so much a part of everyday life, it becomes part of your life too? No wonder she was so determined to leave it behind her.'

I frown. 'I can't believe she didn't tell me.'

'Oh, Noah,' she says sadly. 'That was always the trouble. There was so much you didn't know.'

34

'Oh, Lord, is that the time?' Glancing at her watch, Bea grabs her hat and gets up. 'I'm so sorry, darling, but I have to go. I have a meeting with my lawyer. Then I'm going to look at a flat. I'm moving out as soon as I find one.'

But she can't go, not while I'm still taking in what she's told me. And what is it that even now I don't know?

'Bea, you could at least tell me what you mean by that, before you go.'

Bea fishes in her pocket for her keys, then when she looks up, her face is guarded. 'April should have told you. But maybe she was right. Some things are best left in the past.'

They're almost the same words she used when April walked out just before our wedding. Then, I made the mistake of letting it go. Not this time, though.

'Bea. If you know something that could help prove her innocence, you have to tell me.'

Bea hesitates, then looks worried. 'Oh, Noah. If I thought it would help . . . The trouble is, I'm not sure it would.'

'Come on, Bea. There must be something,' I insist, getting up and following her outside. 'You and I are her only hope. Even Will thinks she's guilty.'

Bea doesn't say anything, just walks, head

down, until we reach her car, a new-looking Volkswagen Golf.

Opening the door, she looks across at me. 'Be careful with Will. April never trusted him, you know.'

Suddenly, it's just too ridiculous. I slam my fist down on the car roof. 'She fucking married him, Bea. She'd hardly have done that if she didn't trust him.'

Bea's eyes widen as she looks at me.

'Sorry.' I take my hand off her car.

'It's not that.' She looks incredulously at me. 'It's April and Will. I can't believe you didn't know. They didn't get married, Noah. She couldn't go through with it.'

★ ★ ★

Far from answering my questions, talking to Bea has left me with more, left me berating myself too, for failing to check on April's past. At the peak of my obsession, I'd tracked her every move until I'd heard she was marrying Will; then I'd stopped hoping and, for sanity's sake, given up.

Having made Bea promise to call me when she can, unsure of the significance of what I've learned, I drive back to Kent, frustrated, because Beatrice and Will know far more than I do. More, too, than they're prepared to tell me.

Will. Everything comes back to Will.

I'd no idea they hadn't married. I'd simply assumed he and April had divorced. And Will had lived happily ever after, as far as I knew, with the famous Rebecca Masters, with their impressive house and no doubt equally talented children, while his professional status had skyrocketed. Will had the life he'd always planned. He had it all.

Only I had to be missing something. I was sure of it. April was in his past. He'd loved her once. He must have. He was going to marry her and for whatever reason they'd parted, but he'd moved on, surely, when he married Rebecca. So why such animosity towards her? Why, all these years later, were they still in touch?

It seemed reasonable enough to assume that their paths might have overlapped professionally, but there must have been any number of other counsellors Will could have referred his patients to. Yet he chose April.

In which case, why was he so convinced of her guilt?

ELLA

I know exactly when my dreams started.

I was nine years old and it wasn't quite autumn. I remember the yellow dress I was wearing that floated round me when I spun round in circles and the pile of leaves smouldering in some distant part of the garden, the air carrying the sweet scent of their smoke. It was dark but it wasn't cold and the double doors in the kitchen were open, letting the night in.

My mother was cooking. At least, that was what she called it. I used to think that was what cooking was, until I worked out she was heating up something Gabriela had made, but then, with her standing at the cooker, that was good enough for me. She had her back to me, and I sat on the doorstep, watching the garden get darker and the sky fainter, staring into the night counting the stars.

I was thinking about the galaxies and infinity, because we'd been talking about them in school. I was trying to figure out how the universe can never end; about how small humans really are. That was when the first moth fluttered in, followed by another, then a cloud of them, until they were covering the doorframe, disoriented by the light but so soft and delicate, their cream wings painted with intricate black lacework. One landed on my arm and I remember I held my breath, not wanting it to move.

I was still watching them when I heard my father come in. Heard him kiss my mother, then come over to where I was sitting. Felt his hand ruffling my hair, then as I looked up, watched him, in one continuous, unbelievable, ugly movement, sweep the moths off the door frame, swatting them onto the floor, deliberately putting his foot on them.

I heard my own gasp, wanting to stop him, getting up and pulling at his arms, felt myself pushed away. Screamed at him that he's a moth too, that there are giants.

I lay in bed that night, hungry because I couldn't eat, haunted by what he'd done, by his callousness towards harmless, living creatures, seeing it over and over, slow motion, in my head. And it was my fault, I knew that, for sitting in the open door, for letting the moths in, for not shutting them out where they belonged, agonizing over it until I drifted away on my tears.

In my dream I made everything right. In the darkness, the moon rising behind the trees illuminating the gnarled fretwork of their branches, those same beautiful, black-lace moths found my open bedroom window, where the walls had grown flowers, where I gave them a refuge from people like my father, with their sprays and rolled-up newspapers and heavy boots; where they gently stirred the air with their wings, blanketing the walls with their softness, knowing they were safe.

Later, they were joined by the pheasants who could still fly because no one had shot them, and the rabbits whose lungs were no longer filled with toxic gas but with pure, clean air, and even the tiniest ants that would never be boiled between the paving stones because that would never happen here. Sometimes Theo was there too, but that's how dreams are. The real and imagined crossing over, until you can't tell who belongs where.

September 2011 was when the dreams started. The first night I knew my father could kill.

35

On my way back from seeing Bea, I call at the hospital. As I walk into ICU, the friendly nurse catches me.

'I'm so glad I've seen you. I don't want you to be alarmed, but your friend has one or two problems. We're running tests . . . ' Her face the mixture of quiet anxiety and concern that comes from having seen it all before.

'What do you mean? What kind of problems?' I'm unprepared, fearful, because since arriving here, I've only allowed myself to think she'd stay the same, maybe for weeks.

'She has a chest infection. When patients are like this for longer than a few days, I'm afraid they're more susceptible.'

'So what happens now?'

'She's on antibiotics. We just have to wait and see.' Her voice is gentle; reminds me that one way or another, this is transient.

As I walk towards April's room, the reality once again hits home, that she may or may not come through this, may or may not die. Remembering why I've come here, my resolve strengthens. I've failed her in the past. This time I can't let her down.

★ ★ ★

Later, as I leave the hospital, I text Will.

Had an interesting call from Ryder, who seems to have me pinned as a liar. But I am curious — April tried to call me the night that Norton died. Do you know why?

I know he's been in contact with April because of recently referred patients. Having a hunch what he'll do, I press send, then wait for him to respond, knowing that unless he's in the middle of surgery, how long he takes is a measure of how much this matters to him.

My hunch is right. Ten minutes is how much.

★ ★ ★

When I get to the pub Will's suggested, he's already there, has been there a while, judging from his half-empty glass.

'Ryder doesn't miss much,' Will remarks casually.

'Ryder's a bully,' I tell him. 'Old school. I know the type. Ought to be put out to grass.'

Will doesn't comment.

'So. Do you know why April called me?'

Will shrugs. 'No idea. I haven't even seen her, Noah. Not for months. But you can't be that elusive. After all, I managed to find you.'

'Yes. And tell me, just how?'

When I've made no attempt to stay connected with the world, how did the person I least wanted to be found by get my number? Then the wheels and cogs in my brain whir into action and I nod wryly. My medical records. 'I should have guessed. But are doctors supposed to go delving into the records of patients who aren't their own?'

'I know it sounds questionable.' Will hedges. 'I felt the end justified the means. And it's as well I did — don't you agree?'

'Yes.' Then I frown, because if I'm going to get anything out of him, I'll have to abandon my preconceptions, my mistrust, and level with him. 'Ryder seems to think I have something to do with Norton's murder.'

'You?' Will looks incredulous. 'That's insane. Perhaps I should have a word with him.'

'I'm not sure that would help.' This is the police we're talking about. Is he really that arrogant? Then seeing his face, I understand. 'I see. You mean the infallibility of the medical profession?'

'Has its uses,' Will says curtly. 'When I'm not busy saving lives.'

But I catch the smallest hint of self deprecation underneath. 'I've heard about that. I was talking to John at the North Star — he told me how you saved his grandson.'

'Not single-handedly. There is a team,' Will says. 'We've been working on a new surgical approach to treating heart defects. It's early days, but so far, the results are impressive.'

'Must be quite something — to save a life.'

He nods briefly. 'But don't forget, it's a job I've trained to do. Like you and law. If you thought too hard about the implications of failing, you'd probably crack. To be honest, it's all part of a day's work.'

'Even so.' Then I pause, because I wasn't

going to tell him. 'I saw Beatrice.'

I watch interest flicker in his eyes. 'How is she?'

'In the process of leaving her husband — but OK. What she had to say was interesting.'

For a single, giveaway shadow of a second, Will freezes. 'Oh?

I think of Bea's words, about how April had never trusted Will. How she'd called off their wedding, but I hadn't known.

'It was curious.' I watch him closely. 'She told me there was always so much I didn't know.'

'What did she mean by that?' From the sharpness of his response, I know I have his full attention.

'That's just it. She wouldn't elaborate. She said it wouldn't help anything. I had the feeling she didn't want to get involved. She's got enough to worry about, with her divorce.'

Will's silent. Then when he speaks, his voice is disarmingly smooth. 'Good old Beatrice. You know, I've completely forgotten where she lives.'

'She didn't say.' Lying. 'We met at a motorway service station. She said her husband would love to catch her with another man and it wasn't worth risking it.'

'Pity,' Will says lightly. 'So she knows about April?'

I nod. 'Actually, I saw April as well. She has an infection.'

'Unfortunately, when someone's in a coma, on a ventilator, it's not uncommon. They'll put her on antibiotics. It should clear up. It's a good hospital.' It's rehearsed, off pat, spoken a million

256

times before like the doctor he is.

'That's reassuring to know, coming from you.'

'She still has a way to go, Noah. There were bottles of diazepam and paracetamol in her house — the police picked them up. The side effects aren't good — we're talking organ damage. Liver, kidneys, brain — it depends what she took and how much of it.' He leans back, his eyes not leaving my face, as he continues.

'I knew she was on antidepressants at one point, but that was years ago. Maybe she had some kind of breakdown.'

Presented with facts that don't match the April I knew, my brain fumbles, trying to take it all in.

'You know, I'd always thought you and April had married. I never knew you hadn't until Bea told me.'

I'm remembering Will's charm again, the easy way he used to draw girls, that the years had worn to a veneer of arrogance.

Will shrugs. 'Just one of those things. It didn't work out.' Looking uncomfortable, he changes the subject. 'So. What about you? Are you in Devon for good?'

'Hard to say. I thought I was . . . But it's quiet.' As I speak, realizing how quiet. Maybe too quiet.

'What do you write?'

'It started with a research project that ran away and turned into a series of novels.'

Will's eyebrows rise. 'You're published?'

'Yes.' I pause. 'Well, the first two are. I'm working on the third. Or rather I was, until I came here. I'm not exactly a household name — unlike you . . . ' I'm not entirely serious.

A ghost of a smile flickers across his face. 'You watch too much TV. The medical profession isn't glamorous, Noah.' He leans back. 'If you want to know, it's non-stop — we try to go away when we can. If Rebecca's on tour, I usually try to catch up with her, even for a weekend.'

For the first time, I look straight at him. 'You did it, you know.'

My sentiment is honest. Uncharacteristically, he looks taken aback. 'Did what?'

'Everything you planned. Look at you, Will. You have the perfect life.'

I wait for him to laugh — to make some joke about how I could have had it all too, but then I was never cut out to be a lawyer. A dark look crosses his face.

'Easy to say,' he says quietly. 'Though as you know, there are always sacrifices.'

I'm about to push him on what he means by that, ask him what he's surrendered to get where he is, but he closes up. Then the look clears. He picks up our glasses. 'Another pint? My shout.'

'Yes. Why not? You do owe me a few.' It's intended as a joke, a reference to days before our friendship went sour, when my lawyer's wages paid for our meals out. A glimmer of a smile plays on his lips.

'I suppose I do, don't I?'

He turns abruptly and I watch him walk over to the bar, curious about the sacrifices he wouldn't elaborate on; not at all sure that even

258

without April coming between us, we could have stayed friends.

★   ★   ★

I have missed something. I'm walking along the street when I work out what it is, thinking of her London attic flat — and the antique box with its broken hinged lid that was inlaid with mother-of-pearl. I used to joke that it wasn't a box at all; it was actually her heart, where she kept her innermost secrets; that if she'd dared to open it and show me, I'd at last have been able to understand her.

Funny how I've forgotten it. Forgotten, too, how its contents had remained hidden from me and how I'd never once been tempted to look inside. I'm wondering if she still has it; if the box that hides April's secrets is hidden away, inside the cottage that's hidden from the world.

As I let myself into my B&B, I can feel the past, almost tangible, as though it's gathering force and closing in with its secrets and unresolved ambiguities, along with an echo of Bea's words, Will's reticence. I pour myself a drink, then, closing the curtains and pulling on a hoody, I shiver.

ELLA

'I've been thinking about the letter,' she says. It's weird, but I kind of don't think of her like the other therapists. 'The one you told me about, that you weren't supposed to read.'

I hope she won't make me tell her.

She waits. 'I know it's to do with Theo, but you haven't actually told me what it says.'

All this time, she hasn't actually asked. She must really want to know — I know I would.

'I know.' I so nearly tell her then, because I'm so tired of secrets and not sleeping — how my head aches nearly all the time — but then I stop myself, because the problem is, once it's out in the open, it will be a storm wave sweeping across the landscape of my family, completely obliterating it.

Biting my lip. 'And I know you're trying to help me, but I don't think there's any way you can.'

She waits, then she says, 'You know, like when you told me about Theo? Sometimes it's better just to get it out there. You feel better.'

She's right. It helped, kind of, but she doesn't know about the other stuff I should have left alone, that's just as shocking. Or even worse.

'Yeah, but the thing is, once you've said things, you can't unsay them.'

'You're the one who has to decide.' She sits back. 'But you know you can trust me, don't you, Ella?'

I nod. It's cool. I really believe her. But it's not about trusting her, it's about me. If I tell her, it'll be real. At least this way, while it's a secret, even for a bit longer I can still pretend.

She looks at me. 'There's another way of looking at this.'

I look at her, surprised. 'How?'

'Well.' She pauses. 'You're the one who knows what it's about, but maybe it would help if you could understand why the person who wrote it kept it secret.'

Oh, Jeez. Why did I even start this?

'I know I suggested this before, but maybe you really should talk to your father.' She sits back in her chair. 'He might be glad to explain it to you.'

Then I'm distracted, because how does she know the letter was from my father? Then I realize she doesn't. I've only told her I think he's Theo's father.

'You don't know my father,' I tell her. 'Absolutely no way would he be glad.'

'Right . . . '

'It's not just about Theo.' I fold my arms and stare at the floor.

'No?' She looks surprised, then realizes she's really pissing me off.

'I'm sorry, Ella. You know I only want to help you. Look . . . There's no pressure here. Not from me. And I can see what this is doing to you. If it gets too much, if you ever need to talk to someone . . . ' She goes over to her desk where she picks up something and writes on the back of it. Then she hands it to me. 'Call me.'

I look at the business card, printed with her

name and the address here, turning it over to look at what she's written.

'My mobile number.' She says it gently. 'Ella, I mean it. Any time.'

36

The call that wakes me the next morning jolts me into sharpness.

'It's John — from the North Star.'

'Hi. John.' Sitting up, I roll my feet out of bed, rub my eyes. 'How are you?'

'Thought you'd like to know I had a visit. From that copper.'

'Ryder.' My head clears, my thoughts coming into focus as I say his name.

'That's him. Don't much like the bloke.' John's dislike evident in his voice.

'What did he want?'

'He was asking questions — about that lass he thinks killed Norton. And about Mr Farrington. He'd been going through CCTV footage. I don't know, the picture wasn't all that great. It was from that meddling git who lives across the road here. Always causing trouble, he is. Had his camera rigged up that night. Caught them going into the pub together, then an hour later, coming out.'

I'm frowning. 'Was he sure?'

'Well, he seems to think it was them. I wasn't there.'

'Sorry, which night was this?' It makes no sense that Will was in the North Star with April; when Will himself just told me, yesterday, he hasn't seen her.

'Couple of weeks back. It was my night off.

That April, he said her name was. She came in with Mr Farrington. Ryder showed me a photo. It was her all right. Same lass who came in with Norton . . . '

Suddenly my mind is racing, because why didn't Will mention this?

'Thing is, after he'd gone, I remembered. Wasn't until he told me what her name was that I knew who she was. But I looked it up to check.' He pauses. 'You see, the next morning — after the photo was taken — when I was opening up, I took a phone call. Young lady had lost her phone and thought she'd left it here, in the pub. Left me her name too. April Rousseau.' He says it triumphantly.

'John, you're sure about this?' I'm elated, my head reeling with this newest piece of information, trying to make it fit. This is the proof I've been looking for, that April didn't leave her phone in Norton's car. She couldn't have. Someone else had it all along.

'Got it right here in black and white,' he says. 'Happens all the time. We keep this lost-and-found book.'

'This is really important, John. Can you keep the book somewhere safe? Does Ryder know?'

'Not yet. I was about to call him.'

But there's a new question, because if April had lost her phone, how did it end up in Norton's car? Someone must have picked it up and intentionally left it there, which indicates she's been framed. But then my elation subsides, because there's another possibility too — that she could have found it again.

'Anyway, thought I'd better tell you,' he says cheerfully.

'Thanks, John.' Then I almost forget to ask. 'Before you go, did the phone turn up?'

'No sign of it.'

* * *

When I call the hospital, they tell me April's condition hasn't changed, that it will take at least twenty-four hours for the antibiotics to start to work. Then I try calling Bea. When it goes to voicemail, I leave a message.

'Hi. Bea, it's Noah. Look, I really need your help. Please call me back.'

Then, fired up by John's call, I pull out the folders and notes on April's clients and start painstakingly working through them, looking for something else I might have missed.

Only this time, because I've met Daisy and Lara and heard first-hand about the agony they've been through, the stories resonate far more deeply. The scale of suffering, the impact on real lives, of losses so devastating that the fallout never leaves, but remains, hidden where no one can see.

Then as I leaf through the pages of the old law book I found in April's house, more pieces of paper flutter out that I haven't seen before. As I start reading, slowly the mist clears.

Several stories leap off the pages at me. They're all of them about mothers carrying babies diagnosed with the same heart defect, yet only some of whom have been offered treatment. Because it's a subject I know nothing about, I google the condition. Check several sources, finding they all say the same. Previously considered untreatable; now, if caught early enough, new surgical procedures offer a cure.

Puzzled, I look up more websites, none of which explain why some babies would be treated and others wouldn't. It leaves me with a question. *Why?*

Other factors aren't clear. For example, whether there were other medical problems. From April's notes, I can't tell. But it looks as though she'd thought the same. There are simplified statistics about mortality rates from several hospitals around the country. I'm no mathematician, but as I scan the tables she's crudely put together, two hospitals stand out for all the wrong reasons.

In both of them, the mortality rates of newborns with heart defects is four times that of any of the others. That much is clear enough. One hospital is in north London, the other St Antony's, where April is, here in Kent.

I check again through the client notes, my heart quickening as I find that with the exception of one, all April's clients with heart-defect babies had been treated here, in St Antony's.

⋆ ⋆ ⋆

That afternoon, I go to the hospital. But this time, instead of the familiar corridors and stairs to ICU, I follow signs to the north wing of the hospital, at the far end of which is the neonatal unit.

It's a contemporary wing, unlike ICU, full of light, a resource clearly considered better spent on those arriving in this world than those leaving it. I pass a window through which I glimpse a row of incubators, hear a fragile, high-pitched cry from behind a closed door, imagine again the anguish of April's clients, as I reach a large desk behind which a nurse sits.

'You look lost, sir,' she says. 'Can I help you?'

'Maybe.' Hesitating, clutching at the ghost of an idea that comes to me just in time. 'A friend of mine had her baby here. Lara Collins.'

I'm bluffing. I don't know where Lara's baby was born and died, but then I doubted the nurses remembered everyone by name. 'The baby didn't make it. I was away at the time. I hope you don't mind — I just wanted to see what it was like here.'

'I'm sorry. It must be difficult.' Her sympathy is genuine. Then she reaches into a drawer under her desk. 'Why don't you have these?'

I take the leaflets she hands me. 'Thank you.'

Then, suddenly awkward in this place of sick babies and grieving parents in which I don't belong, I turn to leave; as I walk, glancing at the leaflets, shocked at the irony of seeing April's name listed on the first one.

★   ★   ★

As I reach ICU, a trolley is wheeled towards me, the figure on it inert, their long dark hair the

267

most recognizable feature, and I miss a heartbeat, only realizing as it passes that it's not April and that she's still there, in the same room, with the same PC. The only difference is that there are more flowers, pale pink roses this time.

'Who was her visitor?' I ask the nurse who comes in.

'You saw the flowers! Family, probably — she was here for quite a while.'

I don't correct her, don't tell her that to all intents and purposes there is no family, only the most distant blood relatives who don't care and wouldn't have thought to bring flowers. Then I frown.

'I didn't think flowers were allowed these days.'

'To be honest with you, they're not — as a rule. But one or two of the more senior staff have what you might call a healthy disregard for the rules.'

She doesn't say who and I wonder if Will is one of them.

'She was a fair-haired lady. She stayed for quite a while. I don't think anyone else has been.' It must have been Bea. If she was here for a while, was she waiting for someone? Then it's as if the nurse reads my mind.

'Mr Farrington came in, too.'

'Oh?' My ears prick up. 'You don't happen to remember if they were here at the same time, do you?'

'Oh, yes,' she tells me. 'In fact they left together — about five minutes before you arrived.'

Which in itself is enough to make me uneasy. I already don't trust Will. He's told me too many lies, but where is Bea in this? Are they friends? Can I trust her?

I'm in two minds, torn two ways, but as I leave the hospital, Bea texts me.

★   ★   ★

We meet in a cafe in the middle of Sevenoaks.

'Were you at the hospital earlier?' I'm relieved she's alone, that there's no sign of Will. But I'm wary, too; conscious that too much is not as it seems.

She nods. 'I'm sorry, Noah — about how I left the other day. I couldn't take it all in — on top of everything else.'

'Are you all right?'

Usually a light dances in her eyes, but today it's dimmed. 'Oh, I will be. I've found a flat, which is the first step. I just need to move — and then sort out the rest of my life.'

'I know how tough it is.' Grimacing, because even scars have a memory, while Bea's wounds are new, her hurt still raw.

'Yes.' Her clear eyes are troubled. 'You do, don't you?'

'There's a question I have to ask you, Bea.'

She already knows. 'You mean Will and April.'

I nod. 'What happened between them?'

She sighs. 'I never understood why they got together in the first place. There was chemistry between them, but it was more like he was obsessed with her. She does that to people. Even

269

me — for a while.' Bea looks slightly embarrassed.

'You and April?' There's incredulity in my voice that I can't help.

But as her cheeks flush, she's already shaking her head. 'Nothing happened. For a while, if I'm honest, I wished it had . . . But anyway, with Will, it was more than that. I think he saw you as a rival. And he couldn't bear for you to win.'

I'm astonished. 'So when I was out of the way and he had her to himself, what was the problem?'

Bea's silent. 'He was obsessed with her, but he couldn't forget about her background. Yet he couldn't change it, either — and he couldn't bear for her to be with anyone else. Just after they got engaged, April discovered she was pregnant. After that . . . I'm not really sure what happened. Maybe she saw Will's true colours, but it was April who left him. It was quite brave, I thought. She could have married Will and brought up their child. But instead, she went away. I didn't see her for about two or three years. I tried to stay in touch, but it was as though she'd disappeared. Then I bumped into her at a party and after that, well. Ever since, we don't see each other often but we've kept in touch.'

'What about the baby?'

'She miscarried. But she wouldn't talk about it.' Bea's eyes are full of tears. 'I think that's why she went away. So unfair, after all she'd been through.'

Maybe that's why she had such empathy with

her clients. 'And as a counsellor, she helps women who face the same.'

Bea nods. I can't help thinking April's clients must constantly remind her of her own loss.

A sigh comes from Bea as she shakes her head, then gazes past me. 'Remember how we were in school? Teenagers who thought we could do anything. Look at us now. Single. Lonely . . . '

'Will isn't. And single's not so bad. Anyway, you'll meet someone, Bea. Give it time.'

Her smile is rueful. 'What about you, Noah? Are you really happy?'

'I tried happiness. Don't worry, there've been other girls — it just didn't work out. And I've lived alone far too long.' Then I hesitate. 'Can I trust you with something, Bea? I need you to swear this will stay between us. Just us — for now, at least.'

Her eyes are wide as she nods.

'I think April had discovered something strange going on at a couple of hospitals. Some of her clients were carrying babies diagnosed with a heart condition. I've read up a bit, and it was something that these days should have been treatable. Only, at two hospitals, the mortality rates were through the roof.'

But she shrugs. 'You read about this, though, don't you? Some hospitals happen to be much better or worse than the others. Don't they call it the postcode lottery?'

'Yes. But this is different. We're talking about reputable hospitals. Westmead in north London and St Antony's, where April is now.'

I watch her blue eyes turn towards me, the

271

flicker of interest in them. 'The obvious person to talk to is Will.'

'No.' The word is out before I've thought it. 'I need to know more before I talk to him.'

'Are you sure of your facts?'

'Almost. Anyway, they're not mine. They're April's. But don't you see? There could be a cover-up going on — and if word gets out, you can bet that all the evidence will disappear. No. What I think I need to do is talk to the families whose babies were involved.'

'What will you tell them?'

I sigh. 'That April was putting together her own research. That it might help other families . . . Unless you have a better idea.'

Bea's hand is conspiratorial, reaching across the table, closing round mine. 'Keep in touch, Noah. Let me know what you find.'

ELLA

My life is full of other people's lies, because it's easier for them to lie than tell the truth. Harmless little white lies to protect someone, and the daffodil-yellow ones that are a cover-up, but that's still OK, isn't it, because no one knows. Even the whopping big blue ones don't count — there's always such a really good reason for them; scarlet-red lies that are blatant. Anyway, you've told so many by now, what's the difference?

Which brings me to the black ones that twist your beliefs about really important things; that are about hidden papers and fake names and overheard phone calls; lost photos that were never really lost; a young life that was stolen — by parents who aren't really parents of a child who was never theirs.

37

There are those who choose to remain silent. Even so, I speak to too many grieving, devastated people. Drink mugs of their tea; hear their stories; am humbled by their fortitude. Come away with notes of dates and consultants' names, know I can only begin to imagine their grief. And still, nothing stands out.

The breakthrough comes as I'm leaving the last family, the Miltons, whose quiet sadness leaves me strangely moved. Having thanked them as sincerely as I can for making me so welcome, I'm walking down their neat gravel drive to my car when, behind me, the front door opens again.

'Mr Calaway?'

I turn to see Tina Milton waving something at me, hear her soft, quick footsteps as she catches up with me.

'It may be nothing, but we thought we should tell you. It was after the last scan — before any possible treatment was discussed. Because our baby died, because we never went back . . . ' Her voice wavers. 'But we were sent a form to fill out. A questionnaire. We looked through it when it arrived, but because of what happened . . . Well, it wasn't until recently I realized we'd both thought the same. For families who face losing their baby, the questions are, well, I thought, insensitive. And not relevant. Like I said, it might be nothing but you're welcome to take this with you.'

But she believes there is something. It's in her eyes, in the spark of anger that blazes there and is as quickly gone, in its place a resigned sadness.

I can't smile, just take it from her.

'Thank you.'

★   ★   ★

After a day of emotions ranging from anger to despair, I wait until I'm back at my B&B to look at what Tina Milton's given me.

As I read, I'm increasingly puzzled. The first questions are innocuous enough, asking about the pregnancy, the baby's birth, the health of both parents. But as I read on, there are more probing questions, about family history, schools, education, going on to ask about occupations and income, which in the case of an inclusive health service and a sick baby, should be insignificant.

There's a note at the start, which states how completing the questionnaire is by no means compulsory, but will help with how ongoing treatment can be specifically tailored to individuals, which sounds perfectly plausible. But as I read through the questions again, I'm not sure. Frowning, I search the form for a doctor's name or the medical department that's sent it, and find an address: 'Fairview Medical Centre, 76 Elm Street, Wandsworth'.

Pulling out my laptop, I type it into the search bar. Fairview Medical Centre does indeed exist.

I find a number of listings and then a website.

It looks impressive — a large, white, double-fronted house which is no doubt worth a fortune. There are more photos of the interior: the grand reception, the stylish waiting area, the consulting rooms. Other than describing the practice as a provider of state-of-the-art medical care and making it clear that appointments are by referral only, the website says little but points me towards a contact form for email enquiries.

I wonder if Will ever works there. Then I pause, deep in thought, because on first sight it looks genuine enough, but the questionnaire still niggles at me. Using the contact form, I send a quick email. Not wanting to draw attention to myself, I don't tell them why, just that I'm interested to know more about what they offer and asking if someone could contact me. But as I send the email, something else is on my mind. It makes sense to visit your nearest hospital, particularly when frequent appointments are involved — which if you lived close to here, would be St Antony's. After all, why go further when the specialist unit was on your doorstep? In any case, it's most likely to be where you'd be referred to.

I'm frowning as it comes back to me. One of April's clients, here in Sevenoaks, had gone somewhere else. Reaching for my list, scanning the names, suddenly I remember who it was. One of the first people I spoke to.

Nina Hendry.

★　★　★

Even though it's late, I call her, but she doesn't pick up. Resigning myself to having to wait until tomorrow, I leave a message, but it's only a few minutes later that she calls me.

'Thanks for getting back to me. I'm sorry it's so late, but it might be important.'

'It's OK. I'm curious. What was it you wanted to know?'

'Forgive me . . . ' I hesitate. 'But your babies . . . I didn't want to ask before, but did they have heart problems?'

She pauses, then says, 'Yes.'

'I saw from April's notes that you didn't go to St Antony's. Was there a reason for that?'

I've considered practical reasons, such as that St Antony's had been full, that the hospital she'd chosen was closer to her parents, that she needed their support, or she'd heard the best consultants were there.

She pauses, then she says, 'I took my first baby there. But by the time my second was born, there were rumours.'

'What sort of rumours?' My heart quickens.

'I'm not sure I should say. St Antony's is a good hospital. But when I was pregnant the last time, I found this forum online. It was a kind of support system for mothers in the same boat as I was. Anyway . . . I read something. I could never be sure if it was accurate, but when you're pregnant, especially when you've already lost one baby, you don't take chances.'

'What had you heard?'

'Just that . . . Well, just that it was a bit of a lottery there. It was probably nothing, but someone posted that not all babies were treated the same. There was a whole thread dedicated to it. You can probably still find it if you want to. Anyway, for the record, I'd never had a bad experience there myself, but I thought losing one baby was bad enough. I needed to do the best I could for the next one.'

Then her voice changes. 'Oh, God. Are you telling me there is something? Is that why I lost him?'

I realize then, the guilt doesn't leave you. 'As yet, there's no evidence, but as April's lawyer, I need to find out. If you can please keep this to yourself, at least for now, I can assure you I'm looking into it. If I find any proof, I'll go straight to the police.

'And I'm sorry I've troubled you,' I add again. Sorry, a pitifully inadequate word for the guilt I've resurrected in her. 'I really am. But what you've told me may be useful. And there's no way you could have known anything. There really isn't.'

'Promise me.' Nina's voice is hard. 'If there is something, you'll get to the bottom of it.'

Her words ignite a spark in me. No longer am I doing this just for April. It's for Nina, Daisy, Lara and all the other mothers I've never met who have been to hell and are still caught there. Who deserve justice.

ELLA

Do you know how cheap it is, to check out who you really are?

'We're doing this project in school,' I tell my mother. 'Like about family history.'

'How interesting,' she says, only not like she means it. You can tell. 'What do you think of this dress, honey?'

'They want me to find out all this stuff,' I tell her. 'Like where I was born. I know it was a hospital, just not which one.'

'I'm not sure.'

My heart skips a beat.

'I think it might be too long for me.'

Then it sinks.

I don't believe it. She's talking about a freaking dress, but that's how our conversations are. I try again. 'I thought you said it was the Royal Berkshire . . . '

She looks at me blankly as she remembers the question. 'Oh . . . You mean the hospital? Yes. It was.' Then she frowns. 'What did you say this was about?'

I roll my eyes, act like it's nothing when this is practically the biggest deal of my entire life. 'I told you. Some really lame school project I'm behind with, because it's so freaking dull.'

It sends her off on a tangent just as I knew it would. I wait for the rant. 'Honestly, Ella, I wish you wouldn't talk like that. Your school fees cost a fortune. And it's such a good school, you really should work harder.'

'Mostly I work really hard,' I tell her, pissed off at her for saying that because she already knows my grades are good — and because she's my mother, isn't she? Can't she see past what I'm asking her — can't she tell there's something wrong?

'I'm going to watch TV.'

She looks relieved then, because she has dresses to think about. Of course, I'm not watching TV — well, it'll be switched on but I won't actually be watching, because my head is buzzing with a million noisy thoughts. But also, there's something I have to do.

It doesn't take long. And it's so easy. All you need is a laptop and your parents' names. The name of the place where you were born, a credit card, and a few minutes. That's all.

What's harder is the waiting. The fifteen days they tell you it will take for that envelope to reach you, which when you open it, will make sense of everything. Tell you how you are the person you think you are; that you were born in the Royal Berkshire on October 30th just as they told you; that your parents are your parents, you're just a regular paranoid teenager with an overactive imagination. Time you learned to keep it in check.

Only after fifteen days, the envelope doesn't come. After seventeen days, you're still waiting. Did you make a mistake? Have they somehow lost you? But instead of the letter I've pinned my hopes on, I get an email.

Birth certificate Ella Vivian Farrington.

We have been unable to process your application.

Please refer to the paragraph below.

We have been unable to find any entry with the details you provided.

Crash and burn, Ella's parents, whoever she is, only you're not her parents, are you? Who's Ella? Really? Or did you make her up?

They'll refund my money. I don't care about the freaking money.

£9.25 — the cost of discovering you don't exist.

38

I'm at the heart of a gathering storm, where clouds of confusion loom overhead and I can't see the way forward because the sunlight has dimmed. Easy then, for Detective Sergeant Ryder to find me.

He looks excessively pleased with himself as I get up from my breakfast table and with a sinking feeling, because nothing to do with Ryder is ever pleasant, go out to where he's standing in the hallway.

Swivelling cold eyes in my direction, he stops talking to my landlady.

'There are some questions I need to ask you, sir.' Deliberately speaking loud enough so that everyone stops, mid-breakfast, to gawp, though I'm the only one who hears his smirk.

'Ask away,' I shrug, as his eyes shift.

'It would be helpful if you'd come down to the station,' he says more quietly.

'I've told you everything I can.' I'm irritated, because I know his game. He must be more stupid than I thought. 'If you have enough evidence, come and arrest me.'

I'm bluffing, trusting my instincts that he hasn't.

'Mr Calaway, you will be coming back, won't you?' My landlady hovers, more anxious about my bill than my well-being.

'I'm not going anywhere.'

For once at a loss for words, Ryder glowers.

Hiding my anger under a veneer of calm, I turn to go back to my breakfast. Feeling all eyes on me, the wave of Ryder's fury as he leaves; sitting down, only to find that my eggs are congealed and my bacon cold.

★　★　★

Again, I go to the hospital, but instead of the familiar police presence just inside, when I reach April's room it's empty.

'Hello . . . ' I'm holding on to the door frame, fearing the worst, as I turn to see the friendly nurse standing behind me.

'Where is she?' Suddenly I'm afraid, feeling the blood draining from my face, because I can't let her down, not this time. She can't *die*.

'She's been moved,' the nurse says quietly. 'If you come with me, I'll show you where she is.'

I follow her further along the corridor through another set of swing doors, where she shows me into a larger room divided into several cubicles with a door into another much smaller room, which is where she is — through the glass, I can see a police uniform.

'I'm afraid she's not responding to the antibiotics as well as we'd hoped. She'll have more nursing care in here.'

My ears are assaulted by an orchestra of electronic noise. I glance around, taking in the inert figures in all of the beds, wondering how it is that no one wakes.

'She's quite poorly. Is there anyone who

should be told?' Against the background noise, the nurse's voice is quiet, but my ears make out each syllable, the intonation of every word.

'I don't think so.' Then suddenly I'm thinking hard, because if I'm on the right track and my investigation is discovered, there's the risk that whoever's involved will immediately destroy all the evidence. And because I don't know who else to ask, I turn to her. 'Look, would you have a moment to talk?'

'Of course . . . Is it about Ms Rousseau?'

'Yes — but not directly.' I glance around. 'Is there somewhere quieter?'

'Come with me.'

I follow her round a corner of the corridor, where she gestures towards a group of chairs. 'We shouldn't be disturbed here.'

'I think I told you I was acting as April's lawyer?' Hearing my voice echo along the empty stretch of corridor, I lower it.

She nods. Her brown eyes are full of compassion and her name is pinned to her dress. Luisa. I've been here almost every day, but until now, I haven't seen that.

'I think she discovered something.' My words are fast, my voice quiet. 'If I'm right, she'd found out something to do with newborns who had heart problems. She collected all this data from hospitals around the country — but at two of them, mortality rates were significantly higher.'

She frowns. 'You're sure about this?'

I nod. 'The question is why. But what seems odd is that one of them was giving families a questionnaire to fill out.'

'That happens sometimes,' the nurse says. 'If we're following up on the patient experience, that sort of thing.'

I nod slowly. 'OK. Well, these were handed over before any treatment was carried out — questions about educational background, occupation, income.' Watching her closely.

She looks puzzled. 'But what would that have to do with anything?'

'That's exactly what I thought.' My brain is whirring faster.

'Do you know which hospitals?'

'Westmead, in north London. And here. St Antony's.'

'You're sure?' Her horrified look reflects the churning feeling in my gut. 'And you said this was before any treatment was carried out?'

I nod. 'The only other thing I have is a list of consultants' names.'

Luisa hesitates. 'Mr Farrington . . . ' She sounds uncertain. 'Is he on your list?'

I'm frowning. 'Why d'you ask? I mean, he is, but what about him?'

She shakes her head. 'I'm not sure why, exactly, but there's something about him I don't trust.' She glances over her shoulder, suddenly anxious. 'I shouldn't have said that — it's probably nothing. You won't tell anyone, will you?'

'Of course not.' Hastening to reassure her, curious to know why she's said this. But there's something else I have to ask.

'One more thing . . . Have you heard of the Fairview Medical Centre? Only it's where these questionnaires get sent to.'

She shakes her head. 'I haven't.' Then she leans forward. 'But I have a friend who's a nurse in neonatal. If you get the names to me, I'll see what I can do.'

Our voices have dropped to a whisper as I type Luisa's mobile number into my phone, hoping my gut is right and I can trust her. Feeling something tangible in the silence between us. Hope.

39

With hope comes renewed urgency. As I let myself into the B&B, almost as if she's been waiting for me, my landlady appears.

'Is everything all right, Mr Calaway?' Ryder's visit has made her twitchy.

'Fine, thank you.' Brushing past her without explanation, I go to my room, locking the door and texting my list of consultants' names to Luisa.

I've a growing sense that what April has found could be bigger than I'd suspected, but I'm no clearer as to where Norton's murder fits into all this.

Then I start to google the parents of the sick newborns, some of whom are high profile, their backgrounds available for the world to see. I find work addresses, jobs, for a few of them, even schools; discover a whole new use for social media. The Internet makes what would once have been days of work effortless. Not that I find everyone, but discovering enough that the delicate trace of what I've glimpsed so far slowly gains substance.

But I need to be sure. Snatching up my keys, I'm running back out to my car, a list of addresses in my hand, the darkest of suspicions in my head, as for the next two or three hours I drive around, checking out each and every one of them. Only when I pull up at the roadside outside the last do I know with certainty I'm on to something.

Out of the babies who died, with the exception of one who was stillborn, all the addresses are modest, low-value homes, the Magnolia Ways, the virtual presence of these families nonexistent. I stare at the facts, black and white in front of me, suddenly chilled, because the inference of the reverse is terrifying.

I'm wondering if April had got this far and she'd discovered that the unnatural selection of the newborns for treatment was based on some form of social hierarchy. If she knew her clients, I'm guessing she at least must have had an idea.

I need to check out Fairview Medical Centre — if necessary, drive there. Then I glance at my watch, because I still haven't heard from Luisa. Anxious, too, about April, I turn my car round and drive back to the hospital.

I go straight to the room April's been moved to and stand at the window, watching her. As always, there's a police constable sitting quietly, away from April's bed. I feel myself lulled into stillness by the mechanical rhythm of her breathing that drifts out through the cracked-open door. And I'm not sure where the suggestion creeps in from, but suddenly I realize that this is no life. To just lie, unable to move, unable to speak. I know without a doubt that she wouldn't have wanted this.

As I stand there, Luisa comes in, catching my eye as she attends to another patient. When she's finished, her eyes gesture to me to follow her.

Out in the corridor, away from everyone, she glances around before she speaks. 'I spoke to my friend. I didn't tell her your name or why you'd

288

asked, just that you were carrying out some research about the distribution of consultants. Who worked where, how many hospitals each of them worked in. Then I asked her if they all worked here. She said they did.'

She breaks off, momentarily anxious.

Knowing there's more, wondering what she's not telling me, I watch her eyes widen as she looks behind me, but when I turn, there are only footsteps disappearing in the direction of April's room.

'It's him,' she whispers, fear written on her face. 'They're all part of his team.'

I frown, wondering who she's talking about. Together we walk back along the corridor. Catch the back view of him looking through the window at April. Then as he hears our footsteps, he turns slowly towards us and sees us watching him.

Luisa melts away and I'm filled with uneasiness as Will strides towards me.

'Noah. Good to see you. You look as though you've seen a ghost.'

And I realize I have, the ghost of a monster who thinks he can manipulate lives.

'It's been quite a day.' I'm not yet ready to explain why. 'Maybe you can tell me how it's looking, really, for April.'

Needing him to believe, a little longer, that I'm still holding on to the blackened, burned-down stub of my candle for her.

Even here, in this most fragile part of ICU, it's there in his eyes — that I amuse him. Like the families of the newborns he makes life and death

289

decisions for, I'm being manipulated too.

Slow motion, more silent questions fill my head, only they're about the moral substance of the man who can do this. About others Will might be manipulating.

'Ryder's been on my back,' I add. 'The man has it all wrong.'

Will's look is cold. 'As you said to me, the truth will come out.'

A shiver runs down my spine as I stand my ground, unflinching.

'I've no doubt whatsoever it will.'

I turn and walk away, leaving him standing there. My unease growing with every step, because if Will thinks I know too much, that I'm a threat, then I'm not safe.

★   ★   ★

As I make my way back to my B&B, I'm recounting all the times I've seen Will in April's room, considering a new, hideous possibility. If April was on to Will, he won't want her to recover. Far easier for him if she were to die. No one will query the renowned surgeon. Once in her room, he could do anything.

Back inside, the door locked behind me, I call Bea, but she doesn't answer. It's the worst possible time for her not to be there. Feeling time slipping away from me, I leave a message.

'Bea? Listen. I was right. April had found something. I need to talk to you urgently. Please call me back as soon as you can.'

Then I can do no more, just wait.

ELLA

Who's the person who loves you unconditionally, would do absolutely anything for you, who you should always be able to rely on?

Your mother, right?

'I don't feel well,' I tell my mother. 'My head really hurts.'

'Really, honey? Take some ibuprofen and have a lie-down.' Barely looking up from typing on her phone. 'I have to get ready to go out but I'll pop in and see you in a minute.'

My mother's minutes are variable, can be an eye blink or long drawn-out hours. Today it's the latter, or maybe she forgets. I think I sleep, while clouds cover the sun and the air grows heavy, so that when I wake, I can't breathe. Then I see the moths.

They're there, everywhere, on the walls, the ceiling, on my bed. So beautiful . . . A huge pale cream moth finds my hand, flexing soft wings, then launches into the air and I remember.

I climb out of bed, but when I stumble, it's not my mother who comes.

'Ella? Are you all right, little one?' Gabriela bursts through the door, her face anxious as she strokes my forehead, then helps me into my bed. Dimly I register that I got it wrong. My parents didn't employ her as our housekeeper, she's paid to love me. 'Por dios! What is this?'

Waving her arms, she disturbs the moths so that the air is full of them.

'Don't hurt them,' I cry. 'You mustn't. Leave them. Please . . . '

It's the panic in my voice. Makes her forget the moths, turn to me.

'I'm hurting,' I tell her, drawing up my knees, pushing my face into my pillow. 'It really hurts, Gabriela.'

'Hush,' she soothes. Takes one of my hands, holds it gently, strokes it. The first drops of rain when I crave a deluge, but no less welcome, as wild, selfish, hateful words erupt from deep inside me and won't stop.

'Why is she like that?' I cry. 'Why isn't she here? Doesn't she care?'

Not waiting for her to answer.

'Why does she lie, Gabriela? WHY DOES EVERYBODY LIE?' I'm sobbing louder now, but I can't help it. 'Where's my mother?'

'She had to go out, little one. She has a meeting to go to. In London — remember? But it's OK, you'll be OK . . . I'm here . . . '

'But it's not OK, nothing is . . . '

My raw, agonizing cry, an animal sound of fear and loss and hurt and betrayal, as I try to stand, because I have to get away from here, only the room is spinning and my legs won't work.

'Help . . . ' I'm pleading with Gabriela. 'Please, help me . . . '

But she's frightened, her eyes full of uncertainty. Has no idea what to do.

Then I remember. And with the memory

comes strength. Enough for my legs to make it across the room, while the moths find the open window. Reach my phone.

40

Suddenly I'm caught in a race. Between Will going to Ryder as I know he will, with a fabricated story containing enough half-truths to satisfy them both and implicate me; and Bea, wherever she is, picking up her messages and calling me; against time itself.

But with a flash of insight, I know Ryder won't call me, and that he'll come here, flaunting his status in front of the same people who watched me openly defy him, because he gets a buzz out of it. Quickly I gather up the files and notes, slipping them into a bag, grabbing my wallet and keys, then as an afterthought a hoody.

On impulse, I glance out of the window just as his car pulls up. Panic surges through me, then I slip out, quietly closing the door. Halfway down the stairs, I freeze in someone else's doorway, out of sight, as my landlady shows him up two floors to my room. Two floors that I've cursed traipsing up and down, but am now so grateful for, as seeing my chance and hurrying down the rest of the stairs, I slip out.

Here, again, I'm grateful. For the anonymity that the bustle of people offers, that in seconds I'm lost amongst the throng of rush hour. As I walk I picture Ryder in my room, furious, searching through my possessions, carelessly, angrily discarding them; and I realize that all along I was right. At the heart of all of this is Will.

I find a nondescript cafe by the station where I wait, increasingly tense, for Bea to call. I need her to know what I've discovered, not whatever lies Will has filled her head with. Another hour passes. It's gone seven when at last the screen of my phone lights up.

'I got your message,' she says. 'I'm so sorry. I've only just got out of work.'

I try to sound jovial. 'Working you hard, aren't they? Where are you working?'

'I'm a receptionist — thanks to April, really. It was she who suggested I apply for the job. And it's fine, there's just a lot I need to learn at this stage.' Her tone changes. 'Your call, earlier on, Noah. It sounded serious. What is it?'

'April was definitely on to something. Look, I know it's a lot to ask, but could you meet me?'

There's a pause. 'In Tonbridge?'

'Would you?'

She pauses again.

'I wouldn't ask if it wasn't important.'

'OK. Yes. I'll be there. Where?'

'If you park in the station car park, I'll wait for you.'

'This sounds very secretive . . . ' There's curiosity in her voice.

'It isn't meant to be. How long do you think you'll be?'

'About an hour.'

★ ★ ★

After fifty minutes have passed, I get up and go outside, watching for the familiar shape of her Golf to swing into the car park, hanging back in the shadows as I hear a distant siren.

She pulls in, five minutes late, bright, apologetic. 'Sorry I'm late. The traffic was terrible . . . ' She kisses me on the cheek.

'Thanks for coming, Bea. Come on, I'll buy you a coffee.'

We sit at a table in the corner.

'Are you going to tell me what this is about?' Bea looks worried.

I sigh. 'I'll try. Most of April's clients were pregnant, only their babies were sick. Most had a type of heart defect, which these days should have been curable. Anyway, she started recording mortality rates — over time, I think she started to question why around here, specifically at St Antony's, so many babies were dying.'

Bea looks shocked. 'Are you absolutely sure about this?'

I nod. 'All the babies were under the same team of consultants.' I pause. 'It was Will's team, Bea. And I've got so far with this — but I'm missing something. Something that links this to Norton. I've no idea what.'

Bea shakes her head, struggling to take this in. 'You're wrong, Noah. You have to be.'

'I'm not,' I tell her. 'But there's another thing. Will's team were selecting the babies they treated.'

'They would, though, wouldn't they? I mean, if it was hopeless . . . ' I can see where she's going with this, but her voice tails off.

'They weren't using medical criteria to select them.' My voice is low. 'I'll tell you what they were using. Parents' jobs and incomes. The families from the poshest backgrounds. Social class, Bea. Will's no better than Hitler.'

Her face is ashen. '*Oh, my God . . .* '

In her drawn-out silence, the stricken look in her eyes, I feel time running out, as I see that Will's got to her too. It was in her throwaway comment about being late; her Judas kiss; her conviction that I'm wrong.

'When's he coming?' My voice rises. I reach across the table, grab her arms. 'Bea . . . How could you do this?'

'He told me you killed Norton.' Her voice is tiny and very afraid. 'That you'd never got over losing April. Never got over what Norton did to her. That all the time, for as long we've known you, you've lied about everything.' Then her voice steadies and she looks at me, deadly serious. 'Think about it, Noah. Like that day you ran into her. You were still a student. You must have known April was pregnant. It was obvious. And you pretended you didn't. She couldn't believe it.'

But I've no idea what she's talking about. 'Bea, you're wrong. We were going to be married. If something like that had happened, she would have told me . . . ' I break off, frowning at her.

'God, Noah . . . Even you couldn't have been that naive. Think back. You were in London. You'd come up from uni for the weekend to go to some law lectures somewhere . . . You must have known.'

The light dawns in her eyes. 'Or were you drinking? Even then? When you were a student?'

'I didn't . . . I don't drink, Bea. Not in that way.'

But Bea shakes her head, sorrowful. Then I'm staring at her, a sickening feeling in my stomach as a fleeting memory comes to me. I'd been in London and, as chance would have it I had, as Bea put it, run into April. At the time, I'd registered nothing, but on a subconscious level, had I known?

'Bea . . . ' I pause, trying to do the maths in my head. 'Oh, God, Bea . . . '

Our eyes meet, mine in horror, hers in disbelief, as behind her I see the unmistakable figure of Ryder enter the cafe.

'Bea, I swear I didn't know. You have to believe me . . . ' Imploring her, because she's all I have.

Leaning towards her, I lower my voice. 'Will's a monster, Bea. He manipulates people. He's manipulating all of this.'

I watch disbelief give way to uncertainty.

'Bea, you have to listen. Fairview Medical Centre,' I tell her urgently. 'The address is here, too. If you have any doubts about Will, check it out.'

'My bag,' I mutter as Ryder draws closer. 'Please. Take it. Read what's in it — if not for me, for April. If you still don't believe me, you can give it to Ryder.'

I stand up, watching her eyes darting, untrusting, uncertain as Ryder looms behind

298

her. His look is pure malevolence. As he starts talking, I know that this time he has something on me.

'Noah Calaway, I am arresting you on suspicion of the murder of Bryan Norton. You do not have to say anything. However it may harm your defence if you do not mention when questioned something which you later rely on in court. Anything you do say may be given in evidence.'

Shooting Bea a last glance of desperation, I'm escorted out.

⋆ ⋆ ⋆

Ryder drives in cold, superior silence. At the police station, after the usual formalities, the custody sergeant shows me into a small room, filled with the stale air of cigarette smoke and unheard truths, as all the reasons I fell out of love with the criminal justice system come flooding back. How the small man in the street lacks a voice. That you are guilty until somehow proven innocent.

I'm expecting to be left alone because there is a system; I know it's only a matter of time before Ryder's back. One foot out of line, and I'll have him for the stereotype he is.

It's three hours before I'm taken to an interview room, a few more minutes before Ryder joins me. I wonder if the younger man accompanying him will temper his obvious contempt.

His nod is perfunctory. 'This is Sergeant Elliot.'

Elliot takes the seat next to Ryder across from me at the small table.

'Right. I don't think you've been entirely truthful with us, Calaway. We'll start with the facts, beginning with the crush you had on Ms Rousseau — or Miss Moon, as she was then — when you were at school and the fact that you were a witness to Norton raping her.'

His words are mocking, slicing like knives into the shroud of my privacy. Twisting the facts to intimidate me further. 'I didn't witness anything. What actually happened was that I found her, after.'

That he doesn't question me further tells me that either from Bea, or Will, he knows this. He clears his throat, then carries on. 'If you say so, sir. And you maintain you didn't know she'd been raped? Even though, years later, you were about to be married? Sounds a little far-fetched, if you ask me.' Making no attempt to disguise his pleasure in demeaning me.

'Sometimes the truth is,' I tell him. 'You're a cop. You should know.'

Ryder glowers. 'A witness has come forward.'

My blood runs cold.

'You were overheard saying you wanted to kill him,' he continues. 'The witness says you had to be restrained.'

I'm silent. The witness has to be Will, only he made it up. It's a measure of the desperation of a guilty man, only no one will believe that. I see us both through Ryder's eyes. The failed lawyer and the almighty surgeon.

'There's also the fact that Ms Rousseau called

you, three times, the evening before the murder — a fact which you deny.'

'She lost her phone. Do you know that?' Interrupting him, wondering if he knows. 'She'd been in the North Star a couple of weeks earlier. She called the pub the next morning to ask if anyone had found it. Speak to John Slater.'

Ryder's stare is full of hostility. 'I'm talking about her home phone. Perhaps she wanted to tell you she'd set up a meeting with Norton. You'd talked about it, hadn't you? Old flames, discussing how to get rid of him. I think you saw a chance to right an old wrong and you took it. That reclusive life you lead, writing fairy tales about serial killers . . . '

As he says that, I know in a flash that someone's checked out my cottage, picturing a stranger going through my home, my desk, my notes for my next book. Containing the rage that flares inside me; knowing too, that here, I'm powerless.

'I think it's messed with your head, Calaway. You drove all the way from Devon, waited in the car park at the North Star while Ms Rousseau got him drunk, then when Norton was the last one out of the bar, you saw your chance.'

Slowly, terrifyingly, I see that in Ryder's insane little world he actually believes it.

'That's ridiculous.' Words that stick in my throat. 'And how would I have had April's phone? Or her gloves?'

He shrugs. 'Maybe she'd found her phone. Left it in the pub with a glove and Norton picked them up. Who knows?'

'It doesn't explain why she took an overdose.'

'I'd say — and I'm not alone here — she's a bit of a fruitcake. History of physical and sexual abuse, depression — not surprising.'

But they're not Ryder's words. They're Will's. Between them, they've done what I dreaded.

Ryder goes on. 'And there's another problem, because on the actual day it happened, no one can say where you were.' He sits back, staring malevolently across the table at me. 'You've got to admit — it stacks up.'

'I can give you the number of Sam — the mechanic. He'll tell you he had my car that day.'

'Yeah.' Ryder's voice is heavy with sarcasm. 'This Sam . . . Let me get this right. A West Country yokel who'd say anything if you slipped him enough. How much did you pay him?'

This time I'm seething, fighting back the urge to reach across the table and grab him by the tie, then punch him in the head.

'Call him,' I say, ice calm. 'You have my phone. It's in my contacts.'

Then I sit, silent, using steel strength to maintain my composure, at the same time reading between Ryder's lines. The subtext.

He's convinced he has proof that I'm guilty.

I'm taken back to my cell, where they continue to hold me on suspicion. Ryder has twenty-four hours, minus the three I've already been here, to make it stick. Twenty-four hours for Bea to work out the truth.

41

Alone, as I'm sitting on the narrow bed at the back of my cell, reality closes in. I think about April's life slowly slipping away from her, about how deluded Will has become, and how dangerous. How my future is in Bea's hands. How the link between Will and Norton has to be April. How, even now, there is no proof.

I think of the lies Will's told Bea, and Ryder too, painting me as the twisted monster who had never got over losing April. Who lost his mind, murdered Norton.

Only it's Will who's the monster. Suddenly I'm cold. Is it Will, too, who murdered Norton? Who never got over losing April? Will, not me, whose judgement is in question, whose arrogance has pushed him over the edge.

And, of course, given the choice between the smooth, accomplished, life-saving surgeon and the reclusive writer who walked away from his legal career, it's obvious who is the more credible, more reliable; who you would trust with your life.

Then I think about what Bea told me. Why would April have lied to me? If there'd been another baby, if it had been mine, she'd have told me, surely, during the time we were together. Then my mind wanders, back to the days when April seemed consumed by darkness, to the memories I've buried away.

I feel a wave of shame as I remember Bea's scathing words, her utter disbelief, because she's right. There are more lies, embedded in the life I've created, away from the eyes of the rest of the world. Lies I've told not just other people, but myself.

42

1996

It was my first winter at uni. Five months since I'd seen her. February, a cold, grey month of heavy coats and woollen scarves. Mine was navy, a double-breasted coat that used to belong to my father, on the big side and not really student attire, but perfect for walking city streets, imagining myself the successful lawyer I would one day be.

London's a big city to search for someone, but I'd had a clue. The name of a diner where she worked, that she'd let slip, never imagining I'd turn up there. There were a few by the same name, but I'd narrowed it down. Not that I'd gone in. I remember I'd lurked in a doorway, watching her in the bright lights inside, her easy smile, her long hair neatly tied back as she took orders and carried trays.

I couldn't tell her how I'd watched her, mesmerized, for nearly five hours, my hands deep in my pockets, shivering as I'd felt the temperature drop, terrified that if I went away for just five minutes, she'd disappear. She wasn't the only one with secrets; I'd been too embarrassed to ever tell her.

* * *

I remember seeing her, just before ten o'clock, pulling on her coat, making her way to the door; called back briefly by another girl, before she finally stepped outside. I remember I'd had to orchestrate my arrival to time it to perfection, crossing the street just as she crossed the other way, as I knew she would. I'd watched her the previous night too.

I remember the surprise on her face, the faint flush to her cheeks that could have been the cold. How she'd kissed me on the cheek, hesitantly, then drawn back. We'd had a trivial conversation, in which I'd told her I'd been up there for a lecture. Only I hadn't. That was a lie too.

Had I noticed under the coat? In the glow of street lamps it was hard to tell, but I'd seen her working, hadn't I? Beneath the apron tied round her waist, her shape had most definitely changed. I'd seen that.

Bea was right. I'd told myself she'd put on weight. Eaten too many meals at the diner, in doing so choosing to turn away. How could I have done that? Here, twenty years too late, I do the maths. And I know.

So many times I told myself April abandoned me. But she'd been pregnant with my child, the time she'd most needed me and I'd abandoned her. My eyes fill with tears of shame, but I'm confused, too, because later, when we were going to be married, when we should have had no secrets, why hadn't she told me?

She must have seen me look, then look away. Heard the silence where there should have been my words, asking her. Felt alone when I should have been with her. It was my doing that our wedding hadn't happened. This was what had come between us.

There was a baby I hadn't known about. My baby. I think of Bea's words. *There was so much you didn't know*. She'd said it twice, the first time when April left me just before the wedding, and again, just recently. All along, Bea had known.

I know I must find Bea. Find out if the baby lived.

Getting up, I pace the small room, agitated, needing answers; more than ever needing a drink, then another and probably another, until the alcohol deadens the memories that have surfaced, raw and bleeding. My inadequacies, my failures, my mistakes, because I've lied to myself about those too.

Within the confines of the cell, my thoughts bombard me, then rebound only to ricochet off the walls to come at me again. Here, there is no fantasy world to escape to, no whisky bottle to numb my mind until they've gone. Just hard, cold reality, staring me in the face, as in the half-darkness, the almost-silence, for what feels like an endless night I'm forced to wait.

ELLA

Time comes unstitched, a pulled thread, as seconds unravel from minutes unravelling from hours, then get tangled, so nothing makes sense. Where I can't think, where night and day, yesterday and tomorrow, truth and lies all merge, are all the same.

'I call your mother,' Gabriela fusses, holding my arm. 'We go to the hospital. She can meet us.'

'NO. Don't . . . I don't want her.' Beseeching her, feeling my eyes fill with tears. 'Not the hospital, Gabriela. Please . . . I know what I need to do.'

She shakes her head — at me? Looking down at myself, suddenly I notice I'm in clothes I don't remember putting on, as if I've lost time. It happens again later, when I'm in the car. How did I get to the car? Gabriela's driving and I stare outside, but my eyes don't focus. I've forgotten where we're going; have no idea where we are.

When Gabriela parks near an entrance to somewhere, then comes round and helps me out, I still don't know.

'Come on, little one.'

I climb out, holding on to her arm, tight, because my legs don't feel like my legs. She slowly helps me up two steps, then through the door.

Inside, behind the desk, someone looks up at us.

'Ella's here to see Julia.' Gabriela speaks for me.

'Would you like to take a seat over there?' The receptionist indicates an area with several chairs. 'She won't be a minute.'

Then something weird happens, because the lady looks at me, can't stop looking at me, her eyes staring into mine, as I notice her fair hair and feel a shock right through my body, as though I know her.

Suddenly there's a buzzing in my ears. Then Julia's there.

'Shall I wait here?' Gabriela's voice is a whisper in the background.

'I think it might be best.' Julia holds my hand really firmly, so that I can feel she has enough strength for both of us. 'I'll call you if she needs you. Ella? Would you like to come with me?'

⋆   ⋆   ⋆

Julia's office is strangely quiet. I don't remember how, but when I look up at her, we're sitting at opposite ends of her sofa.

'I don't know what happened,' I whisper. Then because the time is long past for secrets and lies, I tell her.

My breath is shaky. 'I sent away for my birth certificate. I waited two weeks . . . ' I shiver. I'm so cold. 'But it never came. Then I got an email.'

Then all I can hear is silence, until my whisper fills it.

'I don't exist.'

309

Julia's eyes don't leave mine. 'When did this happen?'

'Yesterday — or the day before.' Looking at her, frightened again, because even the days are muddled and I can't be sure.

'Ella, listen to me. What's happening to you is a shock response. A difficult one, called traumatic shock. But you'll be OK, I promise you.'

But I'm not OK, I know I'm not. I'm frozen, like my brain is shutting down. How can just a shock make you feel like this?

'I think you'd better tell me everything.'

'They were in my father's desk.' I'm trying to remember how it happened. Then I think of the papers, my hands shaking as I pull a bunch of them out of my bag. Time does that weird thing again, little frozen seconds floating between us. My breath thaws them.

'This was the first one.' Passing it to her, feeling how heavy it is.

Very slowly she takes it.

Then I watch her face. Know the words she's reading, off by heart.

. . . You will agree to give William James Farrington full custody of the child known as Ella Vivian Farrington. In addition, you will relinquish all parental rights. In return, all details relating to her half-brother, Theo Moon, born the third of July in the year 1996, will remain in the safekeeping of Alderton Chalmers, for as long as the terms of this agreement remain in place. Should the agreement be broken, they will be placed in the hands of the police.

Signed on this day, the seventeenth of August, 2002, by

Mr William Farrington

Ms April Moon

In the presence of Martin Alderton

(witness)

'I don't understand.' Julia looks confused. 'Why would he do this? And what does he mean by details?'

I've thought and thought about this. Looked for any other explanation. Not wanting to believe my father is capable of such things.

'I think my father blackmailed a woman called April Moon. My birth mother.' I whisper it, as if I can stop the ripple of my words.

'Then he stole me from her.'

43

2016

I must have eventually dozed, because I'm woken by the presence of someone beside me, led back to the same room as before where Ryder's already sitting, his back to me.

I take the seat opposite, my blood chilling as I look at his face.

'Rather convenient, isn't it? How you forgot to tell us you were a lawyer?'

'I don't see it's relevant,' I tell him. 'It was a long time ago.'

He fidgets impatiently in his seat. 'Clarify one thing for me. Are you here in your capacity as a lawyer or, as you told us, an old friend?'

'I can't exactly represent someone who's unconscious. When she comes round, that will be up to Ms Rousseau.' A textbook answer he can't argue with.

'Well, that's looking less and less likely,' Ryder snarls back. 'She's got a chest infection today, tomorrow it'll be pneumonia, the day after that they'll switch the machines off.'

And though I'm hating every word that comes out of his mouth, it's a picture I've already painted, too many times.

'Your prints are everywhere,' Ryder says softly. 'All over her house. How often have you been there?'

'She leaves a key.' I meet his stare, play his game. 'For people who know.'

'There's another thing, too.' He shuffles through the papers on the table in front of him. 'About your Mrs Hayward.'

'Clara? What about her?'

Ryder's eyes narrow. 'Here's the thing. One of the local chaps went round to talk to her. PC Taylor, his name is. He found her in the garden, round the back.' He smirks. 'Next time you pick an alibi, I'd think twice, if I were you. Only Mrs Hayward . . . Well, let's put it this way. She's not your biggest fan. Shall I tell you what she said?' He carries on without pausing. 'She says you're a useless drunk. You've let your house go to rack and ruin and she despairs of you.'

His voice hardens. 'Does the name Paul Rogers mean anything to you?'

As he speaks, I feel the blood drain from my face.

Ryder sounds almost triumphant. 'Got him off a rape charge, according to my records. Only he was guilty, wasn't he? He was convicted a year later, for raping a twelve-year-old girl, it says here.' Hanging on the *twelve*, waving his sheaf of notes at me. 'Not your proudest moment, I'd say.' Across the table, his face looms close to mine. 'But you know that, don't you, Calaway? And you bloody ran away because that's what you do.'

As he pauses, it all comes back. *Paul Rogers* . . . A name I've never forgotten, that I wish I could, that replays over and over in my head, as I think of the brilliant career I'd worked

313

so hard to build. The guilt and the shame that had haunted me since, because if I'd handled the case differently, maybe I could have prevented another attack. As I bury my face in my hands, wondering how much else Ryder knows, he goes on.

'Here's what I think. You're a washed-up lawyer and a flaming alcoholic who lives in a dream world. I've seen the bottles in your room. You only have to look at you. You're a mess.'

'There was more to it,' I tell him through gritted teeth, feeling the sweat on my face, running down my body under my shirt, waiting for him to remind me how the twelve-year-old girl had then killed herself.

'Bet you're craving a drink, aren't you? A nice glass of Scotch that burns your throat and warms you on its way down? Like the feel of it, don't you? Only you want another glass, then another, until it fills your veins. Buries the most sordid memories, doesn't it? Solves everything . . . ' Pausing, he smirks. 'Bit hot, are you?'

As I feel in my pocket for a handkerchief to mop my brow, I notice my hands shaking.

His eyes pointedly on my hands; Ryder's clearly noticed. 'Your Mrs Hayward's got your measure. Says you're a waste of space. She's no idea where you were that night.'

I'm reeling, fielding everything he tells me like blows to my head, because suddenly, nothing is certain. For four years I've known Clara. She's abrasive. Speaks her mind. We might not be friends exactly, but we get on well enough. She doesn't really think so badly of me. I imagine her

314

giving her uncensored opinion the way she does about everything. Wishing just for once, for PC Taylor's ears, she could have moderated it.

'I know your sort,' Ryder says maliciously. 'With your whisky bottles, pouring another and another, knocking it back until your pitiful little life and everyone in it disappears.'

He's taunting me with every word, peeling away another layer of my skin. Under the rawness of my pain, I feel myself shiver.

Leaning forward, he talks more quietly. 'Thing is, Calaway, you've told so many lies, I can't believe a bleeding word you say.'

I don't remember being led back to my cell. I'm not thinking, just feeling, a bunch of raw nerve cells in a world that has imploded, in which I'm trapped.

It's a world in which I failed; one where I defended a rapist who'd lied to everyone; who I'd suspected was guilty, but who'd had contacts. Who walked out of court and later preyed on a twelve-year-old girl who killed herself. The real reason I walked away from my career.

* * *

I imagine it's because Ryder finds no hard evidence that after twenty-four hours I'm free to go. It's late, the night damp with drizzle, but I walk, aware of the entire day I've missed, of time like sand slipping through my fingers. As my strength slowly returns, I feel the mist lift and my mind clear; walking faster, until it comes to me what I have to do first. Pausing for a moment to text Will.

If you have time, I think we should meet. I've
discovered what's going on.

I imagine his stunned surprise as he realizes
I'm no longer being held by the police, the
curiosity he won't be able to resist. But I no
longer care. A couple of hours later, he replies.

I'm in Brighton tomorrow, could be in Sevenoaks
for midday. The White Hart?

Then I text Bea.

They let me go, for now. Have you had a chance
to read the files? I'm meeting Will for lunch
tomorrow, hope to find out more.

Then back at the B&B, I'm met by my
landlady, who's clearly waited up for me.
'Mr Calaway? Could I have a word?' I wonder
how long she's been sitting, fretting, wondering
if I'm coming back. 'This is quite difficult . . .
But you know, about the police and everything . . . '
'I can assure you I haven't done anything
wrong,' I tell her. 'Detective Sergeant Ryder has
his wires crossed, he just doesn't know it. We're
trying to solve the same case, that's all.'
'I don't know . . . ' And I see that her cosy,
chintzy world has been threatened by the
mistrust left in Ryder's wake. Her eyes flit
anxiously. 'It's just that this is a certain type of

establishment. Our guests expect certain things.'

'If it would help, I can pay you now.' I reach into my pocket for my wallet and she backs away, as if half expecting me to produce a loaded weapon. I peel off some notes, counting them.

'I'm terribly sorry if I've inconvenienced you, or any of the other guests. There's enough there to cover what I owe you — plus another night,' I tell her. 'Then I'll leave.'

*   *   *

Upstairs, Ryder's presence is in my room, in my emptied holdall, my clothes spread carelessly about the floor, the pointlessness of the squeezed-out shampoo bottle in the bathroom. Catching sight of my reflection, I see what my landlady saw just now.

I stare at the face in the mirror, for a moment not recognizing it as my own. It's old, world weary; causes anger to rise unexpectedly in me.

Scattered around are the empty whisky bottles that no doubt Ryder found. I look for the half-filled one next to the television, holding it for a moment like a lifeline, about to twist the top off it and drink it straight from the bottle.

Then somehow finding iron strength in my shaking hands, I ignore the voice in my head telling me that I'll only go out and buy another. Taking it into the bathroom, I pour it away.

Something happens to me then and as my body starts to shake, emotions, long buried, clamber to the surface. It's not just how I look. Hating how I'm feeling, I punch the door frame.

317

Twice, three times, focusing on the pain in my bleeding knuckles before clutching them, leaning back against the wall, slipping silently to the floor.

ELLA

How could my father do that? Steal me from my mother?

'Ella?' Julia says gently. 'Do you understand how serious this is?'

Feel myself shrink into the sofa; afraid.

'Reading this, it looks as though he threatened her.' Her voice is serious.

I nod. 'I think she must have had a secret. He knew what it was. And he used it.'

'To do with Theo?'

I pass Julia the next folded page. Slowly she opens it, frowning as she reads, then puts the letter down. 'I don't understand. It's a birth certificate. Why would he have this? Who's Elodie Tara Moon?'

I thought if I believed hard enough, someone else would too. That for a while, it would be real. But it never will be. My whisper reaches Julia.

'I think she's me.'

I nod again. 'My father had Theo's birth certificate too. He kept everything together. Here.' I pass it to her. 'If I'm right, he's still my half-brother, isn't he?'

Holding my breath, watching her frown, trying to take it in.

'We need to find him, don't we, really badly, so he can explain?' I ask, because we have to.

But her face is full of sadness. 'I can't believe

you've known all this time. That you were adopted.'

I shake my head, because I wasn't adopted, not properly. I was stolen. 'I only knew for sure when I sent off for my birth certificate. And then, when I found Theo's.' Suddenly I'm shaking. 'I knew he was my brother. I'd always thought we had the same father. I was wrong. We have the same mother. My father — how could he do that?'

I feel Julia's hand on my arm. 'It's too much to keep to yourself. It's why it's hit you so hard.'

Suddenly I feel numb. There's a knock on the door. She goes to answer it. I hear low voices, then she turns to me. 'Ella? Will you be OK if I leave you, just for two minutes? That's all — and I promise I'll be back.'

I nod. She closes the door softly, and I'm alone. Suddenly I'm so tired. The sofa is soft and I curl my feet up, leaning back against a cushion, closing my eyes for a few seconds.

When I open them, Julia's back.

'Sorry I had to leave you like that,' she says. 'But it's good you slept. You're tired because of the shock.'

Pushing myself up on the sofa, I stifle a yawn.

Then Julia says, 'Ella? We've always been honest with each other, haven't we? You know I would never lie?'

I half nod, then gaze at her, frightened again because I know from her voice that this isn't over yet.

Her face shows how sorry she is. 'I'm not sure quite how to tell you this. But I've just found out something about Theo. Something I think that somewhere, deep down, you already know.'

I can't stop my heart leaping erratically with hope, because something, no matter how bad, is better than knowing nothing.

'Is he in prison?' I ask quickly, because it's the only thing I can think of.

She hesitates. 'Theo isn't in prison. You've never met him, have you?' Her voice is gentle.

I shake my head.

'Oh, Ella, I'm so sorry.' There are tears in Julia's eyes. 'He died, honey. A long time ago. Before you were born . . .'

She's looking through the papers I've given her. My eyes turn towards the window. I see myself running across the grass to the old cedar tree, where I thought of him waiting for me, a ray of sun lighting his face; forcing myself to listen as I hear her say it, over and over, 'Ella, Theo died, honey,' until the rushing of the wind blots it out.

I'd known. From the dreams I still have, where he joined the moths and the pheasants that my father killed, from the letter hidden in my father's desk.

I wanted so badly to be wrong. I wanted someone in my family who'd really care.

Suddenly I can't breathe. It's the spider's web again, only the strands are snapping all around me until I'm left with a tightrope and nothing to hold on to, a yawning abyss below as my body starts to shake. Then it goes dark and suddenly I'm spinning, then falling, down and down.

'Ella, it'll be OK . . .'

The words come from far away. I can't tell where from. Just feel Julia's arms as she reaches out and catches me.

44

I'm tired beyond belief the next morning. Wrung out, empty. Stripping off, I run a cold shower that's like needles on my skin, that takes my breath away. Feel no better.

Desperate to talk to Bea, I know I must confront Will first. This is where it starts and ends. With Will. Has it always been that way? If he's uneasy as I walk into the White Hart, he doesn't show it.

He looks up, not bothering to conceal his interest. 'Noah.'

'Glad you could make it,' I tell him.

'I have to admit I was interested to hear what you'd found out,' he says. 'Did I hear a rumour that our friend Ryder took you in?'

From the lightness of his voice, the coolness of his gaze, it's impossible to read what he's thinking.

'I had a most comfortable night in a small cell, thank you,' I tell him. 'The standard twenty-four hours, after which in the absence of any good, solid evidence, fortunately he was forced to let me go. I'll get you a drink.'

'Another Scotch,' Will says briefly, raising his glass to me before emptying it.

I take my time at the bar, indulging in idle chat with the girl who serves me, letting Will wait, before I take the drinks — his Scotch and my own orange juice — back to our table.

His eyes linger on my glass. I'm ready for his caustic remark, to deflect it with indifference, but today, Will doesn't waste time. 'So. What's this all about?'

'I'm still tying up a few loose ends,' I tell him. 'At least, I was before Ryder got in the way. But I'm fairly sure now that April had discovered something. Most of her clients were mothers carrying babies diagnosed with serious problems. I'm no expert, but I've talked to one or two of them. One had a baby with Tay . . . ?'

I pretend I've forgotten, feigning ignorance, drawing him in, playing on my lack of expertise, because I can never forget what Daisy Rubinstein told me, or the reality of it etched on her lovely face.

'Tay–Sachs,' he says sharply. 'What about it?'

'It wasn't just Tay-Sachs,' I continue. 'There were babies with heart defects. That's your area, isn't it?'

Will looks cagey. 'It's a complicated field, Noah. There are many types of problems and different treatment options. I see a few of them. But anyway, go on.'

'April had gathered statistics.' I'm watching every muscle in his face, every shift of his gaze, every blink of his eyes. 'Her data wasn't conclusive, but it looked as though she'd stumbled across an irregularity. You see, the newborn mortality rates at two of the hospitals stood out.'

'That's news to me.' He says it pleasantly, but I can see that suddenly he's rigid. 'Amateur statistics can be glaringly inaccurate.' He pauses, then asks too casually, 'I'd be interested to take a look, though. Do you happen to have the notes with you?'

'I'm afraid I don't. But that wasn't the end of it. She started to look deeper into why some babies were treated and some were not. I think she suspected a pattern of some kind, but never quite worked out what it was.'

On the table in front of him, Will's phone buzzes and he glances at the number that flashes up. 'I have to get this. Will Farrington.' As he speaks into it, I watch him frown.

'Oh, for goodness' sake. Whatever's the matter with her?'

He listens, irritation written on his face. 'Which clinic?'

Then, 'I can't possibly come now. I'm in a meeting.'

He listens again, then says, 'Text me the address. I'll be there as soon as I can.'

'Sorry,' he says, ending the call and taking another swig of Scotch. 'It's my daughter — only Rebecca's away. Nothing that can't wait.'

'You're sure? This will keep,' I tell him, watching him torn, weighing family obligations against the reality of leaving here, not knowing what I'm going to say.

He shakes his head impatiently. 'You were saying. You think April had found a pattern.'

I nod. 'I went over her notes, then I talked to some of her clients. One of them gave me this questionnaire.'

'That's quite standard,' he tells me. 'These

days, it's all about patient feedback — not that most patients can be bothered.'

'This was different.' Studying his face. 'These were questions asked before treatment was started. And I think I'm right in saying, before any treatment was decided.'

His relief is obvious — he actually laughs. 'You *think*? You need to do better than that, Noah. You call me over here because of something you *think*, but don't actually know?'

'The questions were interesting.' Ignoring his outburst, my eyes still riveted on his. 'About social background, jobs, income, schools . . . You have to ask, don't you, what relevance that could possibly have.'

Then as I watch the faintest tinge of red creep into his cheeks, the tiny muscle twitching in his neck, I keep going.

'In the case of a sick baby, I can understand questions about the health of the parents, and any history of illness in the family, but social background? That's a step too far for anyone — except you, Will. Isn't that true?'

Pushing against his silence. 'And there's the Fairview Medical Centre.'

All the time watching him for a giveaway clue that I'm right. Taking a huge leap of faith.

'Are you accusing me of sending out this questionnaire?' His voice is icy. 'Because I may or may not have. I can't be held responsible for every stray piece of paper that gets handed to patients.'

'As it happens, they were always sent — by post — before each case was admitted. I have the names of staff — as well as patients — who will verify this.'

Then my own phone buzzes with a text. Bea.

Where are you? The police want to speak to him. Can you keep him there?

After the night of soul-searching in the darkness of my cell, drawing together the stories from April's clients with my scattered thoughts, discounting what wasn't relevant — after Will's response, I know I'm right.

'Sorry about this,' I say to him. 'Won't be a second.' Texting Bea.

White Hart, Sevenoaks. Will do my best.

He looks uneasy.

'You've told your ridiculous story to Beatrice, haven't you? Was that her? Well, I've already told her the truth. She knows you've lied — for years, to everyone. The police will get you, Noah. It's a matter of time, that's all.'

'I've made mistakes.' I'm calm as I face my adversary. 'Only these aren't my lies, are they, Will? I can see what you've done. They're yours, twisted round and slipped to me when you thought I wasn't looking. Only now I'm looking. I can see all of them. And you know what? I think Bea does too.'

I'm deliberately provoking him, because I need the truth. 'Come on, Will. That questionnaire . . . Did you really think you could get away with it? Choosing to treat babies of families from wealthy backgrounds, with money, education, class? What were you playing at — buying favours or being God? What about the struggling families, up to their ears in debt, who then have to cope with the death of a baby, because the consultant classified them as undeserving of treatment, unworthy of a chance at life? Who the fuck do you think you are?'

'You have no idea what you're talking about.' Staring back at me through slitted eyes.

There's another text from Bea.

April's the mother of Will's daughter.

I stare at the words; my mind empties as I try to take it in.

'Something the matter?' He's nervous. Suddenly I know I've got him.

I try to focus. 'Tell me about April, Will. Forget I was about to marry her for a moment. Leave me out of the picture. Tell me how it was.'

Suddenly I genuinely want to hear what he has to say, but the look he gives me is full of contempt.

'Leave you out of it?' Words that are loaded with sarcasm. 'You've no idea how many times I've wished I could.'

'Did you manipulate her, too? Like the families who come to you to save their babies? All those lives in your hands — I bet you love that.'

'I save lives, Noah.' His tone is steely. 'I have to make decisions. Everyone thinks there are endless resources. Do you know how over-stretched most hospitals are? How hard we work to make the best of it? There's limited money. If I have five babies who need surgery and can only accommodate four, because that's how many beds we have, I have to make decisions.'

'You don't,' I cry. 'You send them somewhere else.'

He throws his head back. 'Christ, Noah. There's nowhere fucking else. It's the same everywhere — budgets and fixed resources, beds, nursing care. Is it so bad that the kid that's most likely to make something of his life gets the bed?'

'You're aware it's a criminal offence? The wilful neglect and ill-treatment of patients?' I shake my head disbelievingly. 'You can't imagine you'll get away with this.'

But Will hasn't finished. 'Do you know how hard we train, for fucking years? Working all hours, learning skills few others have. Making advances that save lives and benefit future generations. Look at A&E. All that effort wasted on people who have no self-respect. Who abuse their health, the system, waste the time and energy of all of us here. Take the drunks who come in, with their self-inflicted illness. They expect to be treated the same way as the victim of a road traffic accident, because everyone does. It's taken for bloody granted.'

'You're forgetting the human race isn't perfect. It never will be. And you're dealing with babies, Will. Making life-and-death decisions when even in your own warped world, even if you could in some way justify your actions, you have no idea

329

who they'll grow up to be.'

'You can take a bloody good guess,' he says scornfully. 'Someone's background is a pretty accurate gauge of how they'll turn out.'

'Like yourself?' I say icily. 'Do you know what's even more terrifying?' I stare at him, wondering how this man was ever my friend. 'You can't see it.'

Then I shake my head. 'So April's the mother of your child,' I add softly. 'Was that part of your plan, too? Then because she found out what you were up to, you wanted her out of the way.'

'You've no idea what you're talking about,' he flashes. 'For one thing, she wasn't fit to be a mother.'

'It's not up to you,' I cry, feeling the sting of his words, of his judgement of April yet again, as I jump to the only conclusion that makes sense. 'God. You've taken a woman's child from her.'

'At the time — ' Will grits his teeth — 'I remember it suited her just fine. We both know she wasn't reliable. Think about it. She was damaged goods, Noah, not the poor lost little angel you thought she was. Don't look like that. The difference with me was that I saw through her. I knew exactly what she was. A beautiful woman who'd fuck anyone. For Christ's sake, her mother was a whore, her stepfather raped her. Sex was like pissing — just another autonomous body function to her.'

'She was vulnerable and you exploited her.' My heart at once ice cold and boiling.

'Rubbish. She could have walked away, any time she liked. She kept coming back.' He points

330

at his chest. 'To me. Open your eyes, Noah. Wake up to yourself.'

'Bastard.' I mutter the word.

He leers, an ugly, monstrous look as he sits back, folding his arms. 'Face it. You're out of your depth.'

As soon as he says that, it's as though a light comes on. Suddenly it's blindingly obvious. All along, he's manipulated me too.

'That's why you called me, isn't it?' I say softly. 'At the very beginning? The dropout lawyer who you thought was still in love with her. I wouldn't have a hope of winning her case, if it came to that, but you knew I wouldn't be able to resist.'

I'm completely stunned as it sinks in, because I can't believe that until now, I haven't seen through him. Will had never wanted me to help April. He'd brought me here to fail.

'I'm right, aren't I?' I add, catching sight of Ryder outside, walking past the window. 'And the only reason you're still here, right now, listening to me, is because you want April's precious files, because she was right. And which most likely by now are in the hands of our good friend Ryder . . . '

Will opens his mouth to reply. Then seeing me glance past him, turns to see Ryder come through the door. His face visibly pales.

'Why did you kill Norton, Will? Were you trying to set her up?'

He doesn't speak. I sit back, my eyes not leaving his.

'Why didn't you just kill her?' I ask softly. 'Or

is that what you're doing now? Quietly altering her meds while no one's looking, because no one would ever suspect you, would they?'

His face is ashen. Then Ryder's beside him, his hand on Will's shoulder as the PC with him reads him his rights.

Reaching for my keys, I get up. 'Like I said, mate, right at the start. The truth usually comes out.'

I don't even know if Will hears me. Then, nodding to Ryder, I walk away.

ELLA

I've slept for an hour, Julia tells me when I open my eyes, remembering where I am. Feel warm softness covering me. Hear Julia's voice.

'Ella? It's OK. You don't have to get up.'

It comes back to me what's happened. I pull myself up so I'm half sitting. Then I notice a second person and, as the mist clears, I realize she's the lady I saw behind the desk.

'I don't know you, do I?' *I whisper.*

She shakes her head. 'I knew your mother — your birth mother.' *She looks uncertainly at Julia.*

I know then, we have met. When I was too young to remember. Closing my eyes again, because her voice feels like I'm going home.

'Ella?' *Julia's voice through my darkness.* 'I tried to call your mother, honey. Only Gabriela told me she's away.'

I sigh then, but it doesn't matter. Rebecca's not really my mother. She never has been.

'I know he's lied, but I had to call your father.' *Her voice is anxious.*

My eyes open wide, I pull myself upright. 'No, please. I won't go with him.'

'Ella, I had to talk to him. You're not well. He's your next of kin. I didn't have a choice. We'll talk to him together, I promise you.'

But I don't want to talk to him. I don't even want to look at him. I try to get to my feet, because I have to get out of here before he arrives, but my legs wobble and I fall back on the sofa.

'Ella? I want to introduce you to Beatrice.'

The fair-haired lady smiles sadly. 'Your mother and I were at school together. We were friends for many years. When she was fifteen, she looked exactly like you. When I saw you come in, I knew.'

I look at Julia, confused.

'Your birth mother,' Julia says quietly. 'April Moon.'

At last, someone says her name. My mother's name.

'I've just started working here,' Beatrice says quietly. 'A few days ago. It was April who suggested I apply for the job.'

'Is she here?' It comes out high-pitched as my heart starts thumping. If my real mother's here, I have to see her. 'Can you get her?' Trying to stand, I feel my legs go again. I slump back on the sofa.

Beatrice shakes her head, glancing at Julia.

'She's not here, Ella,' Julia says quietly. 'She isn't well. She's in hospital.'

I'm confused. It's too much to take in. I turn to Beatrice, trying to understand.

'I don't usually come here,' I tell her, not making sense, but I'm thinking, do I know her eyes? Can you inherit memories like the colour of your hair? Is this my mother's memory?

'What are the chances?' Beatrice says softly.

I'm staring at her, so that I don't hear the

334

quiet knock, just Julia calling across the room. 'Yes?'

Suddenly I'm filled with anxiety. What if it's my father?

It's a woman's faceless voice. 'Just to let you know, Mr Farrington called. He's been held up.'

And I feel relief as though a huge weight is lifted from me.

Then she adds, 'And the police are here.'

I gasp.

'They've come to talk to me.' Beatrice gets up, then hesitates, looking at me. 'Ella? If it's OK with you, I'd really like to see you again.'

She stands there, as if there's more she wants to say, but then someone calls her away. After she's closed the door behind her, Julia says, 'You have to realize, you haven't done anything wrong, Ella. Other people have.' Her voice hardens momentarily, in a way I haven't heard before. 'But not you.'

Haven't I? And then it comes to me, it's not my own guilt I've been carrying. It's my father's. Thinking of my father, hearing Julia say my mother's name, I know I have to tell her something else.

'I heard him on the phone. He was talking to her. To April.' Then my hand covers my mouth, because now his words make sense.

★　★　★

I tell Julia, about my father's voice, the way it's abrupt when he's annoyed about something, which is most of the time. How he carelessly left the door of his study cracked open; how he spoke to her.

'You'll have to talk to him. He's your bloody stepfather. And she's your daughter.'

Silence, then he's louder. Not caring who hears.

'I'd say all bets are off, wouldn't you? Come off it, April. This is different. You're telling me he's threatened Ella, for Christ's sake. Or don't you care?'

'All right. I'll meet you there.'

The phone slammed down. Silence. Then his laugh. Someone threatens me and my father laughs.

★   ★   ★

'Are you certain, Ella?'

I nod, so freaking word-for-word certain I could recite it in my sleep. I'm still hearing his voice, how callously he spoke, his laugh after he hears someone's threatened me, as Julia hurries to her phone.

★   ★   ★

Much later, when the sun has slipped behind the clouds, when Julia half pulls the curtains, I know that the world I inhabited has gone forever, but that while I've slept, time has somehow reassembled. That the secrets are out in the open. That huddled against Julia on her sofa, my head on her chest, her arms tight round me, her chin resting on my head, while the remnants of

336

my old life are scattered in every direction, I'm safe.

Later still, I remember. 'Gabriela! Where is she?'

'She's just outside, waiting for us. I want a quick word with Beatrice and then, I don't know about you, but I'm starving. Shall we treat Gabriela to a late lunch? There's a little coffee shop just round the corner, if you think you can walk that far.'

As I get to my feet, my legs feel stronger. I nod. I'm shaky, but OK. There are still questions — about my father, and about April — but no longer are they crushing me. They can wait.

Then, as I follow Julia through the door, I step into the rest of my life.

45

Ryder's pursuit of me, then Bea's lack of faith and Will's mocking contempt spark an awakening moment of agonizing clarity. One in which my eyes are forced open and the brightest torch shone into the dusty corners of my life, illuminating my failed career and broken relationships, searing them into my mind. But so, too, is my lack of kindness to myself, so that in the most bizarre way, it's a gift. A moment I know I have to cling to. Have to see for what it is and face head on, so that I'm free.

That same evening — one that, because of my own sea change, feels weeks, even months later — I arrange to meet Bea a few miles out of Sevenoaks at a village pub, a place with trees and empty space, where the cool air is soothing and the weight of the day starts to lift.

'I'm so sorry.' Bea hugs me tight, then sits on the bench beside me.

'Don't be. You were great. Couldn't have timed it better.' I pour her a glass of wine from the bottle I've already bought, that I won't touch.

'Thank you.' Bea takes it, then looks ashamed. 'For a while, I'll be honest, Noah — I didn't believe you. God, Will is such a bastard. I checked out the Fairview Medical Centre.'

'You did? I couldn't get anywhere. I was going to drive over there, until Will did his level best to have me arrested. What did you find out?'

'There wasn't really anything online,' Bea says. 'So I went there. You know how on the website there were photos of that big white house? Well, the real number seventy-six is a red-brick semi, rented out to students. I thought I was in the wrong place until one of them just happened to be coming out as I walked past. Owned by a rich surgeon bloke, was what he said when I asked him. Described Will's car to a T. The medical centre, the website, Will totally made them up.'

'You did well,' I tell her, impressed. 'That was quite brave. You might have run into anyone.' Meaning Will.

Bea shrugs. 'When you've dealt with a bastard like my ex, it changes your perspective on a lot of things. Did he kill Norton, do you think? Will? And set April up?'

'It looks like it. Then when I discovered what he was up to, he tried to pin it on me.' I'm thoughtful. 'He's done a lot of that. I think what happened was when April found out that Will was selecting his patients by unethical means, she challenged him. I don't think it was ever about what Norton did all these years ago. Will just used him.'

Pausing, because I'm guessing, because there's still no proof — not yet. Contemplating how Will could have been so cruel as to stir up Norton when he knew what he'd done to April. 'But what doesn't make sense was if Will was somehow manipulating April out of the way and he was even prepared to kill someone, why not her? How come she's still alive?'

339

Bea looks just as puzzled.

I'm trying to work it out as I speak. 'He really is a bastard. But for reasons he's not saying, I don't think he wanted her dead — just out of the way.' I pause, distracted, because it's still so new. 'I can't believe she has a daughter.'

Bea smiles sadly. 'For a moment, it was like looking at April's ghost. She's so like her, Noah. Her eyes, that hair . . . It was Ella who came up with proof. He'd forced April to sign a document years ago, giving him custody of her. It's why she told me she'd had a miscarriage.'

Hiding Ella's existence from Bea in the same way she'd hidden our baby from me. Counting on the fact that we wouldn't ask.

'She must have told anyone who knew she was pregnant the same thing. Then I suppose she must have gone away.' And, until now, no one had been any the wiser.

'I didn't see her so much around that time.' Bea's voice is sober. 'If only I had. Imagine her dealing with Will on her own, then knowing after — if she'd ever tried to contact Ella — he'd have taken her to court.'

What's incredible, too, is that Will thought he could get away with this. But then he had, for all this time, using his own daughter to get at April, and then Norton to frame her.

'He wanted her out of the way because she knew too much,' I say slowly, as it starts to fall into place. 'I'm convinced he's altering her meds, Bea. He isn't her consultant, but he's often in her room.'

'Surely not.' Bea looks horrified.

340

'He probably believes he can pin it on someone else. That's Will through and through.'

Bea's eyes are sad. 'It must have tormented April, not being able to contact Ella. But when she found out what he was up to at the hospital, why didn't she go to the police?'

'I don't know.' It's another question I don't have the answer for. Then I have to ask her. 'You need to tell me about my baby, Bea.'

She nods. 'I've been thinking the same thing. Several times, April wanted to tell you, then just couldn't. I suppose in the end there didn't seem any point.' Bea looks straight at me. 'His name was Theo.'

Theo. I think of the photo I took from April's house. The woman holding him must have been April.

'He was beautiful, Noah.' Bea sighs. 'When April found out she was pregnant, to begin with she was devastated. She'd just got settled with her flat, her job. It represented hope for a better kind of future, she said. Then, suddenly . . . Well, you can imagine how she felt. After all she'd already been through . . .

'She changed her mind, though,' Bea continues. 'As the pregnancy went on, she decided she was going to give this baby everything she'd never had — love, a safe home. The future. When you saw her that time, in London, she almost told you, then at the last minute she couldn't do it. She thought you'd leave your course. It would ruin your life.'

I lean forward, resting my chin in my hands. She was right. I would have left uni without a backward glance. 'It wasn't her choice to make, was it?'

'No.' Bea pauses. 'Anyway, a few months later Theo was born.'

'My mother's name was Theodora.'

Bea nods. 'I know. April told me. She didn't really know your mother, but it was a small way of connecting the baby to you. He was gorgeous, Noah. And happy. April juggled work with looking after him — I babysat when I could. At one point, I lived there. It was hard, but for those months, it was as though we were in another, totally different world. A baby changes how you look at everything . . . ' Her eyes sparkling sadly as she remembers. 'We would take him for walks, noticing the flowers or the birds. We'd laugh when he laughed. He had this great laugh — like bubbles of sunlight, April always said.'

All the time she's been talking, there's been a light in her eyes, but then it dies away.

'It was April who noticed a change in him. It was when he got more active. He got tired so easily. His skin was really pale and sometimes his lips were blue. There were other signs. She took him to her doctor — her useless doctor — who brushed her off and sent her away. He should have been struck off, because that's another thing — you wouldn't believe it now, but twenty years ago, in some parts there was still a stigma attached to being an unmarried mother.'

Her words strike a chord, filling me with guilt as I imagine April with Theo, as if being alone wasn't hard enough, having to field the bounced-off blows of judgement and condemnation of people who didn't know any better, as if it were her choice.

'Her doctor was old school. April said he used to treat her with contempt . . . '

Bea shakes her head, her face growing distant. Then she continues. 'Talking about it brings it all back. We knew something was terribly wrong, but no one could tell us what. April brought Theo home. We watched him really closely but it was getting worse. Eventually she got him to a different doctor who diagnosed a heart defect.'

I remember Daisy Rubinstein, her harrowing account of watching her baby lose his life. Suddenly I feel sick.

'Go on,' I say quietly.

Bea's face is sober. 'We were told he'd need several operations and, even then, they might not be able to completely cure him. The first one went well enough, but after the second . . . He started having seizures. The first time, April was alone with him. The hospital gave her drugs for him, but there wasn't anything else they could do. I remember them coming home — I'd just got back from work. Both of them were exhausted, Theo crying and crying. It was grim. She took as much time off as she could, then she stopped working altogether so that she could care for him.

'It was horrible, Noah. Theo was so weak that further surgery wasn't an option. I couldn't believe how little they could do for him. We were completely powerless. Then one night, he started crying.'

Bea's eyes are wet with tears. 'I swear I've never heard anything so terrible. There was no way to comfort him. Will came round now and then, but he was still a student. April begged him to help, but there was nothing he could do. That was the worst part of it. Theo's crying, and there being nothing any of us could do, other than watch as he grew weaker.'

Bea breaks off. When she continues, her voice is wavering. 'He died not long after that. I wasn't there — I was at work when it happened. But I was glad that if he wasn't going to get better, that it was over.'

All the time she's been speaking, I've been numb. Then suddenly the realization hits me, this is my child she's talking about, *my and April's baby*, as I feel a searing pain, deep inside, of raw flesh being ripped open and human suffering exposed.

'She was distraught. Will signed the death certificate . . . ' I try to listen, but Bea's voice is distant. While I try to focus through the hot tears that fill my eyes, she pauses. 'I was never sure why she called him. But everything was so surreal then, so completely devastating, I didn't question it. Then after, I didn't want to bring the subject up.'

Not wanting to remind April, or perhaps not knowing what to say.

She's thoughtful. 'You know how a child who loses their parents is an orphan? There's no word for a parent who loses a child.'

Bea goes on. 'It was weeks later, because April couldn't bear to do it, but we took his ashes to one of her favourite places. She insisted we went to the top of Reynard's Hill. I remember the fog. So thick you could barely see in front of you.'

She pauses, then looks me in the eye. 'You must remember, Noah. We saw you.'

46

By now in my second year of uni, I'd resented the trip back to Musgrove for my father's fiftieth birthday. It was January and, having just started the term, I hadn't wanted to leave my friends so soon. It didn't help that I knew what the occasion would be — dull people, the same boring food my mother produced for every gathering — but knowing in my sinking heart that I had to be there.

It was a particularly bleak January, I thought, as I stepped off the train into deadly suburbia. Grey but not frozen, the hills shrouded in mist, with that biting damp that chilled you through. Weather for cosy pubs and lively student bars, not my parents' front room full of my mother's canapés and a whole bunch of neighbours I didn't really have anything to say to, but here I was anyway.

I'd like to say I'd been taken by surprise — that it had been a great day. Fun, even. It wasn't. A dozen times I was asked how I was getting on at uni, while Mr Selway from opposite droned on about the dent in his car and my mother flitted around offering trays of her dreary food. As soon as people started leaving, I seized my opportunity.

'I said I'd meet Will,' I told my mother's

disappointed face. 'I won't be long.'

It was a lie, of course. I'd no idea if Will was at home. Even if he was, I had no intention of seeing him. I'd recently taken up smoking and after hours in the presence of my parents, my body was craving its fix. I stopped at the newsagent to buy cigarettes from a disapproving Mr McKenna, wondering why just because someone had known you forever, they felt they had the right to judge you. Then after lighting up, I'd started walking.

I suppose I walked the streets of my old life. I passed Will's family's house, the darkness through the half-drawn curtains telling me no one was home, then the North Star, which beckoned me in. After buying a pint, not unexpectedly I found myself thinking of April.

As I sat at a table in the corner, I knew I was over the indignity of being unceremoniously dumped, but I couldn't help wondering how my life would be if she hadn't written that letter, if I'd followed her and gone to work in London. Would we have stayed together?

I'd decided we probably would, just as the door swung open and they came in.

To begin with I couldn't move, just felt familiar embarrassment engulf me with the rush of heat to my cheeks, as I watched them unbutton their coats, their hair obviously damp from the mist.

I saw Bea say something to April, then April shake her head. As she spoke again, Bea's hand went to her arm. I waited for one of them to smile, or laugh loudly the way they often did together, but they were oddly subdued.

It was as Bea went to the bar that I got up and made my way over.

'Hi. April?' Her back was towards me and, as I spoke, I would have sworn she jumped.

She spun round. 'Noah! What a surprise!' She glanced around for Bea, but not before I noticed the forced brightness in her voice and the agitation she was trying to hide.

'How are you?'

'Good,' she smiled, only that was forced too, not reaching her eyes, as Bea's voice came from behind me.

'Noah?'

'Hi, Bea. What are the chances?' I couldn't think what else to say.

'What a coincidence.' But Bea's voice, too, lacked its characteristic brightness.

April looked across at Bea — I couldn't see what passed between them. Then she forced another smile. 'I thought you'd be back at uni.'

'A dutiful visit only for my father's birthday.' I'd raised my eyebrows. 'You're the last people I expected to see here.'

It was true. As far as I knew, April was still in London.

'We came back to see my mother,' Bea said unexpectedly. 'Didn't we, April?'

Again, I saw a hint of something between them, but it vanished. I thought nothing more of it, because visiting Bea's mother seemed perfectly reasonable.

We'd sat together for a while, the three of us, talking with awkward self-consciousness about

348

how we couldn't wait to get away from Musgrove back to our respective lives. How it was the same small place it always had been. Then before I knew it, I'd finished my pint, and in the absence of any suggestion that I should stay, I got up and walked away.

47

I'm dumbstruck. When I saw them, they'd just scattered Theo's ashes. The baby I'd fathered. It's a bombshell that blows me apart, so that I no longer know who I am. As the world dissolves around me, I need time to take this in, because inside, I don't know how to feel.

★   ★   ★

It's beginning to get dark when I feel Bea's hand on my arm.

'Are you OK?' Her voice is quiet.

I nod. I am. 'I can't believe I didn't know.'

Bea's silent. Then she says softly, 'It was always there, Noah.'

'Her past? She was a victim, Bea. But it shouldn't have been like that.'

'I wasn't talking about April.' Bea's voice is quiet.

I turn to her. 'What are you talking about?'

'You, Noah. The way you only ever saw what you wanted to see. Couldn't think of her as anyone other than this perfect girl, or woman, who you wanted to live happily ever after with. She wasn't that person.'

'That's not true.' I pull away, stung. 'None of us are perfect.' But suddenly I'm remembering

350

the bird April rescued and took to the woods, where she wove a spell and then it flew away. Only the memory's changed. She doesn't heal it. It doesn't fly away. In a swift, twisting motion, she breaks its neck.

Then I see the tree hung with tiny carcasses. Grotesque, truly a death tree, that I'd convinced myself was a tree of life.

Then the lies that were always there, clear like a layer of mist, revealing the truth. And it's painful. Life's been no harder to me than anyone else. Daisy, Lara, Nina and all the others, they've truly suffered, while I've been a victim only of myself.

'Did you know — ' Bea's voice breaks into my thoughts — 'April believed that there were thin places?'

I'm frowning, shaking my head, trying to keep up with her, as Bea goes on. 'They're places where the door between this world and the next cracks open, letting the light in. Reynard's Hill was one, she always said.'

As she speaks, I consider for a moment if maybe the same thin places had let her demons in. She'd never mentioned them to me. Maybe she thought I wouldn't understand. And so often I couldn't reach her; there'd always been too much we hadn't said.

In recognizing my failure to confront her, I accept my own part in what happened — with the exception of one thing.

'I wish she'd told me about Theo.'

'She was struggling, Noah.' Bea pauses. 'After he died, April disappeared for a while. Next time

351

I saw her, we talked about him, but only briefly. She said she'd never forget him. He was in her heart, her every waking thought, but somehow she had to find a way to live with that. She felt she'd be a better counsellor for knowing what it was like to lose her child. We only talked about Theo the once.'

Bea's eyes are full of sadness. 'I tried to mention him again — when you got engaged. I told her I thought she should talk to you. That marriage was hard enough without ghosts. But she said she didn't think she could carry your grief too.'

We stand, in silence, watching the sun slide towards the horizon, listening to the birds. Such peacefulness wraps itself round me.

'Thank you for telling me,' I say at last, but something's niggling at the back of my mind. I turn to face her. 'Will used everything within reach to get to me. He knew about Theo — you'd think he'd have loved the chance to tell me. So why didn't he?'

Bea's brow is furrowed. 'I really don't know, but once the investigation started, he must have realized there was always a possibility you'd find out.'

I'm thoughtful. 'Or maybe not. With April silenced, with you on his side and me demonstrably unreliable — or at least, that was his plan — there was no reason I ever would.'

'After he signed the death certificate,' Bea says quietly, 'Theo was cremated. April wanted it done quickly.'

'But Will was a student.' Suddenly I'm

frowning, trying to work out the timing as I remember the legalities of reporting a death. 'There are laws, Bea. I'm fairly sure, if Theo was at home, and if he wasn't under the care of a doctor — which from what you've said is how it was — his death should have been reported to the coroner. So why wasn't it?'

Bea looks startled, but it's the million-dollar question. Will's audacity is at once breathtaking, terrifying. He'd been playing by his own rules, even then.

I'm adamant. 'He never should have signed it,' I realize. 'Or maybe he faked someone else's signature. Either way, he broke the law.'

At the same time, condemning himself to silence.

'He probably thought no one would find out,' Bea says.

'Until now, they haven't.' My words are bitter. 'But it's so easy, Bea, to check out.'

'I know. Ella ordered a copy of her birth certificate,' she says thoughtfully. 'Online. Only there wasn't one, not for the name she's always known herself as. It's how she found out.'

Suddenly my thoughts turn to the daughter April must have wanted the world for. Who had Will for a father.

'I'd like to meet her.'

Bea nods. 'I thought you might. You should meet Julia too — she's Ella's therapist. She's just joined the practice where I work. She's wonderful. Ella completely trusts her.'

★ ★ ★

The following day when I go to the hospital, for the first time there is no police presence in April's room and I wonder if Will has confessed. I stand in the doorway, uncertain after all this time as to whether I'm allowed in, when I hear footsteps behind me.

It's Luisa.

'I need to thank you,' I tell her. 'What you found out was really helpful. I hope it didn't get you into any trouble.'

'You're welcome.' She smiles, but it quickly fades. 'I'm so sorry, but she's not doing so well. The drugs she took have affected her liver. The police won't be coming back. You can go in. Take as long as you like.'

Slowly I go inside, trying to digest what she's said as she pulls the door behind me so it's almost closed. Then, for the first time in many years, I'm alone with April. I push the chair as close to her bed as it will go, then sit down, sliding one of my hands under hers, gently closing my fingers round it. And suddenly there's so much I want to say.

'April? I know about Theo. I wish you'd let me share him with you, even for those short months. I'm sorry I wasn't there. But I understand.'

Pausing for a moment. 'I know about Will, too. What he did. The police have him now.'

For a moment, I imagine she responds, as I listen for the faintest change in her breathing, the tiniest fingertip pressure that doesn't happen.

'Bea met Ella. She said she's exactly like you.'

Her hair is like yours. She has her own scars, just as you have yours.

354

'I want to say I'm sorry,' I tell her quietly. 'I wasted so many years. And I failed you. You deserved so much more.'

Then I just sit there, for some time, in silence.

*   *   *

I catch Luisa as I leave. 'What you said earlier, about her liver. Can you treat it?'

'We have tried.' She hesitates. 'I'm so sorry. The doctors have done everything they can, but after her overdose, there was too much in her system. I really don't think she intended to be found.'

The kindest, most softly spoken words can bear the most brutal news, as Luisa explains that with acute liver failure, it's unlikely April will regain consciousness. That most likely it won't be long now. I think of her clients, then Ella. Of the nurses who have cared for her. Are still caring for her, while I watch her for the last time, hoping that when the end comes, it's just an extension of where she is now. That her breathing gradually slows and there is no pain; that Theo will be waiting for her; that there'll be no more suffering.

48

I manage to persuade my landlady to let me stay until after the funeral. I'm expecting a handful of people to be there. Myself and Bea, and maybe one or two others, because Ella's insisted she's coming, with Gabriela, their housekeeper — Rebecca, her adoptive mother, is away on a tour of Russia, which Ella says is probably a good thing.

But, to my surprise, a small crowd steals in behind us. As I glance back, I start to recognize faces — April's neighbour, Lara. Daisy Rubinstein, the Miltons and so many others, to all of whom April made a difference.

And this time the service is personal and full of love, and there are tears and there are flowers.

★   ★   ★

A week later, Bea collects April's ashes. Then on a day where a veil of cloud dulls the sun's glare, she picks up Ella and the three of us take a walk up Reynard's Hill.

'You OK with this?' I ask Ella, clumsy, trying to remember how fifteen feels; how brave it makes you but also how scared.

Glancing at Bea, Ella shrugs. 'It's kind of weird. I mean, I don't remember her, but she was still my mother.' She pauses. 'My birth mother.'

She falls silent.

'You're very like her. To look at,' I add quickly, aware that though she's April's daughter, she's her own person. One I don't yet know, though I would like to.

'Ella's going to board for the next couple of years, until she finishes A levels.' Bea gives me a sideways look. 'And I'm really hoping, when Rebecca's on tour, she'll come and stay with me — for some of the holidays. If she wants to.' Glancing at Ella.

'I'd like that.' Then Ella's silent for a moment and I wonder how it must feel knowing her father's being held by the police, especially on top of everything else she has to face. 'It's weird knowing what happened,' she says at last. 'But it's kind of cool, because I can sort of get to know April from what you both tell me. I think that's OK.'

I'm guessing it's not quite that simple, but she has her mother's courage. Then the implication of her words sinks in, that Ella can see a place for myself and Bea in her life. Another layer of the ice round my heart cracks. And as it starts to thaw, I can believe that with luck, and with love, maybe she'll have what her mother would have wanted for her.

★ ★ ★

We walk to the edge where the ground drops away and Bea points out where Theo's ashes were scattered. Then we sit on the grass and wait until the hikers and dog walkers leave us alone;

and when the sun briefly flares before sinking below the horizon, we scatter April's in the same place.

As Ella steps forward, the wind catching her long hair, suddenly the years fall away and I'm fourteen again, remembering my goddess. Closing my eyes, imagining the touch of her lips and how alive she made me feel. No longer running from the past, but embracing it, as in Ella, I'm reminded that there is hope. As April's did, her parents have failed her, but she has strong people in her life who love her, who will ensure history doesn't repeat itself. That the past stops here. She isn't alone.

★　★　★

With the evidence Ryder already has, Will is held in custody, guilty of forging a death certificate and failing to notify the coroner, as well as abuse of his position in the treatment of his patients. But he continues to deny Norton's murder, even though all the evidence points to his setting April up, stealing her phone, even calling his home number twice, before leaving it in the car when he murdered Norton.

There's a further twist when more forensic tests reveal that fibres from the gloves found in Norton's car have been found in Will's car too. Put together, it's enough for the police to hold him, and enough to keep Ryder digging for more.

★　★　★

Now that April's ashes have been scattered, there's nothing to keep me here, at least until Will's trial starts. I think of the isolation of my cottage, the miles of fields and rolling hills which feel a world away, as I pack my bags and check the room in case I've forgotten anything.

But it isn't over. I'm outside, loading up my car ready to leave, when my mobile buzzes. I glance at the number, which is unfamiliar; hesitate, remembering the call that started all of this, that brought me here from Devon. Then answer it, because what the hell, and anyway, I'm going home. So it ends as it began, in the strangest of coincidences, with Will.

49

'Noah, I need to talk to you.' Will's voice is low, urgent.

'There's nothing you can say that I want to hear,' I tell him bluntly. 'You killed a man and framed April. Sorry, Will, but you deserve everything you get.'

'No! You're wrong. Not about the patients,' he says. 'But everything else. But mostly, you're wrong about April.'

'She's fucking dead, Will. Can't you leave it?' Then seeing alarm on the faces of passers-by, I lower my voice. 'It's over. Accept it.'

'You're so wrong.' His voice is deadly. 'About April. You think she wasn't capable of killing anyone, but she was. Do you know about Theo?'

'Yes. But no thanks to you. You should have told me.'

'For Christ's sake — like it was my place to. She should have told you long ago. By the time I got involved, it was complicated.'

'Yeah. Right. He was sick,' I flare back at him. 'Then he died. Bea told me all about it. And you signed the death certificate. Everyone knows that.'

'Bea? Told you Theo died?'

'Yes.'

'Then you need to call her.' He sounds grim. 'She didn't tell you everything. Theo didn't die, Noah. April killed him.'

360

What he's suggesting is impossible. Suddenly I can't think. Why would Bea have lied? Then I realize, it's Will who's lying. Again. Manipulating me, as he always has.

'Fucking leave it, Will,' I mutter. 'You've done enough.'

'Ask Bea,' he says quietly. 'Ask her what really happened.'

Is Will finally telling me the truth because his own secret is out and he's got nothing to gain from silence? Suddenly I'm doubting everything I've been told. 'Theo was suffering, Will, in pain April couldn't take away, with doctors who wouldn't help. Say she didn't prolong his suffering. It's not exactly cold-blooded murder.'

But it's there now. The question. If her baby's suffering had been so great, would April have been able to bring herself to kill him?

It's not a conversation I want with Will of all people.

'Don't call me again.' I hang up on him before he can reply, then just stand there, reeling. Knowing that, before I leave, I have to call Bea.

★ ★ ★

My burning need gets the better of me. I go out, stopping at the first shop that sells whisky, where I buy a bottle. Start walking back, feeling the familiar anticipation, filled with longing for the oblivion it contains. Then I carry on twenty yards down the road to the nearest bin, dropping it in. Retrace my steps back to the B&B before I change my mind.

I missed it the first time, when Bea told me about Will's obsession with April. How she alluded to, then dismissed, her own feelings for April. Her acrimonious divorce, without ever explaining what went wrong. The letter B squiggled in April's diary, that I'd forgotten about.

★ ★ ★

'It was in her diary. You met up with her, didn't you?'

Under her make-up, Bea's face is pale.

'When, Bea? Why didn't you tell me?'

'I was going to, but in the end, I couldn't.' Her voice trembles. 'She'd been through enough. All I wanted was to protect her.'

'This is serious,' I tell her. 'You'll have to talk to Ryder. Even if it changes nothing, you should tell him what happened.'

'Or what?' she says, with an icy calm I haven't seen before. 'April's dead and Will's being held in custody, which he deserves.'

'You might not have a choice.' She may be right, but I'm thinking of the trial, at which she may well be called to give evidence under oath. And it's tempting, where Will is concerned, to leave him where he is until the legal system takes its course. But there's a more burning issue I have to ask her about.

'You were there when Theo died,' I say quietly. 'You have to tell me what really happened.'

Bea swallows, but the set of her chin is defiant. 'I've already told you.'

'The truth, Bea.'

I'm silent; then she turns and sees my face.

'Will told you, didn't he?' she says, incredulous.

I nod.

'*God*, Noah . . . ' Bea looks fraught. 'All right. If you really want me to, I'll tell you.' She pauses, gathering herself. 'That last night was terrible, so bloody terrible. Theo was in the most awful distress. Nothing we did helped him. I wanted to call an ambulance, but April wouldn't let me. She knew he was dying and she didn't want it drawn out any longer, with an uncomfortable journey, only to be surrounded by strangers in a hospital — all for the sake of a few more hideous hours of suffering. God, it was your worst nightmare.'

She's shaking as she continues. 'I've told you most of it. April gave Theo the medication the hospital had given her the last time. It didn't make any difference. He was still crying pitifully, and if we picked him up it made it worse. His sobs . . . ' She puts her hands over her ears. 'I still remember them. It was the worst thing, seeing him in pain. April gave him more medication, then more. Eventually he became drowsy, then unconscious. That was when she panicked, because she couldn't bear him to wake up and go through it all over again. I remember she kissed him. I think she'd already decided that this was what she'd have to do.'

Bea falls silent, then looks up at me.

'She told him how much she loved him. Then she placed a pillow over his face and suffocated him. And I watched her.' Her voice falters. She turns to me, her face tear-stained, eyes streaked with pain. 'He never woke up.'

As I take in what she's saying, a maelstrom of emotions engulfs me. Shock, followed by horror, grief and finally something that can only be love, for the baby I'd never know, as part of my brain tries to put myself in April's shoes, put all of this into some kind of context. Finding no mental reference to measure it by.

Bea's voice is thin. 'Will knew, but he could never tell anyone, because he'd broken the law before he'd even qualified. It was the most tragic secret that bound them together.'

'Bound the three of you, you mean.' Trying to keep my voice neutral, but my eyes are accusing. 'You were there too, Bea.'

'I know.' She bows her head. 'No one needs to know, do they?' It's more a plea than a question.

'That's up to Will. Now the police have the death certificate, who knows what they'll ask . . . But whatever Will tells them, there's no proof.'

'Are you going to tell them?' Bea's voice is low.

'It depends if they ask me, under oath.' I'm still sore at her.

Because what's to be gained at this stage? The only person who'd be punished would be Bea — and for what? Watching a desperate mother, whom the system had failed, end the suffering of her dying baby?

Then I'm thinking about Will's phone call. 'But just because of how Theo died, it still doesn't mean April killed Norton.'

'No.' Bea's silent. 'I guess the phone call was just Will being Will. He knew something you didn't. It was like you said. He couldn't resist telling you, could he?'

'So you and April,' I say, less roughly. 'The truth, this time. Was there something?'

'The truth?' Bea's silent for a moment. 'Maybe there might have been. We never had the chance to find out.'

I look at her, just for a moment wondering if Bea could have killed Norton. Her way of redressing the past, of avenging the misery Norton had caused the woman she loved.

She feels me watching her and I see her eyes widen in alarm. 'You're not thinking . . . '

But I shake my head and turn to walk away. 'I don't know what to think.'

★   ★   ★

I check back into the B&B. My landlady looks reluctant, but I hide my turmoil under a smile, pay her for another couple of nights. Tell her nothing. Make it up the stairs, locking the door as a different, more brutal truth closes in on me, because it's one thing to end a life of suffering. But harder to understand is April's silence.

Only when my anger subsides does the storm inside my head start to calm. But in its aftermath, the landscape has changed. Surrounding me are doubts, that previously were absent, that have sprung out of nowhere. No longer am I sure about anyone.

50

Only now, with Will remanded in custody, do I finally hear what he's been telling me. But the doubt it leaves, that screams from inside my head, is just the prelude for the crescendo of voices that follows, that have stayed silent for reasons of their own; small voices, that alone are insignificant but that now tell their stories, collectively hold the truth.

When I go to talk to her, the pleasure that flickers in Ella's eyes touches me, but Rebecca misses it. She's flustered. It's in her darting glance, the restlessness of her petite, manicured hands. Instantly recognizable. Fear. She, too, has kept quiet all this time, for her own selfish reasons. Thought only of the glittering career that's everything to her; been terrified of saying the wrong thing.

In her attempt to make sense of recent events, Rebecca unexpectedly tells me what went on. 'April had started calling the house. She was desperate to see Ella. I was petrified she'd just turn up. She seemed distraught.'

I can't help wondering if, without Norton's murder and Will's subsequent arrest, her parents would ever have told Ella the truth.

She rests her head in her hands. 'He was obsessed with her. He always had been, ever since I met him. I put up with it, hoping he'd change.'

366

Talking about Will. I wonder why she's kept quiet about this, but then I see it. She's another unwitting victim. Another person who isn't loved by her husband, by her daughter, only by the nameless masses who flock to watch her perform, who adore her.

'Did Will know?'

She nods. 'He called her. Told her she couldn't see Ella. It was what we'd agreed, after all. But it didn't make any difference. I think it was around the time she found out about Will's selection of patients at the hospital. That was when it started.'

The instant she says this, I understand. April must have known that despite Will's obsession, he'd always looked down on her. She was one of his unworthy, undeserving, bypassed for someone richer, from a better background, who had social standing. Would have detested what Will was doing. Perhaps she feared, too, that he felt the same about her daughter.

★   ★   ★

When I next talk to Bea, she gives me more insight into how April's life really was.

'No one can say for certain if Norton did anything. Not recently, anyway.' I look at Bea.

But she shakes her head. 'How can you say that? Between them, he and Will destroyed April. Will used what she did to Theo to blackmail her, didn't he? To take Ella, then to keep April away from her. As if it wasn't bad enough already.' Then her composure slips, her voice wavers.

367

'After losing Theo, not to be able to see her own daughter — I can't imagine how that must have felt.'

★ ★ ★

But I'm still missing something. I call round to see Lara, who seemed to best understand April and who makes me question everything I think I know. Lara, who I believed was April's client, who was her neighbour and closest friend. The holder of her secrets.

'I know April tried to call you. She was quite upset when you didn't answer, but then she said it didn't matter because you'd find out.'

'Find what out?' Was she talking about Ella? Or something else?

There's a quiet determination in Lara's voice as she goes on. 'I didn't tell you. I couldn't — not until now. And Ryder . . . he asks all the wrong questions, that man. But the truth is, Will had a power over her that she couldn't escape. He used it whenever he felt like it, when he wanted sex, any time he needed to know he could still manipulate her. Then just lately, something changed. She told me she'd found a way to show the world what he was really like.'

'Everyone knows Will's guilty. All the evidence points to it.'

'It does? Are you certain?' As she holds my gaze, as the truth flickers there, my skin crawls. *We can't, all of us, be wrong.*

Lara's eyes are unblinking. 'There's another possibility. April didn't lose her phone. She made it look as though she had. She only used it to make those last two calls to Rebecca — the final pleas of a desperate mother, who wanted to see her daughter. Rebecca hung up on her. It was the only time I saw April lose control.'

I'm floundering. This is no theory that Lara's proposing. She witnessed April making those calls. 'But . . . if it was deliberate, she'd have left everything in order. Paid her bills. Found a home for the cat.' Staring wildly at her, clutching at hope that she's wrong.

Lara shakes her head. 'So everyone would know she'd planned it? You're missing the point.'

'You knew what she was going to do?' My voice is hoarse.

Lara shrugs. 'I wasn't sure, but I thought there was something. I tried to get her to talk to me, but she wouldn't.'

'You didn't even try to stop her.' But my accusation is half-hearted.

'Do you really think she'd have thanked me for that? I'd have condemned her to more years of unhappiness.' Lara sighs. 'Stop thinking like a lawyer, just for a moment. Put yourself in April's shoes. The woman who chose to end her son's life, for his sake, not hers. Risked her own future to end his suffering. It's something she lived with, every moment of every day, ever since.'

Lara looks away. 'I think — ' She breaks off. 'She was tired, Noah. She'd been fighting for most of her life, just to survive. Imagine what that does to a person.'

As I stare at her, I see what's been right under my nose. No one framed April. Will didn't kill

369

Norton. It was April all along. *She set him up.*

'He blackmailed her, stole her child, pierced her soul.' Lara's voice, steady, resolute, breaks into my thoughts, my heart.

And as she says that, only then do I fully understand, how the neglect and abuse of April's childhood had leached into her future, corrupting it even before she'd got there. There'd been no choice in what had followed. It had been inevitable.

She was a victim. Exploited, damaged, ultimately destroyed, by both Will and Norton, each of whom would eventually pay the price.

★　★　★

A day later, I set off for home, though Ryder tells me I'll be needed to give evidence at Will's trial. Will's career is over, the respect of others for him destroyed. He may not be a murderer, but there are other crimes for which he must be tried.

As I drive, I'm still consumed with thoughts of April and Will, then Ella; not yet able to mentally file them away, even hours later, as I pull up outside my cottage. But as I unlock my front door, dropping my bag on the floor before closing it behind me, I'm thinking about myself, then about the last four years, in which I've earned nothing, living off my savings and my inheritance.

I've achieved nothing. Nor have I given anything of myself. Within the walls of this cottage, I've become a recluse who cares about no one, my writing part of a spiralling, self-obsessed descent into alcoholism.

Thinking furiously, I go from room to room. The house is untidy, with a cloying mustiness that pervades throughout. In each room, one by one, I throw the windows open, watching rays of sunlight filter in, lifting the gloom, catching the dust I've disturbed, as I properly see my home for what it is. Somewhere neglected and unloved, the same way I've treated myself.

Not surprising then, that I imagine I hear Clara's voice.

'*About time you got on with living.*'

But even before I turn, I know that the room behind me is empty and she won't be rushing over, happy to see me back; that there are too many empty glasses in the kitchen; that on this occasion, her voice is in my head. She talks sense, Clara. Maybe I'll knock on her door and thank her.

I sit down heavily, the cloud of dust I disturb making me cough. I'd always known I'd come back, but now that I'm here, I'm no longer sure what there is for me, noticing also that the cottage is as it was when I moved in.

I know now, I've been stuck far too long. Leaping up, wasting no time, before I can change my mind I go through to my study and gather the years of notes I'll never use, for the book I know is going nowhere, carry them over to the fireplace, scrunch them up and throw them into the grate. Hunting around for matches, then lighting a fire, watching the flames leap up. And all without regret, because I don't need them. Watching the pages melt into the flames.

★ ★ ★

It's a month later when a box is delivered. I began with good intentions that month, clearing out my cottage, my cluttered study, even my life; yet for some reason my good intentions faltered; I was still caught in the past, unsure what the future held for me. Taking the box through to my study, I open it to find a letter inside, brief, the format familiar.

Dear Mr Calaway,

At the request of the late April Tara Rousseau, I have held in my possession an article she entrusted to me for safe-keeping, until the time of her death. In accordance with her wishes, it is duly enclosed.

Yours most sincerely,
James-Colbert
Colbert, Eddison & Partners

Inside, carefully wrapped, I find the small wooden chest inlaid with brass and mother-of-pearl that I'd last seen in April's London flat.

Lifting the lid, the first thing I see is a letter addressed to me, dated ten weeks and three days ago. It's been ten weeks since Will called here that night, though it feels so much longer; but it means she knew exactly what she was doing. As I read, slowly walking across the room to sit on the windowsill, at last I'm able to understand.

Dear Noah,

After all this time, where do I start? Perhaps with how sorry I am, because it's true, even now. I always will be, but the fault is mine.

I want to start at the beginning — with my so-called childhood, only it wasn't, because when cruelty and abuse are relentlessly drip-fed into your veins, they become your benchmark. Sex and prostitution were as normal to me as breathing, but if you're reading this, I'm guessing you already know.

I wasn't your goddess. I was the whore my brother sold to his stoned friends, the stepdaughter of the man who sexually abused me, before beating me. Remember the woods, Noah? I only survived because when it all got too much, that's where I went. In my mind. Think I'm mad if you like, but you know I loved it there. You knew the rumours too, about how each tree was the spirit of a child who had died. I joined their whispers, Noah, heard their names. Saw the faint outlines of their ghosts encircling me. Felt their frail arms reaching out, pulling me back from the edge.

I don't know if you know, that so much

373

changed because of you. That when I was with you, for a short while, I escaped. I loved your world, Noah. It was a magical place, where there were stars and love, and there was hope. Hope. I don't think you know how it is not to have that. I stole some of yours. It was beautiful, but there were too many secrets between us and I always knew I'd have to give it back.

We're butterflies, Noah. Some of you fly, the rest of us get our wings ripped off. My wings had gone before I knew you. And I'm not sure wingless butterflies have anywhere to go.

But there was something else. Something you deserve to know, that it was wrong of me not to tell you. I'd meant to, one day, but it was never the right time and the longer I left it, the harder it became. I knew also, that if I told you, I'd have to relive what happened, feel how raw my grief was. Still is. Bear yours.

We had a baby, Noah. I called him Theo. He taught me what love is really about — brutal honesty, and putting someone else first; doing what's best for that person, no matter the consequence to yourself.

I pause for a moment, because I know about this, from Bea. Then I read on, because this has only ever been April's story.

374

He was sick, Noah. Really sick. It was his heart. He needed surgery, but after the first operation, something happened. He wouldn't feed and then he got an infection. He was too sick for the surgery that would save his life.

He deteriorated quickly. I think that's when I decided never to tell you, because watching your child suffer is harder than suffering yourself. To not be able to help even harder. To know whatever you do, whoever you go to for help, there is no hope.

One day, he had several seizures. My doctor didn't want to know. There was a children's hospice but it was miles away. I had no money, no car — I couldn't get there. And all just to prolong the agony, when I knew what was coming, and already knew what I had to do.

Imagine for a moment. Your child is dying. What would you have chosen? Drawn-out suffering and pain? Because there was never any doubt Theo was suffering. Or oblivion? What do you think about? Your baby's reality — or your own? If you condemn your child to a lifetime of suffering, even a short one, what does that make you? Moral? A torturer? Is there a difference?

The last evening, I was desperate. I gave

Theo the medication the hospital had given me, then half an hour later, gave him more. When a little later he was crying again, more. Eventually, mercifully, he became unconscious. I was terrified he'd wake up and the whole horrible cycle would just go on — unless I stopped it.

I kissed him. Told him how much I loved him. More than anything, more than my life. Wished with all my heart it could have been different for him. I don't know if he heard me — his eyes stayed closed.

I held a pillow over his face and suffocated him. Out of love, Noah. Will forged the death certificate. I didn't know who else to turn to.

It wasn't enough that I carried with me what I'd done, every second of every day. Will's help came at a price. First it was me. Will was obsessed. He wouldn't let me be with you. But he didn't love me, and I couldn't marry him. When I discovered I was pregnant with his child, I ran, but he found me. Threatened to tell the police I'd killed Theo, then took our daughter. Elodie. But nothing was enough for Will. Even when he didn't want me himself, he couldn't bear me being with anyone else.

I've tried to escape him. Moved away, changed my name, but it didn't matter *where I went. He always found me. He's not a good person but he knew me. And I learned a long time ago that he'll use whatever means are at his disposal. You see, Will always gets what he wants. But not this time.*

I used to think life was cheap. That we were no more than a raindrop or a dandelion seed, but I was wrong. It was Theo who taught me that life is so very precious; that each day is a gift; that there is pain in loss, but a broken, ragged beauty in what it leaves us.

Life at all costs, Noah . . . That's what most of us believe, but have you thought what it really means?

That however great the suffering, the pain, the futility, we must cling on for every breath, every second, whatever the cost, blind to the truth: that if life is truly unbearable, death can only be beautiful.

I put the letter down. It's what Lara was talking about. It's also why April never exposed Will, because he would have told the world what she'd done, without a thought for the most devastating of consequences — for Ella.

Tired of life, April had chosen death, but there's no doubt in my head. For Ella, and for me too, she would choose life. Like the hilltop she pulled me back from a long time ago, it's as though she's saved me again — only this time from alcoholism and apathy.

All those years, April and Will kept their secret, until it was discovered by the one person who stood to lose the most. Their daughter.

In the bottom of the box is an envelope holding a few photos, of April and a baby I recognize now as Theo. Underneath is another photo, of a fair-haired toddler who I guess must be Ella, before Will made her give her up. Looking at it, I try to imagine how that must have felt, handing over her daughter. There's the heart-shaped stone and spotted feather I remember from way back and a few other things, and sifting through I find one of our wedding invitations.

For a moment the past comes back again, then as I read the letter a second time, I hear the echo of April's voice, before it's lost, among the fields, the hills, and beyond. I sit there holding it, my last gift from her, undecided whether I'll show it to Ryder, unsure, now she's gone, what difference it will make to anyone.

If the right questions are asked, it may yet come out at the trial. Or if Ryder finds out how Theo died . . . And at the heart of everything, there's Ella to think of. Ella, the person who matters most. It occurs to me to keep the letter for her, to read at some point in the future, so she will know what kind of woman her mother was.

The breeze finds its way through my open door, fanning the fire I lit earlier so it bursts into life. Noticing the slow curl of smoke across the room, I walk over and throw the window open, as I do disturbing the dozens of moths that have settled there. Forgetting the letter, I watch them, the delicate shading of their wings, the bark-like patterns that camouflage them, as they flutter outside, drifting away, a small cloud that blends into the landscape.

As the last few fade away, I think about April. Much as there are people who'd like to try, chalking up huge legal bills in the process, I'm not sure they'll ever prove she killed Norton. But the way I see it, it doesn't matter. However you look at it, Norton's was a worthless life, just as Will got what was coming to him. You don't need the police and highly paid lawyers to work that out.

Then I think of what she said, a long time ago. Maybe she was right. We'd felt too much happiness. Maybe when you live as intensely as she had, feel such extremes of emotion, you burn out before your time. It's how I'll remember her. A blazing star breaking the greyness of my ordinary life.

★ ★ ★

Carefully folding the letter, I replace it in the chest. Then that afternoon, fuelled by a need for change, I run five miles, hard. Years ago, I used to run, but I'm older, unfit; it's too far, too soon, so that I'm out of breath, damp with sweat, when I reach the point along a wooded lane where the trees open out.

I gaze at the view that lies before me. A cold

379

front has passed through, sweeping away the mist and drizzle, leaving crystal-clear air so that I can see for miles, across hills and fields, to the sliver of sea on the horizon.

As the sun's rays break through the cloud, lighting the lane in front of me, I'm thinking of April. Then my thoughts turn to Ella, only instead of my usual angst at what they've both been subjected to, I feel an unexpected rush of warmth. And with it, a new perspective. April made her choice. What matters now is Ella. And I have the strangest conviction that she'll be fine.

Suddenly, the chains that for so long have bound me fall away. Stepping out from the shadows, I start to run again, without their weight, faster, lighter; feeling the weak sun's touch on my skin, the pounding of my heart underneath.

With each step, travelling further from a past that has held me back; moving on.

Acknowledgements

While the writing of a book is solitary, publishing involves the talent and creativity of so many. I'm blessed to have the insight and guidance of not just one but two brilliant editors, Trisha Jackson at Pan Macmillan and Alicia Condon at Kensington, who gently, patiently and insightfully hone my books into their best possible shape. I'm so grateful to both of you. Natasha Harding, Lauren Welch, Laura Carr and the whole brilliant team at Pan Macmillan, thank you, all of you, too.

Whether because of the expectation around it, not to mention all the people waiting to read it, writing a second book is hard — much harder than the first. After I'd finished, I sat on this one for some time before sending it to my wonderful agent, Juliet Mushens, who, thankfully, loved it. Thank you, Juliet, for everything you do and for always being just an email away. I truly have the best agent!

Terry Skelton and Steve Page, again! Thank you, both of you, for sharing your inside knowledge and patiently answering all my queries.

Finally, to my family and friends, and to everyone who read early drafts, much love and huge thanks to all of you for sharing the adventure — especially to Bob, Georgie and Tom for believing in me and for your support and love.

We do hope that you have enjoyed reading this large print book.

Did you know that all of our titles are available for purchase?

We publish a wide range of high quality large print books including:
Romances, Mysteries, Classics
General Fiction
Non Fiction and Westerns

Special interest titles available in large print are:
The Little Oxford Dictionary
Music Book
Song Book
Hymn Book
Service Book

Also available from us courtesy of Oxford University Press:
Young Readers' Dictionary
(large print edition)
Young Readers' Thesaurus
(large print edition)

For further information or a free brochure, please contact us at:
Ulverscroft Large Print Books Ltd.,
The Green, Bradgate Road, Anstey,
Leicester, LE7 7FU, England.
Tel: (00 44) 0116 236 4325
Fax: (00 44) 0116 234 0205

Other titles published by Ulverscroft:

THE BONES OF YOU

Debbie Howells

When eighteen-year-old Rosie Anderson disappears, the idyllic village where she lived will never be the same again. Local gardener Kate had come to know Rosie well, and thought she understood her — perhaps even better than Rosie's own mother. Rosie was beautiful, kind and gentle. She came from a loving family, and she had her whole life ahead of her. Who could possibly want to harm her? And why? Kate is convinced the police are missing something, and that someone in the village knows more than they're letting on. As the investigation deepens, so does her obsession with solving the mystery of what happened to Rosie.

THE LOVING HUSBAND

Christobel Kent

Fran Hall and her husband Nathan live in a farmhouse on the edge of the Fens with their two children. One February night, when Fran is woken from a dream, she finds the bed empty beside her and Nathan gone. Searching the house for him, she makes a devastating discovery. As Fran finds herself under intense police scrutiny, she and her two small children become more isolated, and she starts to wonder whether or not she really knew Nathan. Was he truly the loving husband she had believed him to be? As police suspicion grows, the questions for Fran begin to mount. Is there something that she is hiding from them — something that she has kept hidden from everyone, including her husband?

THE LOST SWIMMER

Ann Turner

Rebecca Wilding, an archaeology professor, makes sense of the past for a living. But suddenly truth and certainty are turning against her. Rebecca is accused of serious fraud; and worse, she suspects — she *knows* — that her husband, Stephen, is having an affair. Desperate to find answers, she leaves with him for Greece, Italy and Paris, where she can uncover the conspiracy against her and hopefully win Stephen back to her side. There, on the idyllic Amalfi Coast, Stephen disappears. In a swirling daze of panic and fear, Rebecca is dealt with fresh allegations. And with time against her, she finds help in the unlikeliest of places, and uncovers the secrets that stand between her and Stephen — and the deceit that has chased her halfway around the world.

I'LL BE WATCHING YOU

Beverly Barton

A series of threatening letters, phone calls and 'gifts' brings chaos and terror to Ella's well-ordered life. Someone is watching her. Wanting her. Promising revenge. The one person who stands a chance of helping her is the one who could be behind the whole thing: Reed, an old crush who has just been released after serving a sentence for murder, and who has every reason to hate Ella's family. When the unlikely couple join forces to discover the truth, Ella again finds herself attracted to the man who comes with his own danger warning. As the body count in the small Alabama town rises, and long-buried secrets threaten to be exposed, it's clear that the killer is determined to take his secrets to the grave — and to put Ella there first . . .